I0708470

Seas the Dating Coach

LAURA LANGA

SEAS THE DATING COACH. Copyright © 2025 by Laura Langa

All rights reserved.

No part of this publication may be reproduced, stored or transmitted in any form or by any means, electronic, mechanical, photocopying, recording, scanning, for use in training AI software, or otherwise without written permission from the publisher. It is illegal to copy this book, post it to a website, or distribute it by any other means without permission.

This novel is entirely a work of fiction created solely by the author without use of AI. The names, characters and incidents portrayed in it are the work of the author's imagination. Any resemblance to actual persons, living or dead, events or localities is entirely coincidental.

AISN: B0DBJ66CTP

Cover design by: Enni Tuomisalo

By Laura Langa

WILKS BEACH
Holiday Tides
En Route to Romance

LOVE TUCSON
Haley and the Yeti
Date the Alphabet
An Unexpected Roomie

MEDICAL ROMANCE
My Heart Before You
A Guarded Heart
Between Our Hearts

For my beautiful, vivacious mother, who loved the beach

And for *anyone* who's been afraid and done the hard thing anyway. I'm so proud of you. I hope you know how incredibly **brave** you are.

ONE

Vivian

You know the feeling you get when Today You needs to pay up on the promises Past You made? It's a mix of a roiling stomach with a bit of *Why do my lungs itch?* topped with a sprinkling of charred dread. You know...the sensations you have to endure NOW because Past You was a shortsighted dingbat.

Seriously. The *audacity* of Past You.

Avoiding the antique wall clock ticking ever closer to seven a.m., I stare at the neon-yellow, spaghetti-strap monstrosity of a prom dress in my hands. It's probably the wrong alteration garment to distract myself with, especially with my normally dexterous fingers trembling.

"This is such a stupid idea," I mutter.

The needle in my hand slips, poking my index finger. A cosmic admonishment.

You wanted this, it reminds me.

I woke up last Saturday, on my twin sister's and my twenty-seventh birthday, and realized that I've been living in fear. No, not of a shark taking a bite of me on one of my open-water swims, but of really *living*. Of stepping outside my comfort zone. Of just doing something other than what's expected of me. And maybe it's being closer to thirty than twenty, but the idea of waking up ten years from now and being in the same exact spot made me break out in a cold sweat.

So today, I'm doing something about it.

All I have to do is march from my humble tailor shop into my sister, Brynn's, bustling coffee shop and finally talk to the man I've had a crush on for a year. Easy peasy.

Does the idea of checking off part one of my three-part self-improvement plan make me want to throw up?

Absolutely.

Will I go through with it?

...maybe?

Yesterday, I chickened out. The tick of the clock was like a snare drum in my ear as I kept my head down, pretending to be engrossed in a difficult beaded section of a gorgeous cornflower-blue gown instead of doing what I'd promised myself...what I wished for.

Like most locals, I believe in the strange, mystical undercurrent that runs along our modest strip of beach. It only pops into existence occasionally, enough to make you doubt a coincidence or question déjà vu. Either way, it's shown up enough over the decades to be entrenched in our small town's lore. Every local knows that if you *really* want something to happen, you make an ocean wish. Taking one of the flat white stones from the library's landscaping, you write your wish and toss it in the sea.

They almost always come true—almost. Nine-year-old me hadn't understood that the magical power beneath our sandy shores isn't strong enough to bring my parents back to life.

My phone alarm blaring my favorite Raven Sacaria song makes me jump, and I nearly stab myself again. Exhaling, I put down my sewing, turn off my work light, and run my fingers over my springy curls.

"You've got this," I whisper in rhythmic repeats as I slide into the slender back hallway connecting our two businesses. The hallway also holds the staircase to our upstairs apartment.

When I push open the door to Seabreeze Beans my heartbeat is in my throat. The layering sounds of grinding coffee, boppy music, and half a dozen voices are almost overwhelming. I take a steadying breath, inhaling the lightly caramelized, almost nutty scent of Brynn's signature roast. Our two businesses and everything in our apartment perpetually smell of the coffee Brynn hand-roasts every Sunday afternoon. I honestly don't know why I bother applying perfume, because I end up smelling like coffee anyway.

My sister's umber eyes widen when they catch mine, her brow immediately pinching in concern. To be fair, I'm never up this early.

I have a tendency to stay up late and rise just before my shop opens at ten. My sister, on the other hand, is usually in bed before nine to wake an hour before Seabreeze Beans opens at 5:30 a.m.

"I'm fine," I mouth to her before catching sight of the reason I'm here.

The impact of seeing Atticus Williams in my favorite suit hits my chest like a fencepost. The deep navy of the impeccably tailored garment brings out the blue in his eyes. His blond hair is styled off his forehead, and he's wearing his glasses today.

My sister doesn't understand my attraction to Atticus, calling him "nerdy" as if that's a bad thing. Since Brynn's dating history includes a former professional baseball player turned smoking-hot firefighter, she'll never understand that I prefer a more approachable aesthetic. Ridiculously hot men fry my brain, making talking to them impossible.

And speaking, in general, isn't my strong suit.

My heart does an unsteady wobble, like it's wearing heels for the first time, when Atticus scowls at his watch. I've spent way too many hours fantasizing about Atticus's long, lean frame on my octagonal step riser as I take his measurements. I feel a little bad about my imagination firing whoever is doing an amazing job of tailoring his suits now, but otherwise, he'd have no reason to wander in my door. Perhaps when my tape measure is around his chest, my fingertips inches in front of his heart, he covers my hands with one of his.

"Vivian, I can't believe you've been right beneath my nose this entire time, and I didn't see you. How could I be so blind?" Then his long fin-

gers brush back one of my curls. "You're astonishing." Those perfectly blue eyes sweep my face in wonder as he leans down. "Could I— Could I kiss you?"

A forceful cough yanks me back to the coffee shop. I suck in a noisy breath when I realize my fingertips are brushing my lower lip. Flipping toward the door I've just come through, I take two giant steps. "He looks stressed. I should try again tomorrow," I mutter to myself.

"Viv?"

I look over my shoulder, catching my sister's gaze from where she's steaming milk. She flicks her focus to Atticus before returning it to me with a slight head tilt.

My chin dips in a small nod.

I've told my sister and a few locals about my crush on Atticus. I just haven't informed my sister that I'm finally ready *to do something* about it.

A shadow wisps over my sister's cheeks before her jaw tightens, just like it does before she tackles—and usually conquers—something challenging.

"Could you come here a second?" Warmth infuses the question, and it's like Brynn is giving me a hug. She's also giving me a perfect excuse to cross right in front of Atticus, who's next in line and beside the espresso machine.

"This is just like when she helped you learn to drive or be brave enough to try contacts," I murmur to the door. "Sometimes you need a nudge."

Honestly, I need two earth movers working in tandem to get me over this hurdle.

"You've got this," I whisper.

My fingers release their death grip on the door handle as I glance over the wildflower-green sundress I'm wearing. Like almost all my clothes, I made it, so it fits my curvy frame perfectly. It also makes my green eyes pop and cools the reddish undertone of my pale skin. Regardless of my smart clothing choices, my hands shake, and I run one down the bodice before turning.

"Of course," I call out cheerfully.

I take several—I'm hoping elegant-looking—strides forward, passing a handful of two-top tables. But then, Joe Matherson slams his knobby hand on the table where Leroy Bates has just won their morning chess game, and his mug tumbles off the edge. Hot black coffee burns my toes and seeps into my white canvas shoes before the broken handle part of the mug almost slices my skin. I jump back with a yelp, kicking my foot in the air to lessen the pain, and hit something solid.

"Are you okay?" The low-toned question comes a second before my other foot slides from beneath me.

My heartbeats slow to a crawl. The room swirls in a slow-motion twist when Atticus glances up, brows anxious. He's going to watch me fall into a puddle of coffee. This will be his first memory of me. I've orbited around him a thousand times, but this will be the *one thing* he'll remember. Resigned to my fate, I close my eyes. The sooner I'm on the ground, the sooner Atticus can swoop in and pick me up.

Then we can begin our love story.

I slip six inches before two strong hands brace around my ribs, pulling me off the ground and backward until I'm standing beyond the mess. My mind sprints in opposing directions. I'm overjoyed that I'm not in a coffee spill, but I'm also disappointed that Atticus isn't the one rendering aid.

My eyes fly open to catch Atticus stepping forward like he was going to intervene. A hiccup shakes my chest as our gazes catch, because I'm certain—absolutely certain—that this is our beginning. The rest flows so easily. Snuggling on the couch while we both read. Long peaceful walks by the sea. *Finally* being someone's everything.

The moment shatters when Sandy, the barista, calls for the next customer, and Atticus turns to order his double shot Americano with a half-pump of butter pecan flavor syrup.

The mystery hands twitch and then release me as Atticus takes a phone call, paying and moving to the small area near the door to wait for his drink.

Instantly, I feel myself transitioning back into wallpaper. Invisible. Unnoticeable.

"That's one way to start the morning. It's not every day I get to rescue a damsel in distress." The mirthful voice directly behind me hits my stunned brain before the scent of books momentarily overpowers the ubiquitous coffee smell.

I instinctively inhale. The scent of books—particularly that of older books like the ones holding the town's archives—is the best smell in the world. No, I will not be taking questions, and, yes, I will die on this hill.

It's then that I realize that this whole thing *is a dream*. It smells like books because I fell asleep with a paperback Regency romance over my face again. I'm cozy in my tiny bedroom, barely big enough for a twin bed and a dresser, stacks of books in every corner. Any second now, my gray tabby, Pepper, will swat me with her tail. Then my alarm will go off so I can attempt speaking to Atticus.

A relieved laugh tumbles from my mouth.

"I'm so sorry, sugar." I startle when Joe tries to dry my coffee-stained shoe with a wad of paper napkins, but since his ancient spine can't really bend, he's just waving the paper over my knees and fluttering the hem of my dress.

My gaze whips around the noisy shop as a boulder settles low in my stomach.

Not dreaming, then.

"I got it, Joe." Brynn takes the napkins from him, pushing them against my toes as she crouches to place the ceramic pieces in a dustpan.

My cheeks flame, unable to do anything but stand stock still as Atticus collects his to-go cup and rushes outside. He doesn't glance back once. The gentle clink of my sister's seashell door chime reverberates like a nail in a coffin.

"What's your name?" The tone of the deep voice behind me is lower—unmistakably intimate—almost as if his lips are right beside my ear.

An involuntary shiver slips down my spine before I remember I need to thank this man for his quick reflexes. Otherwise, I'd be completely humiliated, forcing me to abandon my plan to talk to Atticus.

I still might. Maybe. We'll see.

"If you have something to say, you can speak to me." The death glare Brynn shoots over my shoulder is enough to sober me.

I rush to her side, turning as both Joe and Leroy try to murder the stranger with their narrowed gazes.

The man is almost as well dressed as Atticus, except he's forsaken his jacket and tie. The white shirt beneath his gray suit vest is open at the collar and rolled to the elbows, revealing tanned skin. He takes a step back, casually sliding his hands into the pockets of his black slacks. The tailor in me approves the black buttons of his vest matching his pants and the silver of his belt buckle complementing his watch. Well-coordinated ensemble aside, the hostile body language of the three people I've known since birth makes me wary of this man.

Though I can feel his gaze on me, I only bounce my eyes to his warm brown ones for the briefest of milliseconds. The sheer magnitude of his gorgeous face snaps the breath from my lungs. He's unnervingly handsome with his perfectly styled black hair; his playful, full mouth surrounded by beard scruff; and an easy, sexy confidence.

In the Regency romance books I'm fond of, they would describe him as a capital-R Rake.

Dangerous.

Devastating.

Brynn rises, stepping in front of me to talk to the stranger, but I miss her words. Everything blurs to white noise as the failed interaction with Atticus surges forward. A crushing weight tugs at my shoulders and brings my gaze to my ruined shoes. I should be proud of myself for trying. I know that's what Brynn will say when she brings me a leftover baked good and a decaf iced coffee at three when her store closes.

Until now, I've only stuck with things that come naturally to me—sewing, reading, and swimming. I'd be in trouble living in a beach town and *not* knowing how to swim. Socializing, dating, and putting myself out there are not on that list.

Leroy has one gnarled finger pointed at the stranger's chest as I try to drift from the conversation. It's usually easy, slipping into solitude, but stepping away this time feels like wading through mud. I'm inexplicably tethered. Brynn catches me by the shoulders, turning and guiding me toward the door to our shared hallway.

"That's the man I warned you about."

Who?

I rack my brain but can't recall who Brynn is referring to. Unlike most Wilks Beach residents, I don't usually partake in our town's cherished pastime of gossip. I'm more likely to know the storyline from the latest Wellington novel than who slighted who at church last weekend.

My forehead creases as I turn to find the stranger's focus locked on me. The jolt sliding over my collarbones as our gazes collide punches the breath from me.

Quickly, I blink away.

"I'm sorry that was a bust," Brynn whispers as she encourages me through the back door.

I should be happy that my sister is helping me escape an uncomfortable situation, but a mossy emotion sludges through my veins.

Instead of analyzing it, I quietly thank her.

As soon as I'm safely ensconced in our hallway, I convince myself that the electrifying bolt I felt meeting the stranger's gaze was nothing. The flush staining my cheeks and sliding down my neck is from residual embarrassment, nothing else. And the tug I feel to reopen the door to Seabreeze Beans is a symptom of my overactive imagination, because there's no good reason for me to ever see that man again.

None whatsoever.

TWO

Finn

"I warned you that those backwater wackos wouldn't take kindly to a...what do they call us?"

"Mainlanders," I answer, rubbing the bridge of my nose. Ever since the altercation in the coffee shop this morning, a migraine has been brewing like clouds collecting at the start of a thunderstorm.

Alec's laugh bursting through my Bluetooth earbuds doesn't help the pinching between my brows. "That's right. And they call themselves *islanders*." He snorts. "Even though Wilks Beach is technically a peninsula."

This two-mile, narrow stretch of beach definitely feels like an island—physically and emotionally—but Alec is correct. The Atlantic Ocean stretches to the east; Back Bay to the west; a wide inlet and the Virginia state border separates the town from North Carolina's Outer Banks to the south; and a large, inaccessible, 4,983-acre wildlife preserve borders the northern edge. Being an hour drive from the nearest city, Virginia Beach, only adds to its remote allure.

"I didn't think it'd be this bad." My neck pinches as I pace the short distance along my desk.

Striding in one direction, my gaze bounces over the upstairs reading area and private study rooms through my glass office wall and door. Like usual, reading patrons fill most of the wingback chairs and the study rooms near capacity. Two older women use the oversized table centering the space to plan quilts. They've even brought an ironing board along with their various bags of fabric and batting.

Up until this conversation, I'd always had my office door open, welcoming visitors. In the three weeks I've been working at Wilks Beach Library, I've received none. Spinning on my heel improves the tension behind my eyes as my exterior window reveals a breathtaking view of the dunes and the long, sandy beach beyond. When I was the collection development librarian for the Central Library in Virginia Beach, my window faced a limp willow tree and a stone wall.

"Face it. You're the stereotypical evil outsider here to ruin all their bizarre town traditions." Alec cackles.

I frown at the waves crashing on the warm sand. Alec's assessment is probably an accurate interpretation of their viewpoint. My library staff stops speaking the second I enter a room, and I'm scowled at while buying milk from the tiny market. I might as well be the boogeyman. The only part of relocating to this town that hasn't been miserable has been moving into my bayside rental house and joining the combination Crossfit/boxing gym beside the fire station.

Crossing my arms, I shift my focus to watch the dolphins swim down the coast. The beachgoers pay them no notice since seeing a dolphin splashing beyond wave break is a commonplace occurrence. The beaches surrounding Virginia Beach are teeming with tourists this time of year, but with its challenging accessibility, Wilks Beach remains locals only.

"I'm not an outsider. Until very recently, I lived in the city where everyone here has to do all their major shopping, or go to church, or school, or get a haircut, for Pete's sake." I hear the rising irritation in my voice and tamp it down.

Besides the library, Wilks Beach only has a small market, one restaurant, the coffee shop, the gym, and a fire station. The rest of the narrow strip of land contains single-family homes except for the condo tower and a park near the inlet.

"It's just a year. You can sip seawater in the moonlight or belly dance to bring good waves for a year, can't you?" My closest friend's voice nearly breaks with laughter.

I roll my eyes. On top of having paltry hospitality, inhabitants of this town are also known for having...let's just say, less than logic-based beliefs regarding the ocean.

In truth, I'm one more negative interaction away from taking part in a mermaid protection ceremony—or whatever I need to do—to be accepted. My staff here—all of whom are locals—need to not only *like me* but support my future application for library director. Only a current branch manager can apply for directorship, and only those managers with glowing reviews from their staff make it to the second interview.

No one but me and another Central Library librarian I've sworn to secrecy knows that Ralph, the current director, is preparing to retire in a year. He let that nugget slip after too much scotch at a recent networking dinner. I was fortunate that the Wilks Beach Library manager retired shortly afterward so I could jump on the opportunity to manage this branch.

Everything needs to fall in line over the next year, or my younger sister's future will be irrevocably changed. At a young age, I vowed to take care of her, and even though we live in different cities now, she will always be my priority.

The pressure builds in my head again, and I take a slow breath to combat the impending migraine.

I'd hoped to break the glacial iceberg this morning by chatting with locals while grabbing my second cup of coffee at the local shop, but no one would even say hello. You'd think that preventing one of their own from falling in a puddle of caffeine would garner a modicum of kindness, but three of them immediately launched into various attacks of how I was destroying their library—as if shifting funds to update the ancient computers in the media room and wanting to properly preserve their historic texts was criminal.

"I've gotta go. My next client is here." Alec lowers his voice. "Not much I can do for this one since she won't stick to the diet I gave her, but if she wants to keep paying me, I'll keep taking her money."

I flinch at my friend's callousness. Being a personal trainer makes Alec more body critical than most people, but women don't need to be waif thin in order to be attractive. In my opinion, it makes them less attractive.

We hang up as movement behind me draws my attention away from the tranquil coastline. The corner of my mouth lifts, seeing the woman from the coffee shop again. She's still in her green dress, but a pair of bright-pink flip-flops have replaced her stained shoes. Almost everyone in the reading room gives her a wave. She wordlessly reciprocates, a shy smile joining her small wave.

A few steps before the glass door to an unoccupied study room, she pulls her cell phone from a canvas bag covered in llamas wearing various sunglasses. Then she's typing the six-digit numerical code that she would have received when she'd reserved the room on the library's website into the keypad lock. Because again, as much as these people want to think they are their own municipality, this little *island* is connected to the larger city beyond. This library is one branch of eleven within the library system.

Curiosity gets the better of me as I watch her unpack a laptop, a spiral notebook, a scratched water bottle, and a pack of Skittles from her tote. My stomach reflexively lurches when she pours the Skittles on the multi-use desktop before popping several in her mouth. There's no way that's sanitary. A custodian cleans the library throughout the day, but I doubt they wipe down the desktops.

She clicks on the decorative table lamp after plopping into the wooden chair that would be better suited at a dining table. Before I can avert my eyes, she kicks off a sandal and draws her foot up on the chair, revealing white polka-dotted bike shorts beneath her dress.

Cute.

The word spontaneously reverberates through my brain for the second time that day. The first time had been when she'd barely been able to meet my gaze earlier. Green Eyes is definitely not my type with her sweet, girl-next-door charm. The women I date are usually the female counterpart to myself—outgoing, career driven, and unafraid to take what they want.

The phone on my desk rings with Patricia from the circulation desk downstairs. "Mrs. Cook is here to speak to you."

Internally, I sigh, though I infuse my voice with cheerful warmth. "Thank you. I'll be right down."

Every other day, Carol Cook visits me to express her opinion that the historical archives should not be relocated to a designated area for better preservation. My goal is to move the ancient texts and artifacts of the island into a dedicated, temperature- and moisture-controlled room to better showcase and preserve their historical value. I truly thought the town would be behind me on this initiative, but it seems I could say "Bless you" after someone sneezes, and they'd still sneer at me.

After a riveting hour of being lectured at by Carol while arduously ignoring the spittle dripping from her smudged lipstick, I decide to take my time looking through the stacks downstairs before returning to my desk.

Fiction and non-fiction stacks divide the main floor, the town's historical books lining the back wall. An open atrium with high, stained-glass windows stretches directly above the main circulation desk and center display tables. The back staircases weave to the right to the upstairs reading area and librarian offices, or to the left to a half-flight portion, which contains several stacks of young-adult books before a set of glass doors leads to the children's room.

I run my finger along a fiction shelf. Half of the stacks bow beneath the weight of the books. Though I appreciate the overall aesthetic of the warm, wooden shelves, metal would be more practical and durable.

Yet another item for the list of improvements.

"What are you doing over here? I thought I put you on the center display last Tuesday?" a quiet female voice says from the other side of the stack. There's a hum and then, "I suppose someone could have borrowed you, read, and returned you in that time. How splendid!"

Stepping slowly, I gravitate toward the voice who's moved on to wondering aloud if the wallflower book should also join the bluestocking book on display. There's something familiar about the soothing tone of her words. The rounded Tidewater accent that Carol berated me with sounds wholly different from her lips. Light and lilting. I'm just about to turn the edge of the stack to see who's speaking when the voice's tone changes.

"Oh, no. No. No. No. Not now," she whines. "I'm not ready."

A frantic figure rounds the corner, and then, for the second time that day, Green Eyes slams into my chest—this time, face first. The two books in her hands clap on the sides of my arms as she tries to plow through me like a linebacker.

"You again." Her eyes are comically large before they shoot back toward the door.

I recognize the man from this morning's coffee shop kerfuffle, suit wrinkled slightly, bee-lining toward the hold shelf.

"Move." She pushes me again, and I step back so the large bookshelf conceals us both.

Green Eyes instantly flips and peers around the wooden edge, using the two paperbacks as a kind of shield for her face. It reminds me of hiding behind a newspaper in an old movie, and I can't help but laugh. Instantly, those eyes are on me again, this time pinched with warning as she puts her finger to her lips. The corner of my mouth quirks, but she doesn't catch it. Her attention is already back on the man pulling his phone from his pants pocket.

Since I'm a full head taller than her, I lean around the edge too. Coffee Shop Guy grabs his hold and uses the library card barcode on his phone to check it out at one of the automated kiosks. At least this branch is on par with the rest of the libraries regarding check-out procedures.

When he stops to adjust his glasses before running his hand through his hair, Green Eyes makes this wistful noise. It's so soft and sweet that a flare of irritation spirals through me.

Really? For that guy?

I quickly check myself because it's not like I should care.

With both books clutched to her chest, it seems she's forgotten about hiding. Coffee Shop Guy recycles his receipt and strides back through the automated front door. The way she slumps against the side of the bookcase swirls an enigmatic emotion that I don't know how to deal with, so I cover it with a quip.

"What is it that does it for you? The glasses? The suit? The general frantic demeanor?"

The look I receive is one of absolute bafflement, like she forgot I was standing twelve inches from her. Seriously? I can't walk into my favorite bar and not leave with at least six phone numbers—even with my new alias. Or at least I could when I used to live in civilization. Now, I have nothing to do at night in this tiny town but spend extra hours at the gym.

"Atticus isn't frantic. He's busy. There's a difference." A tightly coiled strand of chestnut hair springs over her shoulder as she straightens.

"Atticus?" I glance back at the exit. "Okay, he's got a good name. I'll give him that."

To Kill a Mockingbird is one of my favorites. I have a signed first edition, gifted to me from my grandmother before she passed. It was critically acclaimed literary works like that that fueled my decision for this career. Of course, it wasn't until I defied my family's lineage, choosing to earn a masters in library and information studies instead of following my older brother into the family business that I learned that librarianship is about so much more than literature.

"He's also a brilliant accountant."

When I snort, her pointer finger pins one of my vest buttons to my sternum. My cheek twitches reflexively. I did not see this fire coming from her. It's such a contrast from the shy-girl persona she embodied this morning—almost like I'm meeting two entirely different people.

Intriguing.

"Knock it off, mainlander. I've heard about you."

When I pointedly look at her hand with a wry smile, she quickly withdraws it. "Have you? And what have you heard, gorgeous?"

She blinks at the nickname. I know I'm laying it on a little thick, but I'm too interested in her reaction not to. Will she bark at me again for flirting so blatantly? Do I want her to?

"I know you want to destroy this library." The books are dropped into her bag so she can ball her hands on her hips, the stance accentuating her curves. "And I know you go through women like tissue paper."

I frown, taking another step back so her delicious magnolia and coffee-tinged scent will stop messing with my head. "I'm trying to improve this library, not that any of you people will see reason. And the status of my consensual relationships with other *mainlan-*

ders"—I use the word locals are so fond of—"isn't any of your, nor anyone else's, concern."

I have no earthly idea how she learned about my dating life, but I've always been upfront that I'm not interested in serious relationships. Not after...everything. The women I've spent time with over the last few years have been *more than agreeable* with that.

Our gazes are locked in such an unexpected battle of wits that both of us startle when another voice asks, "Excuse me. Could I get that book?"

THREE

Vivian

Come on! I know I made a wish, Ocean, but give a girl some grace. Because of course Atticus is standing right beside us, pointing toward the latest spy thriller that I and this....this infuriating stranger are blocking.

He's exactly as Brynn described when she dropped off a cinnamon roll earlier—self-centered and over-confident. My sister said the only reason he'd caught my fall was to use it as a strategic maneuver to gain town approval. My teeth had remained clenched all afternoon. I may not be able to communicate as effectively as others, but that shouldn't make me a helpless pawn in someone else's game.

The mainlander recovers before I do, stepping aside. "Excuse me."

23

Atticus reaches for the thick hardcover while my mind reels through what he could have heard. It takes everything in me not to pat my cheeks. My blush always makes me look ruddy and splotchy, and I'm sure I'm redder than Webster's Dictionary at the moment. Atticus glances at me as he leans back with his book, doing a subtle double-take.

For a second, I think I'll finally get my moment.

"Oh, it's you." Atticus smiles. "I saw you this morning as you gracefully averted that coffee spill. I'm so glad you're okay." Then he'll glance at the books in my tote. "Are you an Annie Ardent fan? Me too! I love how she brings modern feminism into Regency romance while—"

"Miss, are you alright?"

Miss. Atticus's manners and gentle voice almost assuage the fact that, any second now, I'll die of embarrassment. Because instead of speaking to my crush—who's *right in front* of me—I drifted into another daydream.

A desolate sigh leaves my mouth. At least I'll die in a place I love. I think of all the hours I spent curled up in the window nook as a child, luxuriating in every book I could. Since the nook faces the dunes of the wildlife preserve and not the ocean, it was always unoccupied and, in the afternoons, delectably sunny. The memory sends a pang of longing through me. It's been three years since I've done that.

Since the creation of my shop, I've spent my time trying to prove that it wasn't a waste of money to carve out essential real estate from our family's coffee shop for my business. Now, I only come to the library to rent a study room and go over my finances. It's a task I hate, but being surrounded by books makes it less soul-sucking. If I stayed in my shop, I'd sew until the sunlight waned instead of confirming that my fellow islanders have paid me for my work.

A determined inhale fills my lungs. If I make it through this, I'm going to take an afternoon off and read the newest Wellington novel in the window nook. Annie Ardent's Wellington series isn't as popular as the famed Worthington novels, but I try to help out the North Carolinian indie author as much as possible by subtly relocating her books from the stacks to the display tables whenever I'm in the building. The Worthington series, though older, has resurged in popularity thanks to the trendy Netflix show by the same name.

"She's fine." The stranger's cold tone makes me bristle.

Though I'm not usually bold, my instinct is to glare at this man. How dare he speak for me even though everyone else in town does it all the time? It's different when the people who raised me help me get my words out. They know about what happened, how there was half a year of silence afterward. When they help me, it's out of kindness. This mainlander doesn't have a benevolent bone in his body.

"Oh." Atticus looks at me again, an indiscernible emotion sliding over his cheekbones. "Okay, then."

I open my mouth to protest, but like usual, nothing comes out. Atticus watches me for half a breath before striding away. I don't have the strength to peek over the edge to see him check out his second book. Instead, I collapse against the bookcase, defeat bowing my shoulders. All I want is to dissolve into the ancient carpet, just like the grains of beach sand that people have tracked in. For a long moment, I think the stranger will take pity on me and finally leave me alone.

"Well, gorgeous. I've got good news. I just figured out a way we can help each other."

He's smiling when my chin snaps up. It should be distracting, how handsome he is leaning against the bookcase with those muscled forearms crossed over his chest, but now that I've confirmed the rumors that he's a *massive jerk*, the sheer darkness of his playful hair and the pooling amber of his eyes are less disorienting. I prefer Atticus's blond hair and blue eyes, anyway.

I'd planned on giving him one of Brynn's death stares and walking away but impulsively ask, "How's that?"

"Easy." His deepening smirk makes me want to claw at something the way Pepper demolishes her cat tower. "I need the people of this town to like me. You seem as local as they get. Am I right?"

I relinquish a small nod.

"Excellent." He picks an invisible piece of lint from his shirt sleeve. "You help me get on the good side of your fellow townspeople, and I'll teach you how to talk to him."

Having my sister's prediction confirmed is almost banal. Of course this man would only be interested in what I can do to serve his agenda. Except...if I agree, I'll be getting something out of this deal too. And if all the rumors of his love life are true, I should be receiving excellent instruction.

"I don't know..."

"Why don't I call Atticus back, and you can take another crack at it on your own?"

When he tries to lean past me, my movement is instinctual. My only thought is to keep us hidden. It's bad enough that I'll have to recover from my first two blunders. I'm not sure my battered heart can handle a third.

Rooting my feet, I push both palms against the mainlander's chest to keep him in place. He sucks in a surprised inhale as the fluorescent bulb above us flickers and then burns out. The gentle rustling of other library patrons hushes to silence. We're both staring at my sprawled fingers on the brushed wool of his vest. The weightless moment hovers for three thudding heartbeats until my thumb automatically rubs to appraise the wool's weight. When he jolts back, I barely catch myself from tumbling forward.

"So, um..." He tucks his hands in his pockets, clearing his throat. "Do we have a deal?"

My brows pinch as I blink rapidly, confused as to what just happened.

"I don't need help talking to Atticus."

It's a lie, but somehow I feel the need to defend myself, which is also something I never do. If only I'd been this bold a minute ago when Atticus had been in front of me.

"Yes, you do, gorgeous." The smarm he sends my way makes my nose wrinkle. "If you don't, then explain why you're able to have this conversation with me but can't utter a syllable when he's within earshot?"

I honestly don't know. Normally, I can't converse with strangers like I've been doing with him. My words are usually stilted as I constantly worry about saying the wrong thing.

"Because I don't like you."

That must be why. It's the only explanation.

Something unreadable flickers across his face before he raises a sardonic eyebrow. "Either way, you still need my assistance. With my dating experience, I can help you control those distracting, fluttery feelings that keep you tongue tied."

It's my turn to cross my arms. "And teach me to be a Casanova?"

His laugh sends a fissure of energy crackling through my bones, and I shift my shoulders to dissipate the sensation.

"If that's your term for someone who can be around a person they like without clamming up, then I have my work cut out for me."

"Would you prefer I call you"—I check off on my fingers—"a lothario? Libertine? Rogue? Knave?" All while I'm listing off names, he's shaking his head, a hint of a smile teasing the corner of his mouth. "A debauched rake?"

His large hand covers both of mine, stopping me. "Finn." That weird, fizzy sensation skips over my skin before he pulls his hand back. "My name is Finn. Finn Reynolds."

I tuck my fingers into the pockets of my dress and hesitate. "Vivian Hutchinson."

"Vivian." The smile on his face is more fascinated than conniving.

My shoulders tense as the events of the last few minutes catch up to me.

I should walk away.

I should walk away and chalk this whole interaction up to some odd swell of the tide. Because surely I'm not going to make a deal with this devilish man to win Atticus's heart. The sea is already throwing my crush at me. I just need to garner the confidence to strike up some small talk.

All that comes out of my mouth is, "How exactly would this arrangement work?"

Finn rubs his beard scruff, looking up and then scowling at the broken lightbulb. "It'll be an even exchange. One dating lesson for each time you convince a local that I'm not some sinister monster trying to destroy all they hold dear."

A chuff leaves my nose. My mentor and surrogate grandmother, whom I still call Miss Wendy even though I'm grown, might have used a very similar phrase to describe Finn when I delivered her weekly flowers yesterday morning.

All the snark leaves Finn with one large exhale. What's left behind is deceptively vulnerable. "It's bad, isn't it?"

I roll my lips inward. "People around here don't like change. It didn't help that after being here for two days, you defunded bingo snacks."

"This is a library." His tone hardens as he straightens, the glimmer of what I thought I saw gone. "It should serve the community. Providing snacks for a Friday night bingo game when that money could go toward something more important is reckless."

I meet his gaze, trying not to get distracted by the liquid quality of his irises. "Our library does serve our community. It's the center of our town. Most of us are readers and use the library in its strictest sense, but it's also where we gather. It's where we pass neighbors and catch up in addition to borrowing the latest bestseller. Many of the older islanders don't have a computer and use the media room to pay bills or email their grandkids."

"That's why I eliminated bingo snacks." He slides his hands into his pockets again, but this time, the stance is unmistakably powerful. "I want to update the computers, but that money has to come from somewhere. Not providing chips and soda on a weekly basis was an easy way to work toward that goal."

"I understand you believe that's the best option."

His dark brows raise. "What other option is there?"

The answer materializes instantly, but I don't show my hand. Instead, I close my eyes, taking a long, slow inhale. The potent scent of books and the lingering ocean brine flitting through the front door settles the buzzing at the base of my skull.

What if this arrangement worked? I know exactly how to help Finn Reynolds reach his goal. What if he really could help me win over Atticus? Having a dating coach sounds ludicrous, but it's certainly strange to run into Finn twice in one day after never seeing him before. What if my wish sent this man to help me? I know better than to ignore a gift from the sea. All islanders do.

When I open my eyes, Finn is watching me with a curious head tilt.

"You moved into the rental three houses down from the auto shop, right?"

"The auto shop?" he asks.

"Sorry. It used to be an auto shop. It's a...gym or something now."

"How..." Finn pauses, rubbing the back of his neck. The boyish gesture undermines his carefully coiffed appearance. "How do you know where I live?"

I shrug. "Small town."

"Right." He shakes his head. "I still need to get used to that."

I hoist the tote bag higher on my shoulder, an unfamiliar flush of confidence saturating my skin. "I've decided to take you up on your offer. Tonight, you can teach me how not to freeze in front of Atticus, and I'll give you a crash course in Wilks Beach history. I'll come over at sunset."

Before I can second-guess my brashness, I stride toward the exit. Remembering the books in my bag, I place two of my favorite Regency romances prominently on the central display. The theme is *Hot Summer Reads*, so these will fit right in. I give Patricia a quick wave goodbye as I pass the circulation desk. The desire to look back at Finn is a tangible thing, but I channel my inner-Brynn and march straight into the early evening sunlight.

We'll see each other soon enough.

FOUR

Vivian

I've been body snatched.

That's the only reasonable explanation for my erratic be-havior this evening. It's why I lied to my sister about going for a swim, walking past Dotty's market and the library before meander-ing down the beach. Then, like a madwoman—or a poorly trained spy—I buried my face beneath a hoodie, cut between houses, and dashed across the two-lane road that runs the length of Wilks Beach before trespassing through three bayside yards, ending at the dock behind Finn's.

Sweat drips down my temples as I strip off the hoodie and use the sleeves to mop my face. Our summer season doesn't officially start until Memorial Day, next Monday, but it's been unseasonably warm in the mid-eighties with high humidity. The instinct to jump into Back Bay is nearly as strong as the impulse to hustle home instead of marching up the grassy backyard toward Finn's rental house. I'm wearing my swimsuit beneath my shorts and graphic tee to corroborate the lie I sold Brynn, making the bay's siren song even harder to resist.

Turning my back to the seductive, glistening water, I study the asymmetrical roof of the quaint one-and-a-half-story house. Its yellow siding could use some work, but it looks like Rebecca, our resident realtor and rental property manager, has recently repainted the expansive deck leading to where I'm standing. A mature magnolia presides over the north side of the home, its sturdy branches brushing the exterior and obscuring the second-story window.

My sandals feel stuck to the thick centipede grass, but if I don't move toward the house, someone will see me. I've probably already been spotted. I hadn't thought about how easy it is to be witnessed, because I'd never had to hide before. I waved hello to no less than seven locals on the beach before ducking behind a seaside home's outdoor shower stall to pull the hoodie out of my tote.

A maniacal laugh bubbles from my throat, thinking of this whole escapade.

Clearly, I'm not cut out for covert operations, because I'm losing it. It's just...the idea of people's heads exploding over me—reserved, quiet Vivian—creeping toward the house of the dreaded new librarian for a secret rendezvous is *oddly satisfying*. Unlike my sister, I never snuck out of the house as a teen or gave anyone a reason to worry.

Fortified by my small act of defiance, I march up the deck, pushing the hoodie into my whale-printed canvas tote. The sleeve of the sweater drapes down, covering the waving flipper of the cartoon humpback and his *"Whale hello there!"* speech bubble.

You've got this sails from my lips in rhythmic repeats as I raise my hand to knock on the sliding glass door leading to the backyard. With my shadow cast on the glass, I can finally see through it instead of the reflection of the rose-gold glimmers of the setting sun behind me.

My eyes widen as my movement halts. Actually, halt isn't a strong enough word. I freeze. A full and complete whole-body paralysis. Even my cells cease wiggling, my blood screeching to a stop in my veins.

Finn—completely oblivious to my presence—looks up and does the same thing. And thank goodness, because prior to seeing me, his hands were unbuckling the black leather belt on his slacks. It's bad enough that his vest and shirt are already unbuttoned, showing a distracting sliver of tanned skin.

I know I'm in the wrong here. Okay? Finn is halfway through the single-story, open-concept living room, on the way to the stairs where his bedroom must be. He probably expected me to knock at the front door like a sane person, not surprise him through a pane of *impeccably transparent* glass. Not a streak mars the slick surface, not a single smudged fingerprint.

Finn blinks a handful of times before my stomach flips at the slight quirk of his lips. My brain screams at me to do something—close my eyes, turn my head. *Something*. But a devious flick in the back of my skull keeps my gaze locked on Finn's. I expect him to saunter over to me and prove he's the shameless flirt he'd hinted at at the library. Maybe puff out his chest and slide his hands into his pockets to accentuate the alluring gap in fabric.

When Finn slowly pulls on the buckle, the belt beginning to slip from its loops, I flip and crouch like I'm at the air show and an F/A-18 Hornet just shocked me with a low-altitude fly by. All those frozen body parts jump into action—blood rushing in my ears, heart scaling my windpipe, lungs working double-time.

My eyes are still squeezed shut when I hear the sliding door unlock behind me.

"Calm down, gorgeous. It's just a belt," Finn calls from the other side of the glass.

When I make absolutely no movement, he says through a laugh, "Count to ten then come in. I'm going to get changed."

I count to twenty—okay, forty—and then I take a series of deep breaths. By the time I let myself into Finn's rental, he's busying himself in the kitchen, wearing black exercise shorts and a snug, dark-gray t-shirt, running shoes on his feet. Varied powders enter a mixing cup before he begins shaking them with water.

"I've got an hour before—"

"Don't do that again," I blurt.

Fighting the urge to wrap both hands around the straps of my tote to steady them, I set them on my hips. Brynn once told me as kids that standing in a Superman pose before undertaking difficult tasks helps one to feel more confident.

"Do what?" He cocks a single eyebrow.

"You're not going to play games with me. I don't want to be at the receiving end of whatever you think women are interested in. This is a business arrangement. Don't forget that you need me a lot more than I need you."

I wish Brynn were here right now. I've never spoken to *anyone* this way, and I desperately want my sister to not only witness it but to give me a congratulatory high five. My skin is buzzing like it's lit within from thousands of sparklers.

Finn's eyes widen as something resembling pride wisps over his perfectly dark brows. A warm sensation ribbons through my chest before I give myself a mental shake. I don't need or want this man's approval.

"I apologize for startling you, but I thought it would be best if I wasn't seen knocking on your front door. People talk in small towns, and I don't want anyone knowing I'm meeting with you."

A shadowy emotion flickers over his amber irises before Finn uncaps the bottle he'd been shaking and drops a weird little metal ball into the sink.

"Understandable." He takes a gulp of the beige liquid. "Can't have our precious little lamb frolicking with the big bad wolf."

That description grates, even though I've received some version of it my whole life. I should be used to being the soft, sweet half of the Hutchinson twins, but lately, the idea of everyone thinking of me as a docile nobody makes my skin itch. For years, I'd been happy to be coddled, to be given the easy way out of conversations or social engagements, but now everyone thinking I'm helpless makes bile creep up my throat. I need to prove to the town—to myself—that I'm not.

Talking to Atticus is just the first step. The secrets I've been hiding in the closet of my shop are a mountain-sized leap.

"I'm glad you understand the situation," I say, lifting my chin.

Who even *am I* right now? I've never been so brash in my life.

Instead of apologizing for the biting remark, I change the subject.

"I spoke to Dr. Prescott while he was walking his three Great Danes on the way here. He and his wife routinely donate to the library, and I told him you were looking to update the computers in the media room to better serve our community."

"Oh, really?" Finn sets one large hand on the counter, leaning sideways into it. The casual position shouldn't be enticing, but his raw magnetism forces me to look away.

I focus on Rebecca's interior design instead. Finn hasn't added any personal touches to the space, but that's not entirely unexpected since he's recently moved in and is an unscrupulous bachelor.

"Really," I say with a casual shrug. "If you want to succeed in getting people to like you, then you should get to know them. Dr.

P's benevolence is why my teeth are straight." I run my tongue over them automatically.

"He gives a significant discount to local kids. Most of us wouldn't be able to afford orthodontics otherwise. Dr. P should have retired years ago, but he loves his job so much he keeps driving to his practice on the mainland every day. He's also Santa at the annual Christmas tree lighting ceremony." I drop my bag on the galley countertop separating us. "His wife, Lidia, is an equine therapist."

"A what?"

"She helps kids with autism and cerebral palsy gain confidence through working with horses at a ranch in Pungo. The therapy riding program also works with veterans with PTSD."

Finn blows out a breath. "Starting strong by getting on the good side of the saints of Wilks Beach."

I bristle at his mocking tone. "Most of the people here are just as giving as the Prescotts. It's a good community."

"You'll forgive me if I don't believe you since I haven't exactly been welcomed with warm hugs."

My lips twist to the side, considering—definitely not because I'm fighting a smile. "The town's history does make us standoffish toward mainlanders." He scoffs, rolling his eyes while taking another gulp. "You'll understand once you've heard the stories of how outsiders have tried to take advantage of Wilks Beach residents."

When Finn opens his arms wide, it's a challenge not to fixate on his firm pecs. "I'd love to hear them."

"Our bargain was one wooed townsperson for a dating lesson." I tap my fingernails on the counter in what I hope is a nonchalant way. "I did my part."

"Did you?" he challenges.

"Yes." My gaze narrows on his. "Dr. Prescott said he appreciated your initiative to improve the media room, and he intends to call later this week to discuss providing an additional donation toward your cause. And because us *islanders* protect our own, we've taken steps to maintain as much autonomy as we can. I'm sure you've learned that donations given directly to our library aren't shared with the greater library system."

Finn's eyes don't leave mine, but the tense tick of his jaw muscles confirms that he's already been educated on how our library, though connected with all the other Virginia Beach libraries, maintains an independent budget.

"Okay. Fair is fair." He rubs his beard scruff, setting down his half-empty cup. "What is it about your *dream man* that's making you freeze?"

Ignoring the snark lacing his words, I let my vision drift to the decorations above the upper cabinets. Like most Wilks Beach home decor, they're nautical in nature. Dust coats the square white-washed wood planks painted with blue crabs, shells, and sea turtles.

"I don't know if it's Atticus so much as it's speaking in general." The honest answer stings as it leaves my throat.

"You spoke to Dr. Prescott earlier."

My head gives an annoyed shake, but I don't turn my attention back to Finn. "That's different. I can hold simple conversations with people I know. I have a hard time with strangers."

I can almost feel Finn's argument that he's a stranger, but he doesn't voice it.

"What if we came up with a series of conversation starters for you to use when you feel tongue-tied?"

I huff. "Give me some credit. You don't think I haven't watched public-speaking videos or read blog posts on overcoming extreme shyness? Knowing that I should ask Atticus what his ideal vacation is, or if he had a childhood pet, or about his favorite band doesn't mean that those words will fall readily from my lips."

When I glance at Finn, a bemused expression brightens his features.

"What?"

"Nothing."

"What is it?" I put more grit into the question, which only deepens his smile.

"I like your word choices. Not many people would say 'fall readily from my lips.'"

"Oh." I can feel my cheeks flaming. I often mimic the vocabulary and speech patterns found in my favorite Regency romances, but usually, the only person who hears me saying "To be sure" instead of "You're right" is my sister.

Turning to face the adjoined high-ceilinged living room, I plop into an upholstered accent chair. The well-loved piece faces the long bank of windows, and the water beyond it allows me to get my bearings.

"Any idea of what I should do instead?" I hazard a glance toward the kitchen, noting that Finn has rounded the counter, protein-drink abandoned.

He rubs his scruff again as he steps toward the window. My shoulders settle into the chair while Finn surveys his backyard, thinking. The silence between us isn't stilted like it often ends up being when I converse with other locals, when an uncomfortable pause will drop like a stone, almost as if they're afraid to continue talking, before they make a well-meaning excuse to let me out of the conversation.

When he finally turns, the gleam in Finn's eyes makes my hands grip the wooden armrests. I instinctively know I'm not going to like his next suggestion.

"I think what you need is a high frequency of low-value interactions."

My brows pinch. "What does that even mean?"

"It means, dear Vivian"—my blood pressure spikes when his gaze rakes my appearance in an assessing way—"that we're going out."

"Out?" The squeaky quality of my voice is embarrassing, but I'm too shaken to care. "But you have somewhere to be. You said you only had an hour."

I feel very much the little lamb to his wolf with the way Finn prowls toward me, but I can't seem to convince my legs to lift me from the chair.

"I don't mind changing plans." Amusement colors his voice. "I think what you really need is a wingman. We'll drive to Virginia Beach, hit a couple bars." He lifts a shoulder. "Every guy goes through this, learning how to talk to women, realizing it's a numbers game. You just need practice."

Shifting in my chair, I collect the lumpy mermaid pillow I've been leaning on and hug it to my chest. It makes a measly shield, but I'll take anything at this point. "I don't need to talk to all the men, just Atticus."

Finn chuckles, whisper-breathing *all the men* before crossing his arms. "Talking to men you don't care about is how you garner the confidence to eventually talk to your crush."

My head shakes on its own, my heartbeat pounding in my ears.

"Yes, gorgeous," Finn says through a growing smile.

I'm about to dig in. I'll live in this chair from here on out. It's now fused to my spine. Finn doesn't know it, but I can be incredibly stubborn. I'd like to see him try to get me *and this chair* into whatever he drives—something flashy, I'm sure. A sports car with an obnoxiously noisy engine that draws attention as he zips by.

I almost snort at the audacity before a realization makes my intestines twist.

Tall, muscular Finn has already lifted me. He could easily pluck me from my protective chair if he really wanted to. I'm average height at five foot five, but I'm curvy. Due to the blessing of being raised by my Aunt Tammy—a headstrong, body-positive woman—I never grew up hating my curves. Aunt Tammy celebrated my voluptuous frame while simultaneously assuring Brynn that her natural thinness was perfect for her.

"Everyone is given exactly what they need," Aunt Tammy likes to say.

Of course, we both succumbed to peer pressure as teens. There were a few rocky moments in high school that had me skipping meals and Brynn stuffing her A-cup bralette. And there are still times when I compare myself to "the ideal body type" and feel insecure, but now...one single thought flashes in my mind, insistent and shocking as an alarm siren.

What would it feel like to be tossed over Finn's sturdy shoulders?

"Vivian."

Finn saying my name jolts me back to the room, but instead of looking up like a normal person, I rocket to standing, not realizing that Finn is hovering over me. He reels back, holding his nose, as a stinging sensation radiates through the crown of my head. One hand flies to my forehead as the other grips his upper arm.

"I'm sorry. I didn't mean—" But then blood drips between his fingers, and little gray spots flood my vision.

Self-protective instincts have me fleeing to the door, slipping on my sandals while I talk. "I'm sorry. I really am, but we'll have to go another time. Blood makes me—" I dry heave. Even saying the word makes me nauseated. My hand grips the glass, leaving a sweaty handprint as I double over and suck in an uneven breath.

"It's okay," Finn says as I hear the kitchen sink running. "Go if you need to. I'm fine."

I take his words at face value, nod toward my stricken reflection, and let myself out in the balmy evening air.

FIVE

Finn

Someone is playing a joke on me. Or maybe this is a Wilks Beach hazing ritual? Either way, one of my librarians has some serious ninja skills and a dry sense of humor because books keep *appearing* on my desk each time I return to my office.

I pick up today's third book, *Leading with Compassion*, frankly offended. Being a strong leader wasn't just something that'd been drilled into me since before I attended kindergarten; it's a skill I excel at. I stack the book atop the other two: *A History of Wilks Beach*, which I intend to check out this weekend, and a random book on decor for the seaside home.

Yesterday's books were all Regency romances—four of them, delivered separately but from the same series. After returning from lunch, I'd asked Patricia if there was a particular reason I'd received them. As the head of circulation, maybe she was putting together a collection for a display and wanted to run them by me.

The middle-aged mom of five—see, I *always* get to know my staff—blinked from beneath her wrinkled brow and then told me to ask Robert. I simply returned to my desk, doubtful that the septuagenarian who has a habit of falling asleep at the reference desk was the one giving me bodice rippers.

Maybe the mysterious book giver is Trudy, the children's librarian?

I collapse behind my desk, agitating my computer mouse and bringing up the budget that I'd been examining earlier. Not for the first time since I drastically altered the course of my future, my molars grind at the fact that my father's money could easily fix the funding issues I've spent the last five years trying to finagle through proper channels.

All I want is to keep this infrastructure alive, to ensure that libraries stay open and free, allowing anyone the ability to find *anything*. I want to help them continue to resist censorship and protect knowledge, especially in a world with so much misinformation on the internet. I might have initially chosen librarianship because of my love of literature, but I truly believe it's one of the noblest professions.

Noting the blinking light on my desk phone, I check my messages. The tension in my temple upticks when it's another scathing voicemail from Carol Cook instead of one from Dr. Prescott. He hasn't called in the two days since Vivian and I struck up our unusual agreement.

I sit up straighter as my second voice message plays. Lynnette, the reference librarian from my former library, who—though thirty years my senior—has always had a tiny crush on me, informs me that the timeline for my plan has changed.

Ralph might be retiring sooner than expected. A *lot* sooner. Pressure builds behind my left eye, threatening to fully encapsulate my exhausted brain. When I had a whole year to enact my plan, it seemed feasible. Now, I need all the pieces to fall into place flawlessly, or it's not just me that'll be affected.

My younger sister's life will be ruined.

I ignore the white-hot flare that burns each time I think of how my father tethered our little agreement to Cordelia's future and close my eyes to reorganize my thoughts. I need to focus on what I can achieve right now.

The library voice message system cuts off the rest of Lynnette's meandering phone call, updating me on her ferrets' most recent dental issues. As I hang up the receiver, I allow the other person who's been taking up too much of my mental load to float into my mind.

Vivian.

Surprising, captivating Vivian.

I don't believe she'd lie about Dr. Prescott wanting to donate money, but I hardly know anything about her. Even the contents of her discarded tote—a single magnolia- and coffee-scented hoodie—were unhelpful. There was no wallet. No cell phone. No hint to where she might live.

Nothing.

And since we all know how much the locals love me, my casual questions about Vivian were ignored. An elderly man in the checkout line at Dotty's Market *actually reshelved* his two items and walked out rather than talked to me.

Normally, my cultivated charm would have done the trick by now. Years of practiced charisma almost never fails you. I've never struggled to fit in, because I've known exactly which parts of my personality to subvert, how to play by everyone else's rules, and give them exactly what they want, tell them precisely what they want to hear.

I've got to hand it to the people of this town; their dedication to a cause is admirable. Now, if only I could get them to focus on the necessary library updates instead of hating me.

I sigh, mousing to another page. Vivian's information is sitting right there in the library system—full name, address, phone number, email—but finding her that way feels slimy. Instead, I open a web browser and type in *Vivian, Wilks Beach*.

A laugh bursts from me as I read the first result.

I hadn't noticed that the tailor shop beside Seabreeze Beans is named Vivian's Alterations. With the long hours I've been keeping, the drawn-curtained store had seemed perpetually closed. And according to the photo posted online, the shop's name is only painted in small green script on the glass door.

That explains how Vivian's sundress fit her like a bespoke glove. My fingers twitch, remembering the feel of the soft fabric and the way her ribs expanded as I lifted her beyond the coffee spill. Her business listing states hours from ten a.m. to six p.m. and by appointment. If I leave now, I'll just catch her. After packing up, I lock my office door to stop the ninja librarian from striking overnight.

Robert—looking livelier than I've seen him in days—gives me a curt nod on my way to the stairs. Pools of magenta, teal, and citrine light stream from the atrium's stained-glass windows as I descend. I can't help but open my palm in a shaft of periwinkle.

Almost every pane of glass contains a nautical tableau: mermaids resting on rocks, ships sailing, schools of striped bass frozen in blue glass. This historic building is undoubtedly the most beautiful library I've ever worked in. The urge to protect it and the town's archives makes me pick up speed.

"Mr. Reynolds?" Patricia's reedy voice sounds the second I reach the main floor.

"How can I help you?" I ask. Even though it feels like I can hear the ticking of my watch in my eardrums, I force my shoulders to relax.

"I've got it from here, Patty. No need for formal introductions." A barrel-chested man leans over the circulation counter to pat her forearm, giving a charmingly straight smile. "Hey there. You must be the man who's bold enough to shake things up around here."

Before I have a chance to launch a polite defense, he barks a disarming laugh and slaps my back like we're buddies.

"And it's a good thing. I swear some of the computer towers in the media room still have floppy drives." His proffered hand is roughly the size of a baseball glove. "Dave Prescott."

I match his smile and firm handshake with my own. "Finn Reynolds."

Things are *finally* going my way.

SIX

Finn

After casually walking Dave—as he insisted I call him—to his car in the parking lot behind the library, I glance at my watch, knowing I'm too late. It was six o'clock when I subtly edged us toward the exit. I force my feet to continue on a mildly paced trajectory, though I want to sprint like a crocodile is behind me.

I *need* this unusual agreement with Vivian to work.

Dave wasn't only accommodating; he was downright friendly—all because Vivian had had a simple conversation with him. I hadn't realized how starved I was for a polite interaction after almost four weeks of curt brush-offs. And Dave's donation idea—for me to organize and host a fundraising event at the library, after which he'll match the total amount raised—seems easy enough. I'd been

51

attending galas before I had chest hair, so I'm sure I can come up with something that'll meet town approval.

As expected, Vivian's Alterations is closed when I arrive. A defeated sigh leaves my lungs as I clutch the sun-warmed metal handle and give it a shake. I'll have to stop by during lunch tomorrow. My fingers release the handle a second before the heavy green curtain is yanked aside, and my gaze crashes with Vivian's.

A sharp, tingling sensation cascades down my arms as we stare at each other. Then the memory of the last time we were separated by a pane of glass sails to the front of my mind. Vivian's eyes glaze slightly, almost as if she's recalling that moment as well. A smirk lifts my lips as my gaze sweeps her frame.

Today's sleeveless dress is deep lavender. I'm inexplicably drawn to the subtle way the loose fabric cascades down her body and simultaneously grateful this dress isn't like the form-fitting green one.

Another memory rushes forward, of us between the library stacks as Vivian's thumb brushed my chest, and how that single touch felt...transformative.

Mentally, I give myself a swift kick in the pants—much like I've been doing for the last two days when this particular thought demands my attention. No matter what I think I felt, my relationship with Vivian needs to remain platonic. The chances of finding another Wilks Beach resident to help me with my plans are slim, especially now that I'm in a time crunch.

Still, I can't help quirking an eyebrow and seeing if she'll verbally spar with me again.

"How's that belt memory treating you?" I pause, deepening my flirty smile. "Do you revisit it often?"

The flush overtaking Vivian's face is the most delightful shade. If I was particular to pink, I'd use that color in the guest room of my rental house. My personal books have been in storage for years, but there's something about the layout of the upstairs room overlooking the bay that would make an idyllic home library. The soft-pink color would complement the way the sunset light bends through the windows in the evening.

Then Vivian's eyes narrow, and a bubble of victory slips over my skin. Nothing is as fun as teasing this woman. Her lips dive into a defiant frown before she flicks the curtain closed.

"I can stand out here all day," I say, louder than necessary. "I wonder who would notice the evil librarian waiting for—"

The fabric is cast aside as Vivian quickly unlocks and pushes the door open. "Come in. Come in. Just be quiet."

"Thanks, gorgeous." I wink as I stroll past her, smiling at the slight growl I receive in return.

The shop is chaotic, garments and fabric strewn this way and that. There are two smaller tables containing various types of sewing machines and another long wooden table littered with zippers, boxes of buttons, and fabric scraps. Dozens of colorful bobbins hang from a pegboard on the wall shared with the coffee shop, while rolls of fabric fill the bookcases running along the other wall. A half-clothed dress form, a rolling clothing rack, and three standing lamps fill out the tiny space.

When I turn, Vivian is still beside the door. The very front of the store is so orderly in comparison that my brows quirk. An octagonal step riser rests beside an antique settee. Beyond those, a tri-fold dressing screen provides privacy. Another standing lamp lights the corner, casting a warm glow on the closed drapes. They're elaborate, the drapes. Victorian? A second layer of tan brocade fabric swoops over the curtain rod with beaded accents hanging down like fringe.

There's no natural light now that the drapes are closed. Annoyance runs down my forearms. Vivian shouldn't be sealed away in this darkened space. She should be radiant in the golden sunlight. I have the strangest impulse to take a sledgehammer to the wall facing Dotty's Market and replace it with picture windows.

My hand flexes before I notice how Vivian is standing, shoulders hunched while twisting a silver ring on her pinky finger. I love teasing her, but only because she fires back. I never want Vivian to feel belittled or insecure, especially not in her space.

Changing tactics, I grip my chin and tilt it upward. "As you can see, my nose isn't broken. Thanks for asking."

When she huffs and blows past me, the twisting in my stomach lessens.

"What do you want?" Vivian sits at one of the machines, feeding fabric through the needle at a racing speed.

"I thought you might need this back." I pull her folded hoodie and tote from my leather messenger bag, setting them on the largest table—a tiny pile of order amid her disorganized havoc of boxes of beads and silvery ribbons.

"Also, we need to decide when we're going"—at the last minute, I use her lingo in an attempt to speak on common ground—"to the mainland for our speech experiment. I was thinking tomorrow night."

The sewing machine stops for a second before continuing, its noisy whirr dominating the small space. Somewhere in the background, an old seventies song whispers about heartache.

"About that . . ." She rolls her lips inward, focusing on her work and ignoring that I've moved directly in front of her machine. "I've reconsidered. I've decided I don't need to change."

"Frankly, I agree with you." Her startled eyes only bounce to mine for the briefest second.

Anyone who takes the time to get past that initial quiet exterior would see the enticing spitfire beneath. If I wasn't already under extreme pressure to ensure my sister's future, I'd pour my energy into getting to know Vivian better.

"Regardless of my unwanted opinion"—when I receive a derisive snort, I know I'm on the correct path—"you were right when you said that I need you more than you need me."

I stretch my arms wide.

"Haven't my actions proved that? Here I am, hunting you down at your place of business, throwing myself at your compassion. I am a desperate, desperate man."

The corner of her mouth twitches. I'm so close to winning the adrenaline rush of victory singes my nerve endings.

"Please, Vivian." I rest my hand over my heart. "Take pity."

A sigh accompanies her full smile, and I swear it's the triumph that has me breathless, not the sweet curve of her lips.

"If I agree to help you, can you promise not to be so"—she rolls her hand in my direction—"over the top?"

"Absolutely not." My hand curls into a resolute fist at my sternum. "Dramatics are part of the deal."

When a peal of surprised laughter escapes her lips, my chest threatens to expand past the capacity of my ribs. I rub my knuckles against my breastbone before tucking my hands into my pockets.

She looks to the ceiling as if asking for guidance from above before settling her gaze on me. "Can't I just help you without talking to all the men?"

I chuckle, murmuring *all the men*, before forcefully straightening my lips. "No, gorgeous. Let's make this an arrangement that benefits us both."

Normally, I wouldn't look a gift horse in the mouth, but the idea of taking advantage of Vivian is as appealing as cutting out my own tongue.

She deflates, hunching over her sewing machine. "I'm going to fail."

A laugh punches from me. "Of course you will."

Before Vivian can snap her gaze back to her hands, I catch her chin with my thumb and forefinger, gently keeping her eyes on mine.

"You're supposed to fail. Over and over and *over* again. You're supposed to fail and feel like crap and then try again. That's how we get better. That's how we learn." I gesture to the fabric in her hands, letting my fingers reluctantly fall from her soft skin. "Did you succeed at this the first time you tried?"

She wrinkles her nose, and though I knew she'd be displeased at my words, I didn't expect this small movement to be so endearing. I have to force myself to focus on the rainbow of bobbins to gain control over my breathing.

"No, but I don't remember struggling as much with it. It sort of . . . flowed like water."

"Okay," I say, reaching up to push a precarious spool back on its peg. "You were a natural. So am I at most things. The rest you'll have to work for." I almost tense, realizing I'm going to repeat my father's words, but they're as true today as they were the first fifteen hundred times he told them to me. "Nothing worth having comes easily."

I leisurely peruse her fabrics before returning my attention back to Vivian. The analytical way she's looking at me makes me rub the back of my neck.

"What?"

"No one has ever 'tough-loved' me before." She tilts her head to the side, a cascade of ringlets sliding over her bare shoulder. "Everyone just lets me off the hook. Doesn't expect much from me." A muscle in her jaw ticks.

The need to ease the tension in her cheek is visceral. "Trust me, dating coaches are just as tough as any other coach."

"I wouldn't know." She shrugs. "I've never had a coach before."

Seventy-six questions about her upbringing clamor for attention, but I focus on logistics. "What time should I pick you up tomorrow?"

That darned nose wrinkle again. "Let's meet at the water tower at nine."

"You're kidding."

A curly strand falls over her eyes when she shakes her head, her fingers tucking it away before I can. "It's the best way to ensure that no one sees us together."

I make a show of rolling my eyes and huffing, hopefully drawing attention away from how my hand automatically fisted at her words.

"Until our next clandestine meeting." My heavy wink evokes another annoyed glare.

"Goodbye, Finn," Vivian deadpans.

Though my stroll to the exit is unhurried, my heart is hammering like I've just finished a record-breaking one hundred meters. I hold the door open just long enough to pull Vivian's attention.

"Oh, and, gorgeous? Wear something nice." I allow the heavy door to swing shut, silencing her rebuttal.

SEVEN

Vivian

The only thing keeping me from completely hyperventilating the next night while out with Finn is the sweet, briny breeze flowing through the open floor-to-ceiling windows. Everything else about this bar makes me uncomfortable—the sheer number of people, the rib-vibrating base of the trendy music, and the upscale decor.

Not to mention the bank-breaking cost of the drinks. Clara, the owner of Wilks Beach's sole bar and restaurant, Bayside Table, charges nine dollars for her classic orange crush cocktail as opposed to this Virginia Beach Oceanfront bar's seventeen dollars. Maybe they're upcharging because it's Memorial Day weekend?

At least I'm wearing my favorite dress. It's a muted-teal chiffon with capped sleeves. I'd designed a mini corset into the waistline before letting the flowy, layered fabric cascade to my knee. The corset is purely decorative, giving the garment visual structure while maintaining comfort. Like all my dresses, the square neckline doesn't come but an inch below my collarbones.

Though my mentor, Miss Wendy, likes to say that I'm *blessed in all the right places*, I still prefer to conceal my top-half blessings as much as possible.

"First round is on me." Finn's voice pulls my frowning face from the cocktail menu. "Second round is on"—he glances around, that mischievous smirk deepening—"any number of these gentlemen."

"Or we could go home and—"

He holds up a finger. "Ah-ah. No more of that."

Half of the drive here, I tried to get Finn to turn his understated but undeniably luxurious, storm-gray Aston Martin around and abandon this ill-fated plan.

"Let me find you a willing subject." He lifts his chin, subtly surveying the crowd.

I barely repress my body's traitorous reaction to him. Why does he have to be so beautiful? I'm convinced that storybook heroes are modeled after Finn Reynolds. Earlier, when he'd been casually leaning against the hood of his car, waiting for me, I almost stumbled. Not because I was walking in the dark. The entirety of Wilks Beach is embedded in my brain. I could navigate it blindfolded. It was how breathtaking Finn was in the subtle moonlight.

He'd worn tailored black, head to toe, but forsaken his signature vest and socks. The strange pulse of heat that shot through me upon seeing his bare ankles only confirmed that I'm not right in the head.

Finn is as unattainable as the gorgeous three-story ocean-facing homes. Perfect for someone else but never for you. You can always look as you walk down the beach, but that's never going to be your home.

When I Googled Finn yesterday, double-checking that he wasn't a psycho in addition to being ridiculously hot, there wasn't much on him besides glowing accolades from the various libraries he's worked at after getting his masters. Brynn must have known a woman who he'd personally wronged to have the details about his dating history. Though Wilks Beach residents usually stick to our town, many have family who live on the mainland.

I hadn't asked Brynn for more details about Finn because I knew she'd disapprove of this whole escapade. Brynn's natural state is to protect me, but I can't fall in love with Atticus if I'm always at home, reading Regency novels and watching TV.

Since my sister always goes to bed early, I didn't have to lie to her about leaving tonight. My night owl personality has always clashed with her wake-at-four-thirty lifestyle. Fortunately, our bedrooms are above my shop, so the mainland commuters stumbling into Seabreeze Beans first thing don't wake me at the crack of dawn. That and I have an impressive ocean-waves sound machine.

Finn leans his elbows on the white marble bar, pulling my attention back to the present. His perfect-black shirt is Italian cotton. I just know it. Which designer, I'm not sure. Kiton? Zegna? Either way, Finn isn't exactly hiding that he comes from money. No one with a librarian's salary could afford this caliber of luxury menswear.

"What is it?" Finn asks.

The amusement in his voice doesn't fluster me like it usually does. Perhaps I'm developing an immunity to his effortless charm. Since we've officially embarked on this crazy dating-coach adventure, I suppose that's a good thing.

"Who designed your shirt?"

"My shirt?" The corner of his mouth quirks.

I nod, my gaze flowing from the lapels to the sleeve where it's rolled just below his elbows.

"Brioni."

"Should have guessed," I mutter.

"What's that?" He raises his voice to be heard over the din.

"Can I touch the fabric?"

Expecting Finn to poke fun at me, I'm surprised when he simply extends his arm. My thumb and forefinger pinch the cuff and roll it as I let out an approving hum. Even though the evening is warm, he'll be comfortable in this decadent, breathable shirt. My fingers slide to assess the seam, and the heel of my hand brushes his exposed forearm. Finn pulls his arm back like the slight contact was painful.

"You probably shouldn't do that while you're trying to talk to *all the men.*" His roguish smile lifts. "They'll think we're a couple."

"Right," I say, even though his suggestion is ludicrous.

Someone like Finn would *never* consider dating someone like me.

Before I can fully tailspin, I'm saved by a bartender who's a dead ringer for the actress starring in season two of *Worthington*. The next book being adapted into the popular Netflix series is one of my favorites. Bluestocking Elizabeth begins a clandestine dalliance with a gruff soldier, emotionally scarred from the Battle of Waterloo, only to find that he's secretly a duke. I *cannot wait* for season two to release later this summer.

After we've both had a sip of our cocktails, Finn asks, "See the group of three men at the high top?" He turns his back to the men and points to his left shoulder. I stand on tiptoe to glance over. Since heels are the devil, I'm wearing sparkly ballet flats.

"Yeah."

"The one in the green polo has been eyeing you for the last two minutes."

My gaze catches Finn's. "He has?"

"Yes, gorgeous." This time, his smile isn't flirtatious or teasing. There's this dark, indiscernible undertone. "And the one in the ill-fitting suit at your four o'clock, the two men in dress blues, the bald guy who could be your father at your six, and the—"

"Stop." I frame my face with my hands, closing my eyes.

"Vivian." The amused wonder in my name has me glancing up. "Do you really not know how beautiful you are?"

My lungs can no longer bring oxygen into my body. This seventeen-dollar cucumber-infused gin and tonic must be laced with toxins. My eyelids seem to work, however, since they're blinking like I'm stuck in a dust storm.

Finn's eyes survey my face in a quick swoop before he winks.

Right.

Finn wasn't saying *he thought* I was beautiful. He's just bolstering my ego before I attempt something I've never done before.

Like a good coach.

The fact that disappointment swims in my stomach is so juvenile. I don't even want this perfect specimen of human masculinity. I want Atticus with his glasses and floppy hair and soft demeanor.

Atticus is attainable.

Safe.

Finn is...

"Green Polo seems to be buying the drinks tonight, and they're all getting low." Finn interrupts my thoughts, casually turning his body toward the bar. "Why don't you move down to that end? He'll get thirsty real quick."

The reality of what I'm about to do slams into me like a freight train. My head starts to shake, slowly at first and then with more vigor as my gaze drops to the floor.

I can't do this.

I don't know why I ever thought I could do something like this. I should get used to solo snuggling on the couch because there's no way any of this is going to work. Maybe I should just get another cat. Pepper is ridiculously territorial, but—

"Viv," Finn says, lightly touching my wrist to get my attention. "Just walk down the bar. You don't have to do anything. He'll come to you. When he starts talking, just smile and nod. We'll work on words with the next guy."

I press my lips together to tamp down the swell of nausea.

Finn's gaze is steady on mine. "I believe you can do this. But if this first time is terrible, we can come back another day, okay? Just try this once, and I'll take you home after."

There's an unbearable sweetness to his tone, in the way he gives my wrist an encouraging squeeze before letting go. It's completely incongruent with the suave version of himself he's shown me thus far.

My shoulders collapse with a shaky exhale. "All I have to do is walk down the bar?"

His mouth softens, that wisp of pride resurfacing. "Just walk down the bar."

"Okay," I murmur, turning before I lose momentum.

When I weave past the eighth person, my steps become even more hesitant. But then, the guy separates from his friends, and as I arrive at the end, he finds an open spot beside me.

"Three more," he says to the bartender before smiling at me. "Hey."

My "hey" is little more than a croak, and I can't help glancing at Finn. He's turned so his back and elbows rest on the bar, watching me.

"Is that guy your boyfriend?"

My focus snaps from Finn's flinty eyes to the man's face. I wasn't supposed to have to answer questions. I was supposed to smile and nod. My lips tremble at the edges as I force them up, focusing on the man's features to distract myself. Paying attention to colors and textures usually settles the buzzing that hovers at the base of my skull. The man's beard has some red in it, as does his sandy hair. It complements his green shirt nicely. His features aren't remarkable, but he seems friendly.

I shake my head, hoping it's enough.

"Because I don't want to get caught in between—"

"No." I'm so shocked by my sharp refusal that my teeth chomp on the inside of my cheek. "Um..."

Think. It shouldn't be this hard to think. A bead of sweat slides down my spine beneath my dress, and then an answer pops through the haze clouding my mind.

"He's my brother."

An uneven breath sneaks into my tight lungs.

When the man's brows pinch, I amend, "Half brother."

His face relaxes, kindly not commenting on how I sound like a six-year-old being interrogated by the principal and two seconds from peeing herself.

"That makes sense." He laughs, and I force my lips higher in response. "He's got some serious bodyguard vibes."

My gaze flips to Finn's again. The man is right. My dating coach looks protective and... My forehead wrinkles. I must be misinterpreting the hard set of his jaw, because Finn can't be looking at me *possessively*.

"Nice dress."

I snap my head back so quickly my neck pinches. "Um...thank you."

My mind offers me helpful details to mention like that I made it myself, or that I spent hours getting the bodice just right, but I can't get the syllables beyond my teeth.

"Care for a drink?"

I nod, much too aggressively. Any second now, my head will pop off my body and roll on the floor, ruining the effort I put into my half-up style. "Rosé, please."

While the man orders for me, I turn slightly to give Finn a shaky thumbs up.

He's chatting with a leggy blonde who *does not* think heels are the devil. Can those even be categorized as heels? Stilts, more likely. Her core strength must be insane.

When Finn's gaze snags on mine, I decide to make the gesture overt, lifting my raised thumb to my shoulder.

I'm fine. This will all be fine. I will not die talking to a stranger. And if I do keel over, I'm pretty sure Mr. Librarian Bodyguard could scoop me off the floor with little difficulty.

The man beside me laughs again. It's a nice sound, bright and throaty. "Letting him know you're okay?"

I give—what I hope looks like—a casual shrug. "Yeah."

"I'm Dylan, by the way."

At the last minute, I decide to use my sister's name. She's always been the confident one. The one who can stand up for herself and anyone else who needs it.

Who better to emulate tonight?

"I'm Brynn."

EIGHT

Finn

I try to focus on the blonde in front of me—Amanda? Allison?—but Vivian is on to her second glass of wine and starting to sway. Green Polo steadies her with a palm to her ribs, and I almost shatter the highball glass in my hand. He's practically salivating at her tipsy state.

Like a dog.

"It was nice to meet you, but I've got to go," I interrupt Aubrey. Or was it Alyssa?

"Oh, sure. Maybe we can…" Her words pitter off as I march down the bar.

I know I'm being a complete jerk, but Annabell didn't take my first seven hints that I wasn't up for conversation. Normally, I can chat with anyone about anything, but tonight my job is to take care of Vivian.

Green Polo's lips lean dangerously close to Vivian's ear as I arrive beside her. "We have to head out, Viv."

"Viv?" The man's brows crinkle.

She waves a hand, her silver pinky ring glinting in the light. "Childhood nickname."

His gaze cautiously jumps to mine before returning to Vivian's. "Can I get your number?"

"Sorry, man. We're not from here," I tell him, like the world's biggest scumbag, before sliding my arm around her shoulder and pulling Vivian toward the ocean-facing exit.

I have no logical explanation for my uncharacteristic surliness. The little voice in my head that always reminds me to pay attention to the optics of a situation, to constantly put the most likable version of myself forward, seems to be momentarily subdued. By what, I don't know.

"You gave him a fake name?" I ask as soon as we spill onto the wide cement boardwalk that separates us from the beach.

"My sister's."

The corner of my mouth lips up. "Clever."

To my shock, Vivian leans into me and takes a noisy inhale. "It's been bugging me since I got in your car, but I can't decide if it's cliché for you to smell like books. It's probably because you're surrounded by them all day. Though...fragrance companies should bottle this"—she pokes my chest—"and sell it because all the bookish girlies would lose their minds if their boyfriends smelled like you."

I blink. Utterly speechless.

"Oooh, the ocean. I'm going to say hi." Vivian wriggles from beneath my arm and bounds down the handful of stairs that lead to the sand.

The white crests of the waves are barely visible in the light cast from the huge hotel towers, but the reflection of the waning moon on the water stretches like a beacon. There are a few clusters of people on the beach. A teenage boy runs past us, shouldering a squealing girl as a second boy videos the whole thing. An older couple walks along the water, hand in hand. But I hardly notice any of it because Vivian talks our entire walk to the shore. She's a joyful little chatterbox. I seriously hope Vivian never holds state secrets, because all you need is two glasses of rosé, and she'll tell you anything.

I receive a quick lesson about grain and cross-grain lines in fabric, how she thinks her twin sister, Brynn, and I should be best friends because our names rhyme, and a few tidbits of Wilks Beach lore—including how she made an "ocean wish" on her birthday, and that's why I'm her dating coach. Apparently, the sea "sent me to help her." The strangest thing is that if she'd uttered that sentence even three days ago, I would have written her off as a loon. Tonight, it's endearing, and I *cannot* be endeared by this woman.

When we arrive at the water's edge, Vivian casually mentions that she's never had more than one drink with anyone but her sister. Up until meeting me, Brynn has been the only one she's ever trusted to take care of her. The minx drops that bomb, kicks off her shoes, then skips into the water, having no idea that earning her trust cuts a chunk out of my well-forged armor.

Vivian sighs with delight the second the cool water covers her toes. "I wish I could go for a swim right now."

I shudder. "In the dark?"

The idea of her—anyone—in the dark water makes bile scratch up my throat—not that I enjoy being in water under the best of circumstances.

She glances over her shoulder, eyes flashing with an unexpected twinkle. "I do it all the time. Night is the best time to explore the beaches because no one's around."

"But—"

"Don't worry. I have a light-up bubble buoy I use for open-water swimming."

The ringing in my ears overtakes the crashing sound of waves. I'm eight again, and all I can feel is the burning in my lungs and my brother, Brody's, hands on my shoulders. My riotous heart slaps against my ribs, all other sounds muffled by the—

"Finn."

I startle, finding Vivian in front of me. How long has she been there?

"I'm sorry, did you say something?" My head shakes as I refocus my thoughts.

She tucks her lower lip between her teeth. "I asked if you were okay?"

I attempt a charming smile but feel it wobble. "Of course, gorgeous." I slide my hands into my pockets and pull my shoulders back, needing her concerned look to drop more than I need my next breath. "I'm always okay."

"Are you sure?"

My father's words echo automatically. *Don't show weakness. The second they see you vulnerable, you're as good as dead.*"

I nod.

Life has proved my father's warning true, but the sweet crease between Vivian's brows messes with my head. It's making me want to cup her cheek in gratitude before threading my fingers through those curls and bringing her mouth to mine.

My hands fist in my pockets as I remind myself that kissing Vivian would be completely disastrous—both for my plans to save my sister and for my shredded heart.

Her nose wrinkles in that adorable way before Vivian's expression brightens. "I know what you need." She grabs my wrist and tugs me toward the boardwalk, forgetting about her shoes. "Rosé. Rosé fixes everything."

I stoop to grab her shoes before letting her lead me up the beach. "I think we need some water."

"Boo. Spoilsport."

An unexpected chuckle leaves my mouth.

Her mouth splits wide on a grin, and I try to mediate the effect it has on my heart rate. Part of me wishes Vivian smiled like that more often, but then a selfish part loves that she only directs that particular grin at me.

Vivian stops at the top of the boardwalk stairs, still holding my wrist. "If I drink a bottle of water, can we try another target?"

A snort escapes me. "You want to go to another bar?"

I thought for sure we were going home.

"Yeah, because I realized something." It doesn't seem possible for her to shine brighter, yet Vivian positively sparkles.

"None of this matters. In these noisy bars, I can be whoever I want. I'm never going to see these people again." She points to a man skating by on rollerblades. "You, sir! Our paths shall never again entwine."

The man wholly ignores her, much to Vivian's giddy delight.

I understand the allure of anonymity. After being forced to remove my father's last name from my own, the freedom of being forgettable was dizzying at times.

"My whole life, I've been surrounded by people who know me. That intimacy is lovely, but it's also intimidating. Even in high school on the mainland, the stories followed me. Everyone knew about our past before we'd even stepped foot on campus. But here"—she stretches out her arms—"I'm a mystery. An enigma. What I do doesn't matter because no one will tell Aunt Tammy. No one will tell Brynn. I won't be hurting anyone when I inevitably ruin everything."

So many follow-up questions zip through my mind, but it's difficult to organize them, especially when it feels like someone sucker punched me in the throat.

"You"—my voice is entirely too gruff as I step forward, closing the gap between us—"could never ruin anything. I never want to hear you talk about yourself like that again."

Her mouth opens, sucks in an uneven breath, then closes with a hard swallow.

I ignore everything in the next few seconds, concentrating only on remaining absolutely still. The goosebumps spreading down her arms go untouched. The gossamer sheen of her dress, tempting me to trace my fingers over the corset at her waist, isn't worth my attention. The way her collarbones bounce with each insufficient inhale isn't distracting.

Vivian does that rapid-blinking thing again before her expression smooths. "Got it, Coach. Negative self-talk is not going to help me win Atticus's heart."

Her words shive me in the kidneys, but I let my lip quirk. "That's right. And the next step is talking to him."

"Except, there's a problem with your plan."

"What's that?"

"Atticus won't approach me like Dylan did. We have been hovering around each other for a year. The first time he spoke to me was at the library, and that was only because you and I were in his way."

Irrational anger sweeps my bloodstream before I can suppress it. If my life wasn't a complete mess, if my ex hadn't destroyed me, I wouldn't have waited a year to speak to Vivian. If I wasn't her dating coach and this tentative relationship wasn't purely situational, I would have closed those final inches seconds ago.

"Fret not, gorgeous," I begin, waiting until she's caught my roguish smile before continuing. "Your dating coach has a plan."

NINE

Finn

That's the text I get the Tuesday after our Friday-night talking-to-men session. That night, I'd helped her through another interaction before buying Vivian fish tacos and encouraging her to drink more water. While munching on savory rockfish and crunchy cabbage, we finalized this plan. Vivian closes her shop early every Tuesday to spend two hours organizing the monetary side of her business. She finishes her work around six—the same time Atticus tends to pick up his weekly library holds.

Today, *she's* going to approach *him*.

I glance up from my phone, catching her sitting cross-legged on her study room chair and giving me the saddest puppy dog eyes I've ever seen. Her purple panda tote—how many of those darn things does she own?—is crumpled on the floor. Her laptop and water bottle are in disarray, and her empty Skittles bag hangs halfway out of the trashcan.

I give her a playful eye roll.

Finn

> You'll be fine. Just repeat what we practiced in the car.

Vivian huffs, swiping a few remaining Skittles into her mouth and furiously typing.

After checking the library's study room reservation system, I'd noted that the prior patron was to vacate the room at three. That gave me enough time to scrub the desktop with Clorox wipes, ensuring that Vivian won't catch tabletop botulism, hoof and mouth disease, or something worse. When I was caught by our custodian, Debra, I disinfected all the other open tables in the upstairs reading/study area to waylay suspicion.

Vivian

> It's not going to work. Who goes up to another person at the library and asks, What are you reading? I might as well be asking him if he likes breathing. It's pathetic. Seriously, why did we not come up with something better?

I fire off my text before glaring through the two panes of glass separating us.

Vivian types for a long time, and my shoulders tighten, anticipating a tirade. The slight defiance that shines when we verbally spar became a full-force stubborn tornado when I suggested my plan over dinner on Friday.

A short message is all I receive.

My office suddenly feels vacuum sealed, though my door is open like always. I surge to my feet, texting while walking away from Vivian's study room.

My heart pounds in my throat as I send another message.

It's a struggle not to glance over my shoulder as I descend the stairs, to see that Vivian understands how much I believe in her.

Not wanting Vivian to hunt for me when she's already flustered, I hover in the same aisle we were in last week. A book spine tips into my fingers before I push it back. The process mindlessly repeats until I smell her magnolia-coffee scent. This time, I let a book fall into my hand to read the back cover.

"What…" She hesitates, nervously clearing her throat. "What are you reading?"

I have no earthly idea. I'd planned on scanning the blurb, but when I caught her strangling the life out of the straps of her tote from the corner of my eye, my mind went blank. Trying something new is always hard, but the tremble in her fingertips will be my undoing. It's taking everything in me not to tug Vivian to my chest.

I flip the book, glancing at the cover. With the battling spaceships in the foreground and the glowing planet beyond, it's probably military sci-fi. "I was thinking about trying this one. Do you like sci-fi?"

"I, um…" She pauses again, rolling her lips.

Come on, gorgeous. You can do this.

I keep my face open and inviting, though a noose feels like it's tightening around my windpipe. All I can think about is Friday—how enjoyable dinner had been even with her trying to undermine my every suggestion, how we laughed over stupid things, how *darned easy* conversation was. I hadn't had that much fun with another person in…I can't even remember.

"Maybe?" The word comes out high-pitched.

I lean my forearm against the stack. "Maybe?"

Vivian sighs while flopping her hands to her sides. "This isn't going to work. I keep thinking about how you're *you* and not Atticus. It's tripping me up." Her antsy fingers tighten her ponytail before straightening her shirt.

She'd texted me earlier today, asking what she should wear—probably because I'd instructed her last time. Unfortunately, the request went straight to my head. I liked the idea of dressing Vivian way, way too much. After fighting internal demons I had no idea I possessed, I told her to wear her most comfortable outfit.

Vivian's shallow V-neck shirt tucked into flowy wide-legged pants and canvas shoes gives off an effortless nautical feel with its alternating white-navy-white coloring. Her outfit also unknowingly matches my own navy and white combination.

"And Atticus would never do that suave doorway-lean thing you're doing right now. Do you even see yourself?"

I almost hit my funny bone on the shelf, I bring my arm down so fast. "I need to be more like him?" That question sends a hot poker sliding between my ribs.

She nods. "I think it might help."

I tap the book against my chin, as if I'm casually thinking and not eviscerated by the knowledge that even if we weren't in this situation, I wouldn't be the kind of man Vivian wants.

"Hold this." Handing Vivian the book, I slump my posture before unfastening the top button to my navy suit vest and rifling my fingers through my hair. Once it's flopping down over my forehead instead of in the professional style I always wear, I glance up. "Better?"

Vivian's gaping mouth sends a frisson of panic through me. "What?"

"You messed up your hair."

My forehead wrinkles. "So?"

"You're always so perfectly coiffed. I didn't think you..." Her fingertips drift upward before she visibly remembers herself and slides them into her pocket. "I mean, that's helpful. For our practice." She swallows. "Thank you."

Ignoring the heartbeat deafening my ears, I nod. "Okay, good. Now let's run this again."

Vivian takes a deep breath, but before she can make a sound, another voice draws our attention. "Huh. Small world."

Atticus is neither happy nor upset to see the two of us in his designated aisle—he's completely befuddled. I snap to my full height, running my fingers through my hair. Gratitude blooms when my trusted product locks most of the strands back in place before I extend my hand to Atticus.

"I don't believe we've met. I'm Finn Reynolds, the new branch manager."

"Atticus Beckham," he says. "Nice to meet you."

It takes all my willpower not to crush his hand. Even so, Atticus grimaces at the pressure of my handshake. I subdue the judgmental thoughts flooding my brain about men with weak handshakes and gesture to Vivian with an easy smile.

"Do you know Vivian Hutchinson?"

Atticus falters a minute but eventually extends his hand. "I've seen you around but can't say we've officially met."

The nearly inaudible noise Vivian makes when his hand slides into hers makes my vision blur at the edges. Unexpected anti-Atticus gore races through my mind, requiring a concentrated breath to clear it all. Maybe I should scale back on the boxing classes. I've never been the impulsively angry type before I arrived in this town.

"Happy to have made introductions." I slide the book back into the stack to give myself something to do.

When the two of them wordlessly stare, I sigh internally and add, "Vivian owns the tailor shop beside Seabreeze Beans."

"You do?"

Attaboy, Atticus. Welcome to the conversation.

Vivian blinks for a moment then gives an unsteady nod.

I don't want to speak for her, but I also don't want her to leave this interaction feeling defeated. If they don't keep talking, Atticus will walk away like last time.

My insides revolt when sorrow splashes across the slight freckles dotting her nose, as if Vivian has drawn the same conclusion at the exact same time. The air in my lungs draws thin. Before the excruciatingly painful sensation can trip into full panic, I open my mouth.

"Vivian has—" I take a second to even my punchy voice and plaster a charming smile on my face. "She just confided in me that she's a Tuesday regular in our study rooms because the scent of books helps her get through a task she hates." I huff a good-natured chuckle. "Can't say I blame her. I love being surrounded by books."

I tuck my tongue in my cheek over the popular joke librarians share amongst themselves. The general public thinks librarianship is about the love of reading, but truly, it's about so much more. It's the curation, categorization, and protection of information while vigilantly safeguarding accessibility and protecting the privacy of all who benefit from the library's free access.

But I'm assuming since Atticus makes a weekly trip to check out new books, he likes to read. Hopefully, he'll pick up on the conversation topic I've placed before him.

His head tilts to the side. "What's the task you hate?"

Not where I thought this would go but still helpful.

Vivian bites her lip so hard I'm concerned she'll draw blood. "Bookkeeping."

The smile stretching Atticus's face is so earnest and honest I have to pinch my thigh within my pocket to keep myself from doing something rash. "I love bookkeeping. I'm, uh..."—he tugs on his ear—"an accountant. Numbers are my jam."

My jam? What's next? Jazz hands? My hatred of this man grows every second we're forced to share air, even though that emotion is completely unfounded. By all accounts, he seems like a decent person.

He's also who Vivian wants, my mind reminds me like the unhelpful jerk it is.

"Oh?" Vivian straightens, confidence flowing loosely through her limbs as I see that beautiful brain at work. I know what she's going to do before she opens her mouth. I taught her this exact scenario at bar number two when she was panicked about approaching an attractive Asian man.

Damsel in distress.

A classic.

Men cannot pass up an opportunity to show that *they* are exactly what a woman needs. Their egos won't allow it.

On Friday, it'd been a well-timed kick that launched her shoe a few feet away followed by a demure, "Can you help me?" Vivian had fought me for twenty minutes, but I assured her if the idiot didn't help, I'd grab her ballet flat, and we'd move on. In the end, the man had not only retrieved the sparkly shoe but given Vivian a slight ankle caress while replacing it—something I hadn't been pleased about.

Her gorgeous green eyes lock on mine, a surprisingly wolfish smile flirting with the corners of her mouth. Secret knowledge flows between us, and I can't help the pride radiating from my chest.

"Maybe you can help me sometime? I'm new to the software." A single shoulder lifts as she blinks innocently.

Brava, Vivian.

In truth, she's been using Quickbooks for three years but hates every second of it. She told me the only things making it tolerable are the scent of books and sweet, chewy Skittles. I'd also learned that Wendy Martin, her mentor in all things fabric, had trained her and then handed the business over.

True to her word to teach me about Wilks Beach, Vivian gave me a rundown of the local businesses. Other than the brick-and-mortar stores, there were those run out of homes: two rivaling daycares, a massage therapist who gives beachside massages, a dance instructor who teaches beginning ballet and jazz out of her garage, and the stay-at-home dad who bakes all the goodies for Seabreeze Beans. Most islanders prefer to minimize the number of times they drive into Virginia Beach, so many of them have virtual careers or work for the local businesses. In the short time I've lived here, I've found myself avoiding the commute too.

"Uh, sure. Why don't I get your number?"

While Atticus fumbles in his pocket, I make a swift exit. "Excuse me. Patricia is calling me."

I don't head to the circulation desk where Patricia is gabbing with Trudy, the children's librarian. I bypass it entirely and use the badge clipped to my pants pocket to enter the book-return area and march straight into the compact storage closet. Reams of computer paper stare back at me as I try to collect myself. A mother instructing her child to insert each book one at a time reverberates through the external book drop. Most people don't know we can hear them while they return their books. The two teen volunteers scanning and sorting returns giggle when the child throws a fit about having to return the "poop book."

I press my eyes closed, taking slow inhales through the nose. When my phone buzzes, I know it's Vivian.

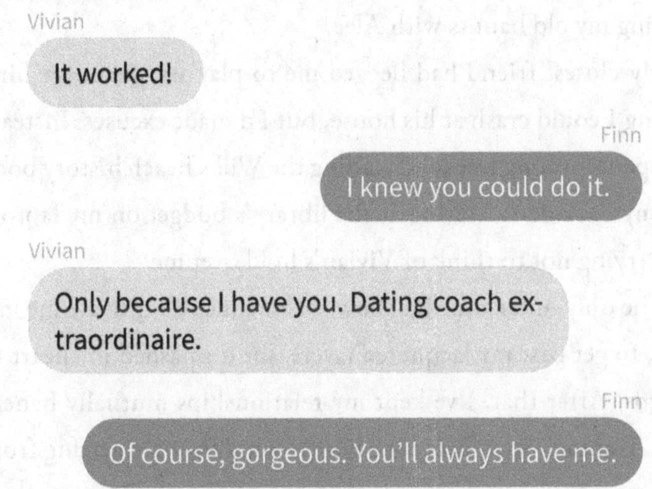

I stare at the words I thoughtlessly sent, realizing how true they are. We met a week ago, but I already know that I'd do anything to help Vivian.

Vivian's text interrupts my tailspin, reminding me to ignore that stupid twist in my chest.

I take longer than necessary to survey the inventory in the closet. It's not one of my duties, but I want to make sure Vivian is gone when I head back to my office. Her influence is already setting my life on its side. I had three whole days to revel in my free time this past weekend. Time I should have spent back in Virginia Beach, hitting my old haunts with Alec.

My closest friend had begged me to play wingman for him, saying I could crash at his house, but I'd made excuses. Instead, I'd spent my long weekend reading the Wilks Beach history book on my back deck, staring at the library's budget on my laptop, and trying not to think of Vivian's hold over me.

The only other time I'd allowed someone to captivate me like this, to get past my lacquered layers, she'd smashed my heart to shards. After that, I've kept my relationships mutually beneficial. Transactional. Everyone knows what they are getting from the start. Vivian lacks Katelyn's ruthless capacity, but I've been fooled before.

I grimace when I find an unopened container of Clorox wipes sitting on my desk. At least I haven't received any wayward book recommendations today.

"Very funny." I raise the container over my head, searching for the culprit through my glass wall.

A few regulars glance at me before quickly returning to their reading. I plunk into my chair, surlier than I've been in a long while. Maybe I should forgo tonight's HIIT class at The Garage Gym and head toward civilization. I could listen to an audiobook to make the drive to Virginia Beach tolerable.

"Mr. Reynolds?" Letitia, the community engagement librarian, knocks on my open door.

I don't have it in me to request that she call me Finn *again*. I've been asking since I arrived, and everyone seems bent on keeping the formality. At least Letitia is kind about it. Since I've arrived, she's been visibly torn over having to regard me as an outcast. I think that's more on account of her affable personality than anything to do with me.

"What can I do for you?" I straighten, setting a friendly smile on my face.

She barely steps inside, keeping her left foot firmly on the exterior carpet. My spine sags an inch, but I try not to let it show.

"No one showed up for tonight's job application class. Since it's been fifteen minutes, I was wondering if I could go home?"

Letitia is two years older than me but already has a husband, a three-year-old, and a one-year-old to get home to.

I glance at my watch. "Sure."

Letitia's shoulders soften, already turning. Before she can escape, my question snags her like a lure. "Why do you think no one attended?"

I'd asked Letitia to organize this class my first week here. This and free classes on resume/CV building were often overfilled at the Central Library. Half of the time, the librarian assisting those in Central Library's media room acted as an unofficial job counselor. The lack of community support classes provided by the Wilks Beach branch is borderline reckless. For many people, libraries are the only place to learn these skills.

She pauses, her hesitation as easy to read as a large-print book.

I rub my temples, pain starting to throb behind my left eye. "Just tell me."

"The community this library serves doesn't need assistance with job applications."

The longer I spend here, the more I realize what a different ecosystem this library is to any I've ever worked in. For example, library closures make me incredibly uneasy. Our free public buildings are a safe haven for so many citizens. I've always tried to connect potentially unhoused individuals with nearby resources during scheduled closings. This past three-day weekend, I checked around the building twice each day and didn't see anyone needing help.

"What do they need, then? Let's give it to them."

Just like before, every expression plays on Letitia's face. Shock at my direct tone. Surprise over the question. Something softer—like approval?—remaining after the first two waned.

"Entertainment."

I lean back in my chair, about to ask for clarification, when Letitia bustles into my office, sits on the edge of my desk, and starts talking.

TEN

Vivian

"I have Atticus's number." The sentence slips from my lips as I clutch my phone in both hands, staring like it's The One Ring. With the way I'm murmuring, singularly focused on the glowing digits while blindly walking home, I might as well be saying, "My precious."

Out of habit, I hook around the back of Dotty's Market, weaving between discarded cardboard boxes and wooden pallets. Cliff, Dotty's grandson and employee, sits on an overturned bucket, vaping. He gives me an upward nod of acknowledgment as I pass.

Before I fling open the unlocked door at the back of my building, I take a breath to process the last half hour. It worked. The wish. Finn's dating advice. All of it. I not only spoke real words—whole sentences!—to my crush, I got his phone number. And more importantly, he has mine. Now I just need to wait for him to ask me out.

I *can't wait* to tell Brynn.

My expanding smile grows as I push open the back door. Once, in middle school, two girls from a group project convinced me to have our planning meeting at my house just to see the only residence on the island that sat atop a coffee shop. I felt a little like an outer space tour guide, showing them the singular entrance at the back of the building, the narrow vestibule holding two doors to the shop and also the staircase. They'd oohed and ahhed over the unusual ingress.

Once we arrived upstairs, my classmates were less impressed. At that time, Aunt Tammy ran Seabreeze Beans, sleeping in the bedroom facing the nature preserve while Brynn and I shared a set of bunk beds in the bedroom facing the road. The compact size of our living room and the galley kitchen that you had to walk through to get to the bedrooms didn't win any awards either.

Toeing my canvas shoes onto the small rack beneath the skinny entry table at the top of the stairs, I call out to Brynn, "Honey, I'm home. What do you want me to make for dinner?"

By this point, she'll be awake from her afternoon nap. After closing shop at three, she and Sandy clean and prepare for the next day, then Brynn usually passes out for an hour or two. Because Brynn keeps me caffeinated and provides me with free pastries—something I indulge in twice daily—I always make dinner.

Some nights, we eat dinner, and then she runs errands, helping out various community members. I provide the food for whoever in Wilks Beach needs a meal, and Brynn delivers it. Whenever people aren't having babies, breaking limbs, or coming home from unexpected hospital stints, we relax together in the evenings. And on Saturday nights, we watch movies, alternating between my favorite—period pieces—and Brynn's favorite—action flicks.

"Hmmmmmrrrrffff."

The animalistic grumble sounds from the couch, and I find a Brynn-shaped lump huddling beneath the gray comforter from her bed. The muted TV on a home shopping channel touts festive summer yard decorations for the low, low price of $12.99. Order now, folks!

"There's no way we can pass up a yard flamingo with a gnome riding on its back." I sit and pull Brynn's socked feet into my lap, massaging her toes. "It's traffic-stopping. That's how cute it is."

Pleased, incoherent muttering comes from the other end of the couch as I continue toward her arches. "Oooh! Now there's a gnome floating on a flamingo raft, holding a pineapple cocktail." I laugh. "Where do they come up with these things?"

When I press my thumbs firmly against her heels, where she's the sorest from being on her feet all day, Brynn flings down the comforter covering her head and gives me a sleepy smile. "You're my favorite person, you know that?"

"Want to buy your favorite person a whimsical tchotchke?"

She blinks at the screen. "That's pretty cute, but we don't have a yard."

"We could put it on the receiving counter at the shop." Though I have my own shop now, we always referred to Seabreeze Beans as 'the shop.' "Give it a fanciful name like Brewster Beanbottom or Java Jingleheimer."

Brynn considers this a moment, staring at the slowly revolving figurine. "It'd be better if it had a coffee mug in its hand."

"Yeah," I concede, allowing my gaze to drift out the window facing the singular road that runs the length of Wilks Beach.

Driving Sand Bend Road into the island, you have two options. Go straight past the water tower, our businesses, and Dotty's, and end up at the small parking lot behind the library. Or turn right and drive for two miles, passing the fire station, gym, a handful of bay-facing homes, and Bayside Table before dead-ending at the larger parking lot for the island's park and public beach access. Along the way, short single-lane roads jut toward the ocean, lined with single family homes. The last offshoot accommodates the condo complex with a residents-only parking garage.

I can only see the corner of the fire station and the flagpole from here, but not far beyond lies Finn's rental. A surge of excitement blazes down my forearms, and I pat Brynn's feet.

"I have news."

"You finally saw a mermaid on today's swim?"

I chuckle, thinking about the childhood dream I often shared with Brynn. "Nope."

"We won the lottery?"

My head shakes. "We'd have to play the lottery to win it."

"Your ocean wish came true."

When I pause, Brynn shoots upright, yanking her feet from my grip and toppling the blanket on the floor. The action startles Pepper, who'd been dozing on the top pedestal of her cat tower. She lets out an annoyed meow, rolling away from us.

"*No.*" I don't think I've ever seen my sister this shocked. I witnessed something similar when Noah, her ex-boyfriend, betrayed her, but the wide-eyed, gape-mouth stare she's giving me doesn't contain a smidgen of hurt.

I bite my bottom lip and nod.

My usually articulate sister stammers for a few seconds, finally eeking out, "How? When?... How?"

"I was at the library. Finn and I were talking—"

"The mainlander? I thought I told you to stay away from him?"

My shoulders deflate slightly, some of my previous effervescence dissipating. I know Brynn is just trying to protect me, but sometimes her need to help, to jump into action, ends up steamrolling me.

A memory from our first year living in this apartment with Aunt Tammy surges forward. Our aunt asked about our school day, and Brynn answered for me. By that point, I'd been working with a school counselor with the hopes that talking about our parents' car crash would help with my self-expression. Though I'd always been more shy than Brynn, I'd barely murmured a word to anyone after their unexpected loss. That night, I'd wanted to talk about the drawing I'd done in counseling while Brynn had been at PE, but I never got the chance.

"Finn happened to be there when Atticus came by. Atticus and I chatted for a bit and exchanged numbers."

The lie about Finn makes me uneasy, but based on her reaction, I don't feel that I can tell Brynn the truth. I'd hoped to explain this whole dating-coach situation, to tell her that she's wrong about Finn. He's helped me more in the last week than anyone in this town ever has. Though, when I think about it...that's not really a fair statement. Cade and Summer—two incredibly sweet and outgoing locals—both tried, on separate occasions, to help me capture Atticus's attention. It just never worked out.

My brows pinch. Why didn't their efforts take, yet holding Finn's gaze in the library earlier, I knew I was unstoppable?

My sister flops back on the cushions. "Wow. That's . . . wow. That's so great, Viv."

I nod, twisting the silver shell ring on my pinky finger. My brain whirs, wondering why things are only starting to work out *now*. It must be my ocean wish. I've just never had one come true before.

Several seconds pass before Brynn's stomach rumbles loudly. "Sorry." She rubs her flat belly. "I missed lunch today."

"I'll get started on dinner," I say, happy for the distraction. "What sounds good?"

"Something light? Pasta, maybe, since it's just for us tonight?" She glances out the window. "Let me get a quick four first."

By "a quick four" she means four miles—two loops of Sand Bend Road. Like many other members of our town who also have a loose grip on their sanity, Brynn loves to run. You couldn't pay me to run in the humid, eighty-degree weather when I could be slicing through soothing water.

"You got it."

Pasta won't take that long to prepare, so while Brynn heads out, I flop on the floral-print comforter in my room. I'm about to unlock my phone and stare at the number I've already memorized when realization that Brynn never asked any follow-up questions about Atticus pricks at my temple.

No "What did you two talk about?"

Or "Did you set up a date?"

Or "Does he have a brother for me?"

Nothing.

Disappointment pools deep in my belly. I'd really wanted a squealy, jump-on-the-couch gab session with my sister. It feels like years since we've done that. We're always so focused on work, only vegging out together after long days. Brynn, more so than me, is perpetually exhausted, always giving too much of herself. That's why I came up with a way to give Brynn a much-needed break. It'll require another huge leap outside of my comfort zone, which is why I've kept it a secret.

A rough swallow struggles down my throat. The next step of my three-part plan to transform my life is Mount Everest compared to talking to Atticus. But after successfully talking to strangers and getting Atticus's phone number at the library, I might just be able to pull it off.

Especially if I have a little help.

Convincing myself that the queasy spiral in my stomach is anticipation and not nerves, I pull up my contacts. I allow myself one breathy sigh at Atticus's number before I tab over to the text conversation with Finn.

Vivian

Hey, Coach. Can you meet up later tonight?

ELEVEN

Finn

It's pathetic the way my heart catapults to the pebbled walkway the instant I see Vivian waiting for me outside Bayside Table. Truly pitiful. I've been in rooms with supermodels and movie stars, and yet, the way Vivian gives her signature small wave/smile combo to the two locals passing her before her face completely transforms when she sees me is enough to end a man. Pair her carefree, luminescent smile with the way Vivian bounces like she's just been given a kitten, and it feels like my armor is melting beneath her joyous gaze.

"You made it."

I give her a practiced, roguish smile. "You had doubts?"

Vivian rolls her eyes. "Can you turn off the charm machine for tonight? I'm going to introduce you to the town."

"Pretty sure the town knows me." I scoff, sliding my hands into my pockets.

Vivian requested casual clothes for tonight's meet-up, so I changed into shorts and a fitted t-shirt. She's switched into a smocked dress, that falls just below her knees, and sandals.

"No," she argues, gesturing for me to follow her away from the Bayside Table's main entrance and to a path around to the left side. "They know Finn-the-mainlander, who's trying to destroy our library."

"I'm not trying to destroy anything," I grumble.

"Exactly." She stops, spinning to face me so quickly we almost collide. "Tonight, we'll show them that."

I tilt my head. "How?"

"By letting them see the relaxed version of you I saw on Friday." The confident smirk on her mouth has no right being that distracting. "Come and socialize with them without having an agenda. Let them see the real you."

My skin burns as if it's been pelted by shrapnel, but I keep my face expressionless. I can count on one hand the number of people who know the real me, and on one finger the number of people who actually like that man. When Cordelia surges to the front of my thoughts, it's a comfort. Grounding. Reminding me of my ultimate goal.

A deep breath fills my lungs as I loosen the tension in my shoulders.

"Alright, gorgeous." I gesture to the path behind her. "Lead the way."

When we turn the corner of the building, the grassy area that's normally dewy and silent during my morning runs brims with life. A group of high school students play giant connect four, their plastic cups of soda resting on a nearby picnic table. Two couples compete at cornhole while three small children—who should probably be in bed, given that it's nearly nine—use giant Jenga blocks to build a castle. Several more groups gather around the remaining tables.

The outdoor bar is filled to capacity—a body on every stool and more on the small dance floor, chatting. A low retaining wall separates the outdoor bar/dance space from the bay beyond, likely to keep intoxicated individuals from falling in the water. In the grassy area, however, you can walk right up to the water's unkempt edge.

I eye the trio of children, hoping that someone is watching them with the proximity of the dark, ominous bay.

"There's also the problem that if I keep talking to locals about your virtuous nature without being seen with you, it might be seen as suspicious." Vivian changes her voice to sound shockingly similar to Carol Cook's. "How could shy, helpless Vivian ever speak to the new librarian, let alone befriend him? She must be making all this up or, worse, be under his evil spell. Burn the mainlander!"

"That went dark real quick." I keep my tone light, even though the idea of anyone putting Vivian down makes my jaw pop.

She shrugs, but her grin wavers at the edges.

"Mr. Reynolds?"

I'd been so absorbed in Vivian—in how I was going to turn that fake smile into a real one—that I missed Patricia standing two feet in front of us. Her gaze bounces from me to Vivian, stalling as she practically snorts her sip of beer.

"Hey, I know you." The man beside Patricia steps forward to slap my shoulder.

I blink up and recognize...Rollerblade Guy. I've given friendly nods to the handful of islanders I encounter on my morning run, and the only one who ever smiles back is Rollerblade Guy. Tonight, he's traded his Rollerblades, cut-off denim shorts, and hairy bare chest for a pair of slacks and a too-big polo.

"Hey." I smile back. "It's good to see—"

"What are you doing here?" Patricia asks, eyes narrow.

My left temple ticks, but before I can answer, Vivian speaks.

"He's with me." Vivian pauses, chewing on her lower lip.

That simple sentence shouldn't feel like an EMP blast within my ribs, but I struggle to keep my breathing even.

"It turns out Brynn had it wrong," she starts, quietly at first but growing in strength with each word. "Finn only wants to do the right thing for our library and our town. Once I found out, I offered to show Finn the town's nightlife since I know..." She swallows, green eyes darting to mine for only a millisecond. "I know what it's like to be on the outskirts."

Patricia's standoffishness dissolves instantly as she wraps one arm around Vivian's shoulder, giving her a maternal squeeze. My lungs have decided to stop functioning, but Rollerblade Guy just barks a laugh, gesturing around us.

"If you wanted nightlife, you found it. This is the only place in town. It's not all bad, though. They've got music trivia on Tuesdays, karaoke on Thursdays, and live music and dancing on Saturdays."

"Don't forget Friday night bingo at the library. Though"—Patricia releases Vivian, lifting her brows at me—"Letitia said there might be other evening programs added to our calendar soon."

During our impromptu meeting, Letitia floated a multitude of possible events—from puzzle swaps, to gardening lectures, to paint nights, to tai chi, to scanning home photos for digital storage. The library already has a popular book club that meets once a month and a Saturday afternoon knitting/crochet/embroidery circle in addition to its storytime programs.

"Really?" Vivian asks.

I try not to interpret the soft look in her eyes, keeping my smile congenial. "We're considering new ideas."

"This town could use them." The man laughs again before offering his hand to me. "I'm Greg, by the way."

Patricia and Greg dissolve into conversation on what's missing in Wilks Beach as the bartender pushes an orange crush cocktail Vivian's way. "Here ya go, love."

I don't miss the slight wince before Vivian responds with a small smile and smaller thanks.

"Newcomer, what'll it be?" The woman points at me, her tattooed arms a blur of different patterns.

Newcomer? I suppose that's better than *Mainlander*.

"Whiskey, neat, please."

She gives me a curt nod, turning away to pour my drink.

Deafening mic feedback has everyone wincing and covering their ears. "Sorry about that," a voice booms before the volume is quickly lowered. "Welcome to music trivia. I'm Izzy, your host." Several enthusiastic *wooooos* go up from the crowd. "Grab your score card if you haven't yet. We start at the end of this song."

"HandClap" reverberates through the speakers. After collecting my drink, starting a tab, and saying goodbye to Patricia and Greg, we grab our laminated score cards and dry-erase markers and make our way to two vacant Adirondack chairs in the grass. The double-sided card doesn't contain answer slots like I'd expected but a Motown-themed bingo card.

"Isn't this music bingo?"

Vivian kicks off her sandals and folds her legs criss-cross beneath her. If I was a betting man, I'd wager there are bike shorts beneath her flower-patterned dress.

"Technically, but Izzy didn't want to ruffle Ida's feathers and compete with the library's bingo night, so she named it something else." When I stare blankly, she adds, "Ida was the activities librarian before she retired five"—she squints at the star-speckled sky—"six years ago."

Vivian takes a sip of her cocktail and grimaces.

"Is something wrong with your drink?"

Conflict skirts over her brow before she focuses on her score-card. "It's fine."

"It's not fine," I tell her, seeing through the lie.

Those green eyes peek at me, her thumbnail scrubbing at a marker remnant. "Brynn ordered this drink for us when we turned twenty-one. It's Brynn's favorite, but I'm not fond of it. Every time I come in, Cynthia makes it for me. She thinks she's doing me a favor by not making me order. She probably assumes twin sisters like the same thing." Vivian lifts a helpless shoulder. "She's trying to be nice."

The speed with which I stand, snatching the plastic cup and flinging its contents onto the grass, startles us both. After a beat, I ask, "What do you really want to drink?"

"I—" She twists her ring. "I've always wanted to try their strawberry Moscow mule."

Antsy energy surges through my veins, but I don't move. The fact that Vivian has been politely consuming a drink she doesn't enjoy for *six years* makes me want to burn down this whole establishment. "And if you don't like it?"

A slow smile lifts her lips, blindsiding me. "I'll let you dramatically throw it in the grass?"

My surprised laugh has the dual effect of broadening Vivian's grin and easing the pressure behind my breastbone. "You knew that dramatics were part of the deal."

She rolls her eyes, but her smile doesn't slip. "Fine."

"Yes, I am. Thank you for noticing." I wink just to get her to huff in exasperation.

Vivian shakes her head. "Go get my drink so we can get down to business. I did my part in making you look less vile to the townspeople. Now I need your help with something."

"Sure thing, gorgeous."

I give her a second wink before turning to the bar, knowing that Vivian could ask me to walk barefoot over shards of glass, and I'd do so with a smile.

Vivian

"How is it?" Finn's eyes seem darker beneath the string bulbs and starlight, more intense. I need to be careful, to remember it's only a trick of the light. Because the focused way his gaze traces the column of my neck as I swallow the sweet, strawberry-flavored cocktail is more intoxicating than the light splash of vodka within.

"It's tasty."

"You're sure?"

I sigh as dramatically as I can. "A most delightful creation. It's been many years since I've had such an exemplary libation."

My use of Regency wording seems to break whatever weird spell we're in. Finn's grin grows in mesmerizing degrees, reminding me of the blur from blue to dusty pink to bright orange as the sun rises. He leans back in his chair, undeniably satisfied, his fingers loose around his plastic cup.

"Then let's get down to it. Do you want to practice first-date conversations?"

That isn't exactly why I asked him here, but it's a good idea.

I take another sip of my delicious drink. "I had something else to discuss, but maybe we can do both? I can talk to another townsperson on the way out to make it even."

Finn shakes his head, and I'm disappointed when his hair doesn't shift from its styled position. I want it to tumble over his forehead like it had earlier today. "Let's just focus on you right now."

I pull my phone out of my dress pocket—because of course it has pockets!—unlocking the screen before handing it to Finn. "It might be easier to show you. Just don't say what you see out loud. I want to keep it a secret."

His brows pinch upon seeing the webpage for the Oceanside Artisan Fair that happens every summer. Artist tents cover the entire boardwalk of Virginia Beach while various musical acts play on stages every few blocks with food trucks nearby. Finn glances up, eyes bouncing to my twisting ring before his thumb powers off the screen to my phone.

"Okay."

"I have a tent," I say on a quick exhale. "For my clothes. Not *my* clothes"—I tug on my skirt—"but dresses I've designed. I've been sewing lots of different styles and hiding them in the hopes of selling them."

I reach for my phone, ignoring the zip of energy that slides up my arm when our fingers brush. I tab into my email, finding the confirmation for my booth at the Oceanside Artisan Fair next Saturday. The severe wave of nausea that usually accompanies reading this congratulatory email is slightly subdued tonight. I have until Thursday to get a partial refund on my booth fees. That would allow the festival staff to reach out to a waitlisted vendor. Before this afternoon's success with Atticus, I'd been thinking about forfeiting my spot.

But now...

What if I succeed? What if I can tackle this? I heard a saying—*Whatever you're not changing, you're choosing*—that really shifted the way I thought about things. I always saw myself one way, but the confines of that persona have started to itch. Making changes in the love department was an easy choice, but *this idea* grew unexpectedly stitch by stitch.

Last spring, after finishing my alterations that day, I'd mindlessly sewn a dress that was two sizes two small and yellow. I'd heard Brynn scraping around upstairs, awake from her nap, before I'd even realized what had happened. In the following weeks, I began sketching styles I would never wear in colors that wouldn't complement my skin. When I'd stashed away sixteen dresses, I had to admit I was building inventory.

But even then, I wasn't sure why.

After I'd completed thirty dresses, a plan materialized like lace from strands of thread. I could sell the dresses at the Oceanside Artisan Fair and see if anyone would want them. If they did, then I could decide what my next steps would be.

A huge bonus to this idea? I could use the profit to pay two baristas to take over Seabreeze Beans for a Saturday and give Brynn a much-needed day off. My sister hasn't had a full day off since Aunt Tammy transferred the business to her at twenty-two. Even when the shop is closed on Sundays, she uses the afternoon to hand-roast her signature blend.

If I made enough profit, I could even treat Brynn to a spa day at one of those fancy oceanfront hotels on the mainland. Brynn needs a ninety-minute massage like a free diver needs air.

Benevolent intentions aside, choosing to sell dresses at a craft festival that boasts 400,000 in attendance will be extreme talk therapy. My heart thrashes against my rib cage as I think about speaking to various attendees.

"Why is this a secret?" Finn's question brings me back to the present.

A rough swallow squeezes my throat. "The thing is, if I went to the fair and succeeded, then I'd tell everyone. But if I fail, I want to do it quietly." I catch his gaze and dare to hold it. "If islanders found out I was selling dresses, they'd come and buy them out of solidarity. I'm pretty sure the only reason I'm in business is because of the way we fiercely support each other. It's wonderful, but I want to see if I can make it on my own."

He nods, waiting for me to continue.

"I was also hoping to use the profits to help my sister." I explain how hard Brynn works and my plans to help her out.

His mouth relaxes as I speak, a slight smile hinting at the corner. "I get it. I'd do almost anything for my sister."

When that little diamond winks in the starlight, it dawns on me just how little I know about Finn. I'm suddenly ravenous for details.

"What's her name?"

Finn hesitates. Or maybe he's just listening to Izzy's instructions that she'll take a quick break before starting game two. Usually, I'd be completely invested in winning one of the two twenty-dollar Bayside Table gift card prizes, but telling Finn about my secret dress collection and my impossible plans to talk to *all the strangers* in order to sell said dresses is more important.

"Cordelia."

"That's a pretty name."

His full smile lights his face. "She'd love to hear that. Cordelia thinks it's a bit old-fashioned, but all our names are like that."

"All our names?"

His large hand rubs at his beard scruff as his gaze drifts out over the bay. "Yeah."

AJR's "Bang!" is the only sound between us for several beats. I'm not unaccustomed to silence. I tend to spend most of my day with just the whisper of my playlists in the background, but Finn being silent feels...odd.

He takes a large breath, straightening and drawing my attention to his wide shoulders. "What can I do to help?"

"With what?"

My gaze lazily traces from his strong deltoid toward the dip between his collarbones, barely peeking out of his collar. What would it be like to slip my fingertips into that subtle notch?

"With your secret ess-dray ollection-cay." The slight quirk at Finn's mouth as he speaks Pig Latin tells me I've been caught staring. I snap my attention to the muddled strawberries in my drink.

"Umm...nothing?" I jostle the ice in my cup before glancing up. "Be the person who knows, I guess? The secret has been eating me alive. I share everything with Brynn, but lately..."

My stomach twists. I haven't just been keeping this collection from my sister because I want her to have a day off. A small part of me knows that if I let Brynn in on my plans, she'll take over. Her strong, take-charge personality wouldn't allow her to stand by helplessly. And this is something I have to do on my own.

I owe that to myself.

At least I won't have to keep this strange agreement with Finn to myself anymore. Our unlikely friendship will be all over town by morning—that's how the Wilks Beach gossip mill works. When Brynn asks me about it, I can finally explain how Finn is helping me to win Atticus's heart.

"It's just hard for me to keep secrets," I admit.

Finn dips his chin, his grin softening. "I've noticed that. Once you start talking, you're an open book."

I wrinkle my nose.

Finn slides his hand off the edge of his armrest so his fingertips graze my forearm. "That's not a bad thing."

My shaky inhale would have been audible had Izzy not returned to the mic at that exact second. "Who's ready for round two?"

"I...um..." I bring my drink to my lips to break the electrifying contact.

My traitorous body's reactions are out of control. Seriously! This is getting ridiculous.

Atticus. We like Atticus.

Speaking of Atticus, Finn's earlier suggestion would be more than helpful since I've *never been* on a first date.

"Could we practice first-date conversations? Like you suggested?"

A shadow passes over Finn's eyes, but it's gone in a blink as his charming smile overtakes his face. "Sure, gorgeous."

THIRTEEN

Finn

"**M**y Girl" kicks off the second round, and though I've never attended music bingo, I instantly see its appeal. Patrons can quietly check off their squares while continuing to chat, drink, and play yard games. Having seen Vivian tapping her fingertips on the arm of the chair, happily sipping on her new cocktail while politely smiling at those who wave at us, it's obvious why she comes here every Tuesday.

"You should bring him here."

That sentence feels like a punch to the kidneys, but at least I kept the man's name out of my mouth.

"I should?"

No. You should only be here with me.

I ignore the unhelpful internal objection and let my gaze sweep our surroundings. "It's a perfect first-date place. You've got enough activities to occupy your time but not so much distraction that you can't get to know each other."

That idea makes my neck pinch, so I keep instructing—like a good *coach* would. "I'd avoid all the taboo date topics—money, your exes, politics, negative experiences."

"So you're saying I shouldn't start with my orphan status." Vivian clucks her tongue. "Good thing I have you to set me straight."

The gentle ocean breeze feels like it's sucking the air from my lungs. "You're an orphan?"

"Not technically." Vivian checks off a song box, but I can't hear anything but blood sloshing in my ears. "My aunt adopted us after my parents died in a car accident when I was nine."

"I'm—I'm sorry." My fingers collect hers atop her armrest, the rest of my words failing me.

My dad is an insufferable jerkwad, and my mother was never part of the equation after their divorce, but at least they're still alive.

Vivian's gaze drifts to the moonlit bay, her thumb sweeping the inside of my wrist like she's the one consoling *me*. "I had a hard time dealing with it—their loss, my grief, the shock of it all. I didn't speak for nearly six months afterward. I'd always been shy, but..." She shakes her head, lost for a moment.

"But afterward, no one pushed me. No one required me to speak. Allowances were always made. It became a pattern, being silent. By the time I entered middle school, I believed this was all I could be."

Needles feel like they're stabbing every inch of exposed skin, but I remain quiet. There is no pain on this earth that could make me interrupt Vivian when she's talking.

"Instead of following Brynn downstairs to learn the details of our aunt's business, I was encouraged into quieter pursuits. Miss Wendy took me on as an apprentice, and fortunately, I loved working with fabrics. But...sometimes I wonder what my life would have been like if I'd had an insistent English teacher"—her green eyes find mine—"or a coach who'd held me accountable."

A thick pulse radiates in my chest.

"I've gotten better over the years." The corner of her mouth lifts, but the smile doesn't reach her eyes. "As you've seen, I can converse with most locals, but I want to show them I can be more. I need them to understand that I deserve more than the little life they expect from me."

My lips part to tell Vivian that she's right. She does deserve more. She deserves *everything*. In the short time I've known her, I have no doubt she can tackle any obstacle, but Vivian snatching her hand back with wild eyes silences me.

"That was the wrong thing to say." Her fingers fly to the sides of her face. "You told me not to dive into personal tragedies, and"—she mimics diving into water—"there I went. I should top it off by sharing an embarrassing fact like, 'I pee in the shower.'"

An unexpected chuckle bursts from me, dissipating the tension in my spine. "Everyone pees in the shower."

"But do you blow your nose in the shower?" At my puzzled expression, Vivian places her thumb beside one nostril and her index finger beside the other. "Then blow."

My shoulders shake from the restraint required not to double over with laughter.

"You don't. Obviously." She groans, glancing skyward. "I might as well get all these taboo subjects out of my system so I don't say them on a real date."

Her off-handed comment reminds me that this is all practice for her. That as much as each of her shared confidences burrow deeper beneath my skin, I'm not the man she wants. Nor should I be. I'm too swept up in my own chaos to give Vivian what she deserves—absolute, focused devotion.

"You're doing fine, gorgeous." I wink, the gesture feeling smarmy instead of flirtatious in light of all that she's shared with me.

Vivian—oblivious to my mental distress—rolls her eyes before pointing to a square on my card. "You missed one."

During the rest of trivia, we discuss safer first-date topics—hobbies, pets, and music—all while trying not to wheeze-laugh over our growing list of taboo first-date topics. The shape of one's skull, your home shrine dedicated to a soccer star, and potty-training preferences for future children all contend for first place. When Bayside Table closes at ten, we slowly meander toward the main road.

"Let me walk you home, Vivian. It's late."

She snorts. "It's late and completely safe. Island teens run wild at night without worry of being harmed. You forget that things are different here."

Before I can destroy my dental work, I loosen my jaw. "Then let me walk you home for practice's sake. Atticus would offer to do so."

She tucks her hands into the pockets of her dress. "That's true."

A companionable silence settles between us. There's only the distant sound of the waves, cricketsong, and the soft crunch of our shoes on the sandy road shoulder. Fragrant magnolia blooms fill the humid air, stirring my thoughts.

"Vivian," I begin, keeping my gaze on the pools of amber streetlight on the road ahead. "Though I wouldn't recommend bringing up your family history on the first date, I'm glad you told me. And about your plans for your dress collection...I like being the person you share your secrets with."

Realizing that the last sentence is way too intimate, I quickly add, "I mean, in that it's helpful. As your coach."

"As my coach." Her hushed tone draws my attention. A beat passes before Vivian nods to herself decidedly. "Right."

When we arrive at the coffee shop, I follow Vivian behind the building. I hadn't noticed that the second story holds a living space. The knowledge that Vivian not only works but sleeps so close to me sends a fission of energy stinging my fingertips.

"Goodnight, Finn. Thanks for the dating practice tonight." Vivian takes a loose key from her dress pocket, stepping into the soft light of the sconce beside the solitary back door.

"Of course." I feel each inch of her moving in the opposite direction, like a hot iron slowly pressed to my skin. "Text if you need anything else."

Her hand freezes halfway toward the lock, and it's that momentary pause that shakes my insane question free.

It's a terrible idea. The worst I've had in a long time. But I find myself saying, "Do you also want to practice a goodnight kiss?"

FOURTEEN

Vivian

My eyelashes flutter, blurring the view of my door. There's no way I heard him correctly. "I—I'm sorry?"

Finn's forceful exhale is audible. "Neverm—"

"Yes," I cut him off, turning to face him and pocketing my key.

I expect flirtatious Finn to hit me with that roguish smile, but his jaw tightens. "You're sure?"

"I think it would be good practice. Don't you?"

The tendons in his neck strain as he shakes his head. "It doesn't matter what I think. What do you want, Vivian?"

You.

The unwieldy thought escapes before I can catch it.

But honestly, who could blame me?

Finn is masculinity perfected—all hard lines and muscles while still managing to be charming and kind. The way his eyes seemed to sparkle whenever I spoke left me heady earlier. And the stupid thing about it is that I've seen him pay that same rapt attention to others. It's a practiced skill. I *know* that. I know I'm nothing special. The connection I feel with Finn is a figment of my unwieldy imagination, a byproduct of reading too many romance novels. Tonight was all an act because I would never register on Finn's radar had we not concocted this unusual alliance.

Regardless, I'm not ready for the night to be over. And I really *could* use help. My only kissing experience had been from one of Noah's baseball parties during high school. It'd felt like Noah's teammate had been two seconds from unhinging his jaw and swallowing me whole. I know kissing can be slobbery, but surely that guy had a glandular disorder.

There's no doubt that Finn's kiss will be extraordinary—a triumphant culmination of years of experience.

Something I am desperately lacking.

"I want you to kiss me."

I don't tell Finn about my lack of experience. He'll likely notice. And if I say anything other than the daring sentence that just left my mouth, I'll chicken out.

The leisurely way Finn closes the distance between us is entirely too predatorial. Though I'd expected fierce, focused intent, the way he's looking at me has the potential to make my heart implode.

When my back bumps against the door, I almost ask him to stop. But then Finn pauses, and the intense pressure vaporizes.

The hesitant way his breath skirts over my temple doesn't feel like a suave maneuver. His broad chest heaves at an erratic frequency, matching mine. It's not until Finn wavers as our noses brush, a thick swallow bobbing his throat, that I finally understand.

He's being slow and cautious because that's how Atticus would kiss me.

My dating coach has thought of everything.

The slight tremor in his fingertips as they slide up my bare arms is intentional. The broken-glass-in-a-cement-mixer quality of his voice as he murmurs "Vivian" is above and beyond showmanship. I almost smile at how easy he's making this for me.

By the time Finn kisses me, I'm ready. The slight press of Finn's mouth to mine isn't what I was expecting, though. Indescribable energy cracks down my bones, righting my organs in its wake. I don't feel flustered anymore. Instead, a sensation of wholeness straightens my spine. I'm somehow stronger with Finn's whiskey-tinged lips on mine. The overwhelming sense of rightness flooding each and every nerve ending is so satiating that a breathy sigh escapes me. I feel Finn's smile rather than see it, and the spike of joy pistoning through me threatens to knock me sideways. Because...

This feels like a memory. Like something we've done before.

Which makes absolutely no sense.

Finn's face lifts from mine, and my body seizes control. It's a hostile takeover. My brain is duct taped to a chair somewhere with a purple paisley handkerchief over its mouth. It knows I should allow that chaste kiss to be the end of this particular lesson, but the rest of me vehemently disagrees.

I chase after Finn, unabashedly capturing his mouth while my hands grip the shirt over his stomach as if it's made of the finest silk. Finn, it seems, needs little encouragement to continue our practice session. One of his hands slides into my hair, expertly tilting my head as he deepens the kiss. Light fragments and re-fracts behind my closed eyelids, leaving blazing phantom streaks in its wake. This is so different from anything I've experienced before that I don't know how to catalog it.

Finn's pace remains unhurried. It's almost as if he's relishing every small touch, every sensation. He gives me time to absorb each movement, and when I reciprocate, a soft sound of en-couragement vibrates his chest. I feel savored and priceless, but not fragile or incapable. The way Finn is kissing me spurs the impulse to take, to demand what I want. It's new and dizzying, but suddenly, my hands fisting Finn's shirt feels like a waste. Why would I touch cotton when I could be exploring the hard panes of muscle from hours of dedicated gym time?

I release the fabric, my fingertips pressing firm and sliding up-ward until they're just below where I'd take his chest measure-ment for a garment. A surprised inhale slips into Finn's mouth as he breaks the kiss. Our gazes lock, and a thundercrack slices through the air, leaving thick electricity trailing in its wake.

My brow tightens. The forecasted summer storm isn't supposed to hit Wilks Beach until Thursday. I glance up, expecting clouds but seeing an open, endless sky. Maybe the skull-shaking sound was a figment of my imagination? Maybe Finn is such a good kisser he gives women auditory hallucinations?

Quite possible.

Finn's gaze falls to my fingertips, transfixed. A surge of power zips through me at his open-mouthed expression. He's even more breathtaking with a glimmer of devastation alighting his dark beard scruff, his thick eyelashes flickering against his tanned cheek, and his firm chest rising and falling beneath my touch.

Good gracious, he's a pretending pro. I feel like if I were to slide my palms over his heart, it would be his end—plain and simple. Before I can test the theory, Finn steps beyond my grasp, wiping his mouth with the back of his fist.

"Was that your first kiss?"

I want to joke, say something flippant that will make the both of us laugh like we'd been doing all night, but all I can manage is a simple "No."

An emotion flits over his cheekbones before Finn tucks it away. Disappointment? No. That doesn't make sense. Why would he be disappointed?

Finn slides his hands into his pockets, his roguish smile tugging his lips. "I'd say you're well prepared for your first date now."

A sensation of déjà vu overwhelms me, my brain racking to remember when I'd seen this before. That slight glimpse of a vulnerable underlayer before Finn threw charm upon it. It's undeniably intentional, and I suddenly want to dig into what Finn is hiding like pirates searching for buried treasure.

"Right." My forced chuckle sounds as hollow as it feels. "Thanks, Coach."

I'm rewarded with a tiny wince before Finn composes himself. There! I wasn't imagining it. My gaze drifts off while I think of why Finn would be unhappy...

Oh my goodness!

It has to be me.

I must be a terrible kisser.

That's why he's frowning now that it's over. I probably slobbered all over him like an untrained puppy, and Finn was so accurate with his portrayal of Atticus that I didn't even notice. My skin flames, and I nearly rip a hole in my dress pocket, searching for my key.

"Thanks again for everything,"—I turn my back, failing twice to put the key into the lock—"but I need to get to bed. Long day tomorrow. It's prom season, and well, you don't know what that means, but it's busy."

"Vivian."

"I love sequins as much as the next girl, but they make alterations so much harder."

The sensation of the lock releasing beneath my shaking hand almost makes me sob. And I plan on crying—*hard and messy*—but not until I'm safely behind not only this door but the door to my shop. I'm going to burn through an entire box of tissues in five minutes flat.

"Vivian." This time, a firm hand grips my wrist and flips me before I can turn the handle.

How it's possible for Finn to be breathing harder now than he had while kissing is unfathomable. His gaze bounces all over my face, his grip on my wrist loosening but not yielding.

"What is it?"

I shake my head at the soft question, pressing my lips tight and willing my eyes not to spill their sheening tears.

"Please tell me." The tender way his free hand frames my face sends goosebumps over my skin.

I hesitate, goldfishing for several heartbeats. "It was bad, wasn't it? My kissing."

Finn closes his eyes with a hard exhale. "No."

The honesty in his gaze when Finn focuses back on me steals my breath. "It was good. *Too good.* You made it easy to get swept up in that kiss, to forget who we are, but it's my job to make sure no lines get crossed." He releases me and steps back. "We've got a good thing going here, helping each other out. My colleagues are finally regarding me with something other than disdain, and you not only talked to Atticus today, you got his phone number. That's huge."

With him beyond the reaches of the wan lamplight, it's harder to scrutinize his features. "I'm glad I was able to help you tonight, but in the name of our friendship, I don't think it's a good idea to practice kissing again."

"Our friendship?"

"That's what we are, right?"

As much as my imagination would like to apply the completely inappropriate label of *lovers* to our fledgling relationship, I say, "I don't know when we switched from mentee/mentor to friends, but I'll take it."

I make sure to lace my lightly toned sentence with a toothy smile.

Finn's tense shoulders finally relax. "Goodnight, then."

"Night, Finn."

I tell myself that watching Finn walk home from the living room window until I can't see his sturdy shadow in the distance is something a *caring friend* would do. So is double-checking that said friend made it home safe via text.

Vivian

Any ruffians give you trouble on the way home? Apparently, the island is teeming with them.

Finn

Har. Har.

Vivian

I'm serious. Apparently, safety is a real issue. Should we move?

Dots blink for an inordinately long time before Finn's message comes through. I can't blame lack of service for the delay in his answer. Wilks Beach might be out of the way physically, but its cellular service game is strong.

Finn

> **If I get the directorship, I'll be leaving at the end of the summer.**

I knew that. He'd be coordinating the entire library system from the Central Library in Virginia Beach. The whole point of our arrangement is for him to get that position. The gnawing pinch in my stomach is probably hunger related. I open and stare blankly at the fridge contents before grabbing the container of grapes. Delicious sweetness crushes between my molars as I type out an answer.

Vivian

> You're absolutely going to get that job. By the time we're done, everyone on this island will love you.

And if I'm not careful, I will too.

FIFTEEN

Finn

Here's what I expected on a cloudy Wednesday morning: a peaceful walk to the library, work as usual, and that's about it. What I hadn't anticipated was how being out with Vivian last night would sprinkle a layer of golden sunshine over my day.

Every single library staff member reciprocated my daily "good morning." Patricia even invited me to join her and Greg for karaoke on Thursday. My voicemail was nearly full of messages offering suggestions for ways to raise money for the media room.

Had I thought of a shirtless car wash at the fire station?

No, but Carol Cook had. Complete with detailed descriptions on which firemen should do the washing and which should run the cash box. Receiving a non-vitriol voicemail from her was so refreshing that I even *smiled* at the stack of Regency romances left on my desk by the ninja librarian.

I've just finished clearing the messages when Brynn sails through my open door. If I didn't recognize her from our brief interaction at the Seabreeze Beans last week, her coffee ground-stained apron over her t-shirt and running shorts gives her away. Unlike the other locals I've interacted with today, Brynn's pinched gaze could cut glass.

"Did you go on a date with my sister last night?" Her raised voice draws the attention of Judith and Bonnie, two lovely patrons who offered to make me a book-themed quilt when they arrived a few moments ago with their bags of fabric.

My affable smile doesn't waver as I stand. "No. Vivian kindly allowed me to accompany her to music trivia, but it wasn't a date." I move from behind my desk. "I don't think we've been properly introduced. I'm Finn Reynolds."

Brynn stares at my outstretched hand for two beats before closing my office door. "Listen, Mainlander. My sister has been through a lot and—"

"You both lost your parents at a young age." I barely keep the flaring irritation out of my voice. It's clear that Brynn only wants to protect her sister, but it's overly cautious responses like this that contribute to Vivian feeling so small. "Vivian told me. My condolences to you as well."

Brynn takes a half step back, her brows crashing together. "She...she told you."

"We've become friends," I say, suppressing the memories from last night—of what happened right before I drew that line in the sand.

I'd been able to keep up my confident persona until Vivian had been inches from me. Then, I'd completely forgotten who I was supposed to be. Vivian's soft scent dismantled the intricate layers I keep tight around myself until all I could do was trace my fingers up her warm skin and bring my mouth to hers.

It'd been the sweetest torture to pace myself, to give Vivian the gentle first kiss she'd needed. Even when she'd demanded more, I held back out of self-preservation. But then Vivian had touched my chest, and I'd been lost, structurally rearranged, and given a soul-satiating sense of belonging in the span of three seconds. It'd taken all my willpower to step back when all I'd wanted was to possess her mouth with the same ferocity that her fingertips had captured my heart.

My fingers flex as my brain drags the rest of me back to my office. "Friends?"

I nod, tucking my hands into my pockets. "Vivian is helping me find ways to connect with patrons who want to improve this library. Dave—or Dr. Prescott, as Vivian calls him—has already offered to match the sum of donations brought in through a fundraising event. I'm working to determine what kind of event would best serve this community."

Her scrutinizing gaze slides from my Oxfords to the gloss of my hair. "You're up to something."

"Yes." It's been a while since I've needed to use this much effort to remain cheerfully neutral. "I'm trying to improve the media room. I'd also like to establish a preservation space for Wilks Beach's historic books, but..."—I lift a casual shoulder—"one step at a time."

Brynn shakes her head subtly, her right fingers fisting. "You held her hand."

Vivian hadn't been lying when she said that word travels fast in a small town. Though I silently curse myself for not thinking about what holding Vivian's hand must have looked like from outside the conversation, I can't seem to conjure a single speck of regret over the action.

"Briefly, yes, while she told me about your parents' deaths."

Brynn's facial features soften.

"I don't mean Vivian, or anyone in this town, harm. I'm simply here to do my job."

I don't add that, after last night, I'd reroute the ocean if it'd help Vivian achieve her goals.

The only thing I *can't do* is kiss her again.

Brynn opens her mouth as if to retort, but I'm rescued by Trudy knocking and then cracking open the glass door. "I'm sorry to interrupt, but it's urgent."

"You shouldn't come to the library smelling like crab cakes and cigars," a woman's brassy voice drifts through my office door. It sounds like she's shouting from downstairs.

Judith and Bonnie have abandoned their project and are leaning over the short half wall that separates the upstairs reading area from the first floor.

"Yeah, well at least I don't smell like an overgrown hothouse," a man's voice retorts.

"People like flowers!"

"People like cigars!"

"You better get down there before they start throwing chairs," Trudy says, worry etching the subtle lines that bracket her hazel eyes.

I slip past both women, thundering down the stairs and arriving on the main floor just in time to catch a fluttering hardback mid-flight. A bleach-blonde woman—whose head was the book's intended target—snatches up a corner-gnawed board book from a nearby reshelving cart and holds it aloft. I stop her heavily perfumed forearm with my open palm, halting her throw.

"That's enough! I don't know what's going on here, but it stops now." My voice is entirely too loud for the library, but tossing books like they're opened pudding cups in a cafeteria food fight is completely unacceptable.

Carol Cook snorts from beside the circulation desk. "It will now that you've acknowledged these idiots." She leans heavily on the desktop to use her cane to point at the tank-top clad man. "These two just need to brawl it out publicly every few weeks or so."

As if Carol's words had been a switch, remorse floods the man's face. He rubs a hand over his unkempt beard, stepping forward. "I'm sorry, baby. I'll ease up on the cigars."

The woman crosses her arms over her mesh swimsuit cover, tucking the board book against her side and looking away with a defiant chin lift.

"Honey, angel. What I gotta do? I'll do anything," he pleads, moving forward.

"I'd kick them out before they get to the next part if I were you." Carol's tone is sharp with warning.

Not wanting to know what *the next part* entails, I extend my palm, pinning the woman with a stare. "Please exit the building."

Her glittered fingernails slap *The Very Hungry Caterpillar* into my hand before she runs toward the man she'd just tried to maim. When she jumps and twines her legs around the man's torso, I get an idea of what's coming.

"Outside, please!"

They listen but while devouring each other like starving piranhas. A nearby mother attempts to cover the eyes of her two children while the amorous couple slams into the side of the automatic door before finally stumbling out.

I set the board book on the circulation desktop. "Who in the name of—"

"Karen and Todd," Carol cuts me off with a disapproving huff. "You'd think since they're both pushing fifty, they'd know better. Usually, they keep their antics tethered to the bar, but there must be some serious tumbleweeds in the romance department if they felt the need to have it out at the library."

Bile flicks the back of my throat at her colorful description, but Carol simply shrugs. "Marriage is long and hard. You've got to spice things up from time to time."

When all I can manage is to blink, a slow smile curls her mouth, causing the hairs on my neck to stand on end. "I can't believe I've bested Mr. Charm. What? No witty retort? No appeasing sentence to smooth things over?"

"Excuse me?" Even when I'm saying the words, I straighten my spine, even my facial expression, and mentally run through the last few seconds to see exactly where I let my veneer lapse.

Carol waves me off. "Never mind about that. What did you think about my fundraising idea?"

The rest of the day continues with the same strange trajectory. A patron comes in looking for a lost wetsuit, which, oddly, Patricia had set aside for him last week. Two misguided seagulls find their way into the stacks, and it requires the five of us on staff to coax them outside with croutons from my lunch. A pair of teens decides to use the staircase as a rehearsal space for the balcony scene from *Romeo and Juliet*, but I can't bring myself to stop them because 1) it's literary related, and 2) their portrayal is surprisingly moving.

By the time I'm wrapping my hands for my evening boxing class, I give myself a mental high-five for keeping it together, especially since, every three seconds, I'm distracted by the memory of Vivian's breathy sigh against my mouth, or the feel of her curls draped over the back of my hand, or how her incredible magnolia-coffee scent seemed to seep into my skin.

"Dude." A man with curly brown hair playfully knocks me in the shoulder with his gloved hand. "I heard you got our Vivian to laugh last night. Usually, I'm the only one who can make her laugh in public. I'm impressed."

My exhausted brain can't recall this man's name. I've been memorizing the names of the other gym members when the owner yells at them—something she's fond of doing. We've been partnered up before, but this is the first time he's spoken to me. What's his name? Nathan? Niel?

"Noah! Less chit-chat, more hitting. You should already be on your bag." Geneva's sleek pony-tail swings as she turns to harass two other attendees of the popular boxing class.

Noah chuckles. "She yells at me almost as much as my ex does when I try to buy a cup of coffee. It's not my fault that Brynn's is the only shop in town, and sometimes I want something nicer than the road tar they brew at the fire station."

All the pieces fall into place. Noah. As in Brynn's ex, the former flamed-out professional baseball player turned local firefighter whom Vivian affectionately calls her long-lost brother-in-law.

"That's something we have in common."

Noah's eyebrows rise a second before his shoulders bounce in a casual shrug, lifting the WBFD logo on his ocean-blue t-shirt.

"Makes sense she'd lay into you." He begins to warm up on the bag. "She warned us you were one of *those* mainlanders weeks ago."

A spiny black sea anemone pricks at my temple. "It was Brynn who told everyone to give me the cold shoulder?"

Noah nods to the bag, placing a few well-targeted hits dead center. "She's incredibly protective not only of Vivian, but this town."

I slip on my gloves, switching spots with Noah as he holds the bag. "You'd think she'd get to know me before making a judgment."

Noah chuckles, bracing punches that are much too hard for a simple warm-up. "Brynn shoots first and apologizes later. Actually"—his gaze drifts to the exposed metal cross-beams above us—"she isn't big on apologizing either."

"Sounds like a real peach."

"Careful." Noah's sharp tone draws my attention.

The fire in his gaze reminds me that I never speak ill of anyone in public, especially when I don't know everyone's alliances.

Suffice it to say, I might as well be an island here.

"Sorry, man."

Noah's jaw visibly loosens. "It's fine."

We're quiet for a few punches before he adds, "I know what it's like being at the receiving end of Brynn's wrath. It isn't an easy place to be."

I stop. "How'd you get back on her good side?"

He twists his lips. "I wouldn't say—

"Noah! My chickens cluck less than you do. Shut it!"

Noah surprises me by shaking his head at Geneva before sticking out his tongue. Geneva growls, low and animalistic, making the two women on the bag next to us shudder.

"Aren't you worried that she'll disembowel you?" I ask quietly once Geneva's impaling gaze focuses elsewhere.

My first few weeks in class, the tough-as-steel gym owner put me through my paces, working me twice as hard until one night she simply nodded and treated me the same as everyone else.

Noah's mouth tips at the corners. "Mom would never allow it."

My clarifying question is cut off by Geneva calling out our strike patterns with the threat of weighted burpees upon anyone who utters a syllable until the end of class. Wisely, Noah and I seal our lips. But as soon as we're dismissed, I'm asking my new friend if he'd join me for a beer at Bayside Table.

SIXTEEN

Vivian

"There you are." Amanda Ratchack's saccharine-sweet voice slides beside me in Dotty's compact freezer aisle.

I barely trap my ragged exhale. I'd wholly underestimated how many people would want to talk to me—someone they *never* engage in conversation with—after being out with Finn last night. The second I opened my shop this morning, folks rubber-necked while passing my glass door. Bolder citizens, like Carol Cook, barged right through.

When she asked if I was dating Finn, I almost stabbed myself with a needle. How absurd! There's no world in which a man like Finn would be interested in me. I assured her that we're not dating, sticking to my story that I was simply correcting my sister's bad reconnaissance.

After Carol left, I expected Brynn to charge into my shop, wanting to talk. With Seabreeze Beans being the mecca of town gossip, it'd been shocking that my sister didn't pull me out of bed before my alarm went off at nine. People certainly spoke to her more than they were stopping in my store.

But Brynn never came by, not even after the coffee shop closed. And after her nap, she silently stewed, making our dinner awkward. I get that my sister hates being wrong more than she loathes adjusting her rigid schedule, but the cold shoulder?

What are we, ten years old?

I couldn't take the tension in our small apartment a second longer. That's why I'm staring at Dotty's limited frozen section, hoping ice cream will solve everything. It has an eight out of ten success rate, so I'm optimistic.

"I'm so glad I caught you," Amanda says, every word dripping with insincerity. "I'm still waiting on my alterations. Or have you forgotten?" A sharp, fake laugh punctuates her sentence, and I have to fight the urge to flinch.

Every generation has what my aunt likes to call *a duplicitous charmer* since she says *a wolf in sheep's clothing* is uninspired. I've had the good fortune of my high school bully living abroad for the last few years, but Amanda popped into my shop a few weeks ago, announcing her return to Wilks Beach, with an armful of dresses that are too big now that she's lost weight from living a healthier lifestyle in Sweden.

"I haven't forgotten, but since you said 'no hurry' on the return time, I prioritized the prom dress clients," I say, debating between getting The Tonight Dough or Phish Food. It's been such a weird day I should get both.

Amanda's overfilled lips pout before the corner of her mouth quirks in a devious smile. "Is it that time of year again? Remember our senior prom? So fun. I loved the masquerade theme and trying to figure out who was behind the mask. Of course, it was easy to pick you out with that dress."

Amanda's thinly veiled insult doesn't land because my prom dress was incredible. While everyone else had worn store-bought dresses, I'd constructed a Victorian-inspired gown from midnight-blue velvet. Miss Wendy and I had worked on it for weeks after school. It'd been in the quiet moments of working on my mentor's dining room table as sunlight shone through the large windows when she'd asked if I'd be interested in taking over her tailoring business.

Seeing she's missed the mark, Amanda taps her cheek with her index finger. "Who did you go with again?"

My face stings as if I'd been slapped. Amanda knows full well that I played the unwilling third wheel to Brynn and Noah. I'd planned on staying home after Zach Hineman stood me up, but Brynn would have none of it. Instead of enjoying a romantic evening with her then-boyfriend, she'd insisted the three of us remain inseparable.

The only thing that'd kept my twin from joining me at the hip had been my hoop skirt.

My heart clenches. Even with Brynn's childish behavior tonight, she's always looked after me. I snag a pint of Cherry Garcia—Brynn's favorite—as a peace offering.

"No matter," Amanda continues. "I wanted to ask you about your friend. I've seen him running since he moved here."

"Atticus?" My stomach sinks to my exposed toes as I let the freezer door shut.

Brynn commenting on how she passes Atticus in the evenings was how I learned he was also a runner. Over the past year, I have occasionally—in a completely non-creepy way—snuck into the living room to watch his long, confident strides eat up the asphalt.

"Who?" Her forehead creases before she actively smoothes it out—almost as if remembering that facial expressions cause wrinkles. "I'm talking about the new library manager."

Oh. I didn't know Finn ran.

I must have put too many red pepper flakes in tonight's pasta aglio e oilio because a flare of heartburn surges in my chest. I rub at my sternum, but the stubborn sensation persists.

"Finn." Why does his name taste like sawdust?

Amanda lights up. "Yes. What can you tell me about him?"

"He...uh..." I pause as my brain spirals.

Amanda is exactly the type of woman Finn should be with—gorgeous, confident, athletic. She doesn't even sweat like normal humans. She gets this preternatural glow after running. Meanwhile,

I end up with goggle impressions around my eyes and streaks of red on my shoulders from where I misapplied sunscreen after my open-water swims.

The spiral continues, unrelenting. Amanda is wearing bike shorts too, but she doesn't need them under everything to evade chub rub. Her elastic waistband doesn't accentuate existing rolls since there isn't an inch of squish on her. They effortlessly pair with her sports-bra-as-a-shirt and her ultra-sleek ponytail.

Mentally, I pinch myself.

I shouldn't compare myself to Amanda.

"Everyone is given exactly what they need." My eyes close as Aunt Tammy's words reverberate through my brain.

And besides, it's not like we want the same man.

Before I can stop myself, the memory of Finn's kiss slips over my vision. The tender way his fingers grazed up my arms. The approving hum each time I mimicked the delicate actions of his tongue. The way his eyes looked almost black, staring at my fingertips as they rested on his chest.

"He's..." I pause to collect myself, opening the freezer door again and dropping The Tonight Dough into my hand basket. "He's great. Really outgoing. Very passionate about the library."

Inexplicably handsome.

Not helpful, brain!

"He, uh...he's a..."

An incredible kisser.

STOP THAT!

"He smells amazing, if you like books."

Amanda's serene expression wavers with that last description, and my cheeks blaze as I push past her toward the register. "You should stop by the library and talk to him."

"I will." She gets in line behind me, unloading nothing but carrots and celery, but blessedly leaves me alone as I quickly check out with Cliff.

When I return from the market, Brynn is locked into her room—either avoiding me or already asleep. Since it's only eight, I assume the former. I put away her pint of ice cream with a heavy sigh. My eyes fixate on the condensating lid of The Tonight Dough before adding it to the freezer. The only emotion I can't eat through is sadness. Sugar helps quell nervousness, boredom, irritation, but sorrow hollows out my stomach every time.

Suddenly, I miss Aunt Tammy with a fierceness that shortens my next inhale. No one deserves to be living her best life more than our aunt, but I miss her not being a short walk away. When she transferred the business over to Brynn, Tammy moved in with her long-term boyfriend. The two of them were married last fall and are still enjoying their global honeymoon, currently sailing off the coast of Spain.

A deflated sensation zaps what was left of my energy. Collapsing on the couch, I tap my phone against my thigh and think about Finn. I shouldn't. I should only be thinking about Atticus, but thoughts of Finn's lips, the soft noise he makes in his throat, and the scratch of his beard scruff have haunted me all day. I wonder what kind of day he had. What did he eat for lunch? Things I have no right to know.

There *is* one thing I can ask him, though.

Vivian

> When should I expect Atticus to text me?

Finn doesn't respond immediately. He's probably at The Garage Gym for his evening workout.

Loneliness sweeps from my collarbones to the tips of my unpainted toes. I curl beneath the pink couch throw, clicking on the TV. I'm usually alone, but I don't feel lonely. Tonight, the sensation is disintegrating my bones.

Before my misty eyes spill into unnecessary tears, I cue up my favorite Netflix show—mine and eighty-two million other's. Since the television series' second season is scheduled to drop mid-July, now is the perfect time for a rewatch of season one.

I'm fifteen minutes into the second episode when Finn answers my text.

Finn

> Probably Friday. If you don't hear any-
> thing by Monday, let me know.

My fingers race, typing things I don't intend to send. The first season of *Worthingon* is centered around young Jane from an up-and-coming society family becoming the unfortunate scapegoat for sinister Lady Fitzroy's scandal. That is, until the eldest Worthington—his grace, the duke—swoops in and rescues Jane by way of a fake proposal, becoming fiercely protective of her.

I chuckle to myself, rereading my message, but then the image of Finn boxing in buff breeches and a rolled-up linen shirt makes my smile fall. My imagination runs wild, envisioning sweat sliding down that distracting notch between Finn's tanned collarbones, his black hair flopping over his forehead, and his toned shoulders heaving from exertion. He'd saunter toward the ropes after winning, his gaze possessive as it rakes me from head to toe.

Pepper leaps from her cat tower, startling me. My finger—which had been hovering over the delete button—punches the send button instead.

"Shoot!" I jump from the couch, nearly tripping over the blanket that's still half-tucked around me. "Shoot! Shoot! Shoot!"

A horrified, high-pitched sound escapes me. Pepper lovingly winds herself between my legs as I type.

Finn

So someone else named Finn? How many of us are in your roster, gorgeous?

I slap my forehead with my free hand, my cheeks flushing. I've been thoroughly caught. At least Finn isn't here to witness my humiliation with that devious little smirk of his. All I need to do is put my phone in the freezer and pretend I don't have cellular service. Yup. That should work. I take a stride toward the kitchen when another message pops onto the screen.

Finn

But to answer your question, we don't speak of She-Who-Must-Not-Be-Named.

The starburst shining from my chest is so unexpected it takes me a few seconds to catch my breath. I tuck back onto the sofa, holding my phone in two eager hands. Finn is an accomplished conversationalist. Other than talking about his ambitious drive for the directorship or plans for the library, he evades personal questions like dodging punches. All I got out of him yesterday was his sister's name.

Ask about the rest of his family? Bob and weave.

Childhood? Slip to the right.

It's almost as if his life didn't exist before he got his masters. This admission that there's an ex who did damage feels monumental.

Vivian

So there was someone...

Finn

Everyone has a someone.

I huff, my fingertips racing over the screen.

Vivian

I don't have a someone.

Finn

That's because every man in this town is an idiot.

My heart sprints as I type and send my next message without thinking.

Vivian

Where are you?

The dots blink and recede. Like last night, it takes too long to receive his answer.

Finn

I'm walking to Bayside Table with Noah.

My head tilts back against the back of the couch. Of course. He should be making friends, not sitting around texting with me. Finn seems like the type that's usually out every night. I try to picture Finn snuggled beside me on the couch, watching *Worthington*, reading next to me on his deck chairs as the sun slips below the bay, or holding my hand as we take a quiet evening stroll down the beach. A social creature like Finn probably prefers being out to such docile activities. He practically lit up while being surrounded by others at music trivia last night.

Finn

Want to join us?

I blink at the invitation for three seconds. I *had* told Finn that I wanted to do more with my life. Maybe going out twice in one week is the perfect start.

It's not until I'm outside my apartment that I realize I'm wearing a pair of gray bike shorts and an oversized *Made in the 90s* shirt with cassette tape design. My hair is pulled into a messy bun, and I'm wearing my tortoise-shell glasses. I take a step backward before I realize that Noah—and this whole town—has seen me exactly like this thousands of times before. Amanda and Cliff *just saw* me like this at the market.

If I change now, I'll be changing to impress Finn. And there's no need to impress Finn. He was very clear in defining the lines of our relationship last night.

Just friends.

I'm rounding the building when a delivery driver rolls to a stop in front of Seabreeze Beans. Though it's past nine, it isn't unusual for deliveries to our island to be the last of the day.

"Vivian Hutchinson?"

"That's me." I take the proffered envelope. "Thanks."

Though online delivery is helpful everywhere else in the country, the extra delivery charges applied to Wilks Beach residents means we order less than the general public. And I certainly didn't order this package.

Curiosity bubbles as my hand dives inside, finding a gift receipt first.

I didn't want you to lose your key. -F

Upturning the envelope, a bronze music note keychain falls into my palm. I stare at the small paired eighth notes glinting in the lamp light. I love it. It's so completely perfect. But then I turn it over, and goosebumps slide over my skin. My favorite Raven Sacaria lyric is engraved on the back.

Rock me like the rolling sea.

During music trivia, we discussed our favorite musicians—mine being Raven Sacaria. The aging singer-songwriter who has transcended music through the decades by constantly adapting was also my mother's favorite. Mom used to hum her songs as she entered data into spreadsheets while working from home, or while weeding our small vegetable garden, or while playing board games with us on rainy nights. Listening to Raven's music helps me feel connected to her even after all this time.

How did Finn know? I never spoke about any particular song, just that I loved her music. My shaky fingers reach into my shirt and pluck the loose key from my bra. With how much my hands are sweating, it takes two attempts to secure the key to the attached ring. Unconsciously, I fist the gift to my chest, noticing for the first time how erratic my pulse is.

This can't be my response to a simple, thoughtful gift. Finn wants us to be friends. Friends who don't kiss. I need to clobber these romantic fantasies like a teenager raging on whack-a-mole.

"He's so out of your league he might as well be another species."

I make myself say it two more times before I pull out my phone to respond to Finn's invitation.

SEVENTEEN

Finn

"**W**hat's with the face?" Noah asks, as we sit at an empty picnic table at Bayside Table.

I lock my phone screen to hide Vivian's polite refusal, sliding it into the pocket of my sweat-damp athletic shorts before reconsidering and placing it face down on the table. "It's nothing."

Earlier, when we'd been walking here, I'd answered Vivian's question about Atticus, not telling Noah who I was texting with. Then I'd had to keep from grinning like an idiot as we'd gone back and forth.

Vivian's last message, thanking me for the invitation but saying that she's staying home makes sense. It's late. She's not used to being out multiple times per week since she usually only goes to music

152

trivia. It probably wouldn't be best for town gossip if we were seen together two nights in a row, anyway.

Especially since she's interested in Atticus.

These are all logical, valid reasons, yet none of them assuage the dull ache along my ribs.

"Nothing, huh?" Noah gives me an unconvinced look over his club soda and orange.

My new boxing partner was happy to accept my invitation for a post-workout drink with the caveat that his be non-alcoholic since he's six years sober. Drinking after Geneva practically beat the crap out of us didn't seem like the best idea, so I ordered the same.

"It's just...women problems," I tell him, shocking myself by actually telling the truth instead of coming up with a complex web of lies. It's second nature when someone asks me a question about myself at this point. I must be *really* exhausted for the truth to wiggle through.

"With someone on the mainland," I add quickly when Noah's eyebrows shoot up.

"No offense, but I can't imagine you having women problems." His boisterous laugh draws the attention of the middle-aged couple nearest us.

"What's that supposed to mean?"

"My dude." He pulls off his backward baseball hat, runs his fingers through his hair, and replaces it. "You own a mirror, right?"

I grin at the table, shaking my head. "It's never that simple."

"True." He nods, his gaze drifting out over the calm bay.

Sensing an opening, I ask, "What's the story with you and Brynn?"

Noah sucks a breath through his teeth. "Come on, man. We just met. Don't hit me with the hard punches at the beginning of our bromance."

I laugh for what seems like the seventeenth time in ten minutes. Before Vivian and I began texting, Noah had been playfully goading Geneva after class ended. We helped put away equipment as Noah tried to get Geneva to crack a smile—unsuccessfully, I might note.

My hands lift in surrender. "Got it. Women are off the table. Want to talk sports?"

Noah's grin broadens. "Please tell me you're a baseball fan."

The remainder of the week is almost bland in its simplicity. Don't get me wrong, I'm glad the locals are finally being pleasant, and no one else attempts to jumpstart their marriage in the library. Even the wild rainstorm we were supposed to receive yesterday ended up being a light sprinkle.

It's not until Vivian rushes through my office door late Friday afternoon that I realize it's *her* that's been missing. I struggle to keep my expression even, to conceal the way my mood lifts as she tosses her butterfly tote on my desk with complete disregard for my neatly stacked folders. I've missed Vivian's quiet chaos, her freckle-dusted cheekbones, her—

I cut off the thought, leaning back in my office chair with an air of nonchalance that's in direct opposition to my sprinting heartbeat.

"Isn't this a pleasant surprise."

Vivian tucks a springy curl behind her ear, coming around the desk. "I need help."

Her quick motion sends her azure skirt billowing, her coffee-tinged magnolia fragrance perfuming the room. If I thought my heart was racing before, it's malfunctioning now. She's going to kill me sitting on my desk like that, legs crossed at the ankle. I know there are shorts under her tea-length dress, but that doesn't make me want to slide a hand up her calf any less.

I let an easy smile lift my lips and interlace my fingers over my stomach to keep them from misbehaving. "With what?"

"Petunia finally clunked out," Vivian tells me, biting her lip and twisting her ring.

I bolt upright in my chair. "Who's Petunia?"

A great-grandmother? A townsperson I've yet to meet?

"No, Finn." Vivian settles both hands on my shoulders, her head subtly shaking. "Nothing like that. Petunia is my car. Brynn's, technically, but we both use it. I drive to the mainland less than her, so we share one."

"Oh." I should lean back now that she's clarified, but then I'd miss the gentle weight of her hands.

"This is going to sound silly."

"I doubt it." I make sure to quirk the corner of my lips, even though I'm being completely honest. "Nothing you say is silly."

Vivian wrinkles her nose, and I nearly implode. Death by cuteness. Is that a thing?

"Just listen." She playfully pushes me back, breaking contact. "Do you remember when I told you about the Oceanside Artisan Fair?"

"Of course, gorgeous. It's tomorrow."

Her mouth opens and closes a few times before she swallows. "Right. Well, what I didn't tell you was it was part two of my ocean wish. Officially, I only wished for the ability to talk to the man of my dreams, because everyone knows you can only ask the ocean for one thing."

"Naturally." My fingers clench the armrests at the reminder of Atticus.

Vivian narrows her eyes at my dry comment but continues, "Having that first wish granted gave me the confidence to move forward with part two of my plan."

She breathes that wistful sigh of hers, and darn if my chest doesn't clench.

"Honestly, the last few days have felt like an upbeat montage. All that was missing was Natasha Bedingfield's soulful voice as I boxed up dresses to secretly put in the trunk overnight, coordinated online with a clothing store on the mainland to borrow some garment racks, and got a credit card reader for my phone for cashless transactions. But when I drove to get money for a cash box this afternoon,

Petunia broke down, and I had to hitch a ride with Dr. Prescott to get home."

"So you need a ride tomorrow," I say, tamping down annoyance that Vivian didn't come to me sooner. If she had called, I would have picked her up.

Vivian nods. "The mechanic said he can't get to it until Monday. I know it's asking a lot, but would you mind driving me?"

Unable to keep from touching her, I give her forearm a quick squeeze. "Of course. I'd be happy to."

"And you don't mind coming over late tonight—like ten-thirty—so we can load up the dresses? You'll have to park beside Seabreeze Beans so no one recognizes your car."

I run a hand down the buttons of my suit vest to dissipate the sting from her comment. "I thought that since I'm no longer the town villain, we can be seen together."

"Yeah, but being together that late would look like we're dating." Her lips twist as if that idea is as appetizing as sucking raw sewage through a straw. "Atticus still hasn't texted me. Do you think it's because of music trivia? Maybe he thinks we're—" She flicks a finger between us.

"Facing each other?" I ask, lifting a single eyebrow.

Vivian huffs. "No. You know..." She widens her eyes pointedly.

I'd planned on teasing her a few more times but change tactics. Since the library is scheduled to close in ten minutes—except for those in attendance for bingo in the meeting room downstairs—the upstairs is empty.

I stand, my smirk broadening. "Friends who practice kissing?"

A shaky inhale lifts Vivian's shoulders as her cheeks flush. I unconsciously follow that cotton candy stain as it streaks down her neck, my gaze stalling at her thrumming pulse point. Several seconds pass as the air around us grows thicker. Electrifies.

"Finn."

My name is a breathy whisper, but I can't drag my eyes from her neck. There's a spray of freckles over her left collarbone that I want to trace with my lips.

"Yes, gorgeous?"

All the lights in the library click off except those in my office. Patricia is probably closing early.

"You..." A swallow bobs her beautiful throat. "You said—"

"Just wanted to double-check that—" Letitia's voice cuts off as she looks up from the thick stack of bingo cards she's been organizing, freezing in my doorway.

It takes me three stumbling heartbeats to realize that I'm pressed between Vivian's fabric-covered legs, and that her right hand is gripping my hip. When did I move forward? How did Vivian touch me without me noticing? Probably because I'd been consumed by the insatiable need to kiss her again. Another second and I was going to start at that frantic pulse point at her neck and work my way up.

"Um." Letitia's dark skin pinks slightly before she flips. "Never mind."

A handful of bingo cards slips from her arms, but Letitia doesn't even look back. In fact, she uses the pink cardstock to shield her face until she descends the stairs.

I want to laugh, but the impulse swiftly dies once I catch Vivian's panicked eyes. "Shouldn't you go after her?"

"And do what?"

"Tell her she didn't see what she thought she saw."

My step back is so forceful I send my rolling chair skittering. For a second, I thought—

No. Nothing's changed. Vivian has been very clear about her desire to date Atticus. I was the one who pushed things by flirting when I shouldn't have. This is my fault. I barely resist the urge to fist my hands at my own idiocy.

"You're right," I say, heading toward the door. "I'll go talk to her."

Once I attempt damage control with an unconvinced Letitia, I return to my office. To my surprise, Vivian is still here, hugging herself and staring at the ocean. I clear my throat so as to not startle her and lean against the doorjamb.

"Everything's sorted."

I hate that her brow softens at my words. "Good. Thank you."

A casual nod bobs my chin, though it feels like all my tendons are a half inch shorter. Everything in my body is tight.

"I've been thinking..." Vivian twirls her pinky ring. "Maybe I should take the first step with Atticus. Text him and ask him to Bayside Table? It's not the 1950s, right? I don't need to wait for him to make the first move."

"You don't." I cross to my desk, packing my things for the night. I need to get out of this room, out of this conversation, more than I need oxygen.

Blessedly, Vivian takes the hint and gathers her canvas bag. "Okay, I'll do that."

"You should." It takes all my strength not to fling those words at her like a moody teenager.

I just need some space to get my head on straight. Atticus is who Vivian truly wants. She's just practicing with me. I need to understand that I'm here to help, not for keeps. I shouldn't be upset. This is how I like my dating life. I've always kept things short term so I didn't have to open up, because my life is overly complicated.

That and the one woman who got beneath my layers didn't want the real me. I'm not putting myself in a position to be shattered again. It isn't worth it.

I slip on a carefree smile and slide my messenger bag over my shoulder. "I'll text once I'm parked tonight. I'm assuming you'll want to pack the car without waking Brynn."

Vivian's brows are furrowed, her gaze fixed on a gray carpet square. "What?" She glances up. "Oh, yes."

We walk shoulder to shoulder down the stairs until I break off with the pretenses of checking in on Letitia.

A splash of disappointment skirts her face, which is confusing as heck. "Okay." Vivian bites her lip. "See you later, friend."

That last word was a dagger I really didn't need, but message received. From now on, I'm keeping six feet of space between us at all times.

"Bye, Vivian."

I wait a minute before leaving, but instead of going home, I head to the small market. After buying all the cold sodas in Dotty's refrigerator section and twenty bags of chips, I return to the library meeting room to raucous applause. They even pause the game to receive my gifts—something Letitia assures me *never* happens.

Bingo is apparently very cutthroat in Wilks Beach. A table needed repairing last week after being flipped in a dispute of who called "Bingo" first. They don't even play for prizes, just clout and their name on a winner's circle poster that hangs in the corner.

A handful of locals invites me to play, but I make excuses. What I need more than anything is to remind myself who I really am. I'm no one's forever. Vivian wouldn't make a cosmic wish for someone to date for a few weeks.

I check my watch: twenty after five. Just enough time to get off this island for a few hours. Pulling out my phone, I call Alec.

"Please tell me you're coming out tonight," he answers. "I've had such a crappy week, and I need to bury my sorrows in a dumb blonde."

I force a stale laugh, ignoring how his words chafe. Has Alec always spoken so callously about women? "I am."

"Yes!" He aggressively hoots into the phone, forcing me to pull it away from my ear.

"But I can only stay out until nine-thirty."

Alec grumbles, calling me a few emasculating names before we make plans on where to meet.

I intentionally lower my tense shoulders as I walk home. It doesn't matter how I feel about this situation. Vivian and I are only friends, so maybe I should find someone else to kiss.

EIGHTEEN

Vivian

I don't realize that I'm standing on Miss Wendy's doorstep until I see her seashell welcome mat beneath my sandals. Since I don't usually visit on Friday evenings, I knock instead of letting myself in like I would on a Monday morning when I deliver her weekly fresh flowers.

My lips downturn, hearing heavy cane-assisted steps toward the door. Wendy didn't tell me she was having issues with mobility. I hadn't thought to ask since she'd been seated in her cozy sunroom with a cup of coffee when I'd been by earlier this week.

"It's about time." The door flies open, Carol Cook's tattooed eyebrows slashing low with disapproval. "Vivian." Her expression softens. "I didn't mean to startle you. Come in."

I shouldn't be surprised to find Carol here on a Friday evening. Her and Wendy have been best friends since their moms used to sit on town council together. This was before the town was fully absorbed into the larger city beyond and council members became social figureheads instead of those who held elected power. Young Wendy split her piece of gum in half, and they've been inseparable ever since.

Carol pulls me inside with a surprisingly strong grip, the door closing behind us with a snick. "Wendy's waiting for Nick to stop by and fix her bathroom sink, but he's late." She grumbles something unintelligible that sounds a lot like *good-for-nothing louse.*

"Carol, stop." Wendy breezes around the corner in a bespoke sundress similar in color to the one I'm wearing. It effortlessly complements her faded blue eyes and the long white braid over her shoulder. "Nick added me on after he finishes work for the day. He'll get here when he gets here. You know that boy won't charge me, anyway."

Nick Watson, a foreman for WB renovations, has a notorious soft spot for sweet old ladies. He's even fond of Carol, though she'd rather run him over with her white Pontiac.

Carol harrumphs, pushing back the lace curtain to peer into the lane.

"What brings you by?" I'm enveloped in a rose-water-scented hug so warm and firm that my eyes mist.

It's not until I'm wrapped in Wendy's comforting embrace that I realize I'm here to spill my guts about everything. My ocean wish.

The whole situation with Atticus. The covert dress collection. My weird entanglement with Finn. The still-secret plan to get off the island for the first time *ever*.

I can't talk to Brynn without spilling the beans about the Oceanside Artisan Fair and ruining everything. Wendy has always been a good listener. It was her who I first started speaking to after Brynn and Aunt Tammy, though I've never fully unburdened myself like I want to now.

"It's, um…"

Wendy pulls back, surveying me with a soft gaze.

"I'm just so confused."

I thought Finn and I were friends. But a friend wouldn't press into my space with a flirty smile, or stare at my skin like it's buttercream icing, or call me gorgeous in a way that vibrates into my bones.

What's a woman to do?

No, what am *I* supposed to do? Because an average woman might have a ghost of a chance in this situation, but I have absolutely no defenses against someone as inconceivably attractive as Finn, especially when he's acting like I'm the person who lights up his day.

Because in that moment, I *wanted* his lips back on mine, his hands in my hair, his firm chest flush against me. And I'm not allowed to want those things. Those things are impossible. Finn is not mine to have.

Thank goodness Letitia showed up and stopped me from embarrassing myself.

Fiery indignation licks at my agitated muscles the more I think about it. I've asked Finn not to toy with me—more than once. And what's with him pretending to be upset whenever I mention Atticus? As if Atticus isn't the whole reason that we're even spending time together. It was Finn that suggested this...this arrangement, not me. I'd call the whole thing off right now if I wasn't dependent on him to get to the fair tomorrow.

The words are seconds from exploding from my mouth. Who cares that the town's gossip queen is within earshot?

My lips part, but I'm saved by the literal bell when Miss Wendy's old-fashioned doorbell rings. Carol—it seems—had been solely focused on us and missed Nick's truck pulling up in front of the house. When I catch her hovering beside Wendy's antique tea table—obviously eavesdropping—instead of by the window, she simply shrugs before marching toward the door.

"You're late," Carol barks in greeting.

"Carol. Always a pleasure." Nick's broad grin widens as he steps into the house with his tool bag.

The sight of Nick makes me suddenly bereft for a relationship I've never had. Nick's girlfriend, Summer, has tried a few times to connect with me, as have a few others over the years, but I'd always stuck to my old patterns of solitude and silence.

What would my life be like if I had even *one more* person to lean on? So when I have things I want to hash out, I could? Summer had once confided in me when things were murky between her and Nick, and now look at them. They're so sweetly in love it makes your teeth ache.

A single thought jolts to the front of my mind. I should add a part four to my plan—make new friends. I've got Summer's phone number from when I replaced the zipper on her favorite holiday dress last Christmas. I'm sure she wouldn't mind an invitation to meet me for coffee next Saturday.

"Hi, Vivian." Nick's smile relaxes into something gentler. "Good to see you."

"You too."

"Wendy, I hear you have a misbehaving sink." He runs his fingers through his hair, displacing sawdust.

"*Nicolas*," Carol scolds. "Can't you dust yourself off before coming inside?"

"It's fine." Wendy collects Nick by the elbow, tugging him toward the downstairs bathroom. "Tomorrow is cleaning day, anyway."

They're halfway down the entry hall when Wendy looks over her shoulder. "Vivian, do you mind waiting a minute?"

"Actually, I need to get going." My hands grip the tote bag still slung over my shoulder.

"Stay, dear. It won't be any trouble." Carol's smile is just short of devious.

Though Carol has always been kind to me—or kinder to me than she is to most—I know that speaking to Wendy with her present will only spread my news faster than a fire in a paper factory.

I'm *this close* to selling my dress collection, to everything being different.

My lips clamp tight as I shake my head.

Carol tuts as I take my exit, but once I'm back outside in the fresh sea air, everything feels clearer. The answer to this crazy day is right there, waiting. I trade the asphalt of Wendy's street for the deck boards of the dune cut-through leading to the beach. Seeing the steady roll of the waves as I crest the walkway loosens my nervous tension.

I kick my sandals off and tuck them next to the beach posting with all the other shoes. Several beachgoers pack up while those who just got home from working on the mainland take their evening walks. I set my tote in the dry sand and wade straight into the waves, fully clothed.

It's not the first time I've sought solace in the sea. Brynn won't even blink when I come home sodden, I've done this so often. Once I'm deep enough to dunk my head below the waves, true calm sluices down my spine. I push beyond the wave break and tread water, thinking about everything. My dress billows up around my arms, but the soft sensation of the fabric brushing my fingertips is soothing.

A squadron of pelicans soars along as I tilt to float on my back. The sky is endless while drifting like this—a bright, beautiful blue. Water fills my ears, limiting extraneous sound and softening the noise inside my head. A slow exhale leaves my open mouth as I revel in the buoyant calm that comes with being supported by water.

Some people find peace by hiking through trees or clinging to rocks, but my first love will always be the ocean.

The water swells beneath me almost in a reciprocating caress, and an easy smile splits my lips, my confidence returning. I can keep my secret one more day. And if I freeze up at the fair or something goes horribly wrong, I'll deal with that then. I've done all the preparation and planning I can. Now, I need to believe in myself. I've already done things I've only dreamt of over these last two weeks. I can do this.

And when flirty Finn texts me at ten-thirty tonight, I know just how I'll set him straight.

NINETEEN

Twenty minutes into weaving through the lush farmland that separates Wilks Beach from the outskirts of the city, my sister calls. My mouth loosens into a smile as I answer the phone, not realizing how tight my teeth had been clenched.

"Hey, Cordelia."

"Did you know?" The question is a watery plea followed by a heavy sniffle.

My shoulders tighten as I sit up taller in the driver's seat. "Know what?"

"That dad is taking away my trust?"

A string of expletives rushes through my mind, but I keep my voice even. "Who told you that?"

"So it's true?" She wails when I don't immediately refute it. "I can't live without Dad's money, Finn. I'm not like you. I'm not smart enough to make it on my own. Maybe I could if Dad let me say yes to any one of the reality shows, but he won't because that would 'taint the Otto name.'" A hiccup echoes over the line. "All I'm good at is socializing and parties, and I—I can't make a living off that. I guess I could get married—"

"Cordelia, listen," I say gently, though my hands are strangling the steering wheel.

I want to smash her every doubt to dust, to tell my sister that she's so much smarter than she or anyone else in our family gives her credit for, and that she certainly doesn't need to marry for money at nineteen, but I focus on the bottom line.

"Dad's not taking anything from you. I'm handling it."

"You are?" She sniffs again.

"Yes. I've got you."

It's been a personal rule I've upheld since Cordelia was born. I'd been ten and beginning to understand some of the seedy under-workings of my father's world, though I didn't have the strength to rebel against them. My live-in nanny, Magda, liked to make phone calls to her sister within earshot, divulging everything.

My father largely ignored Cordelia, and therefore, my older brother, Brody, followed suit. In my father's misogynistic mind, a woman wasn't fit to follow in the family business, and therefore, Cordelia never received the same rigorous education that Brody and I did. My father groomed his sons to join him in running one of the largest luxury hotel companies in the world, our grandfather's company—Otto Hotels.

"How?" she asks, her voice still shrill but her breathing a bit calmer.

The question pulls me back to a time I don't like to revisit. It'd been late spring, and I'd been days away from finishing my MBA at Yale when I discovered that first contract—the one my fiancée, Katelyn, had with my father. After confronting Katelyn, I took the family jet to the historic Otto Hotel in Virginia Beach to brood, residing in the penthouse suite and subsisting on sea air and gin and tonics. It was a complete shock when my father showed up five days later.

"Enough." Dad scowls at the wet pool towel on the ornate rug before stepping over it. "This is enough."

I ignore him, taking my mid-morning cocktail out on the sunny terrace and plopping in a lounge chair.

My father shocks me by following. "You want to throw a tantrum. Fine. You can rage all you want...after you complete finals next week. Finish out the school year, and I'll send you wherever you want in the world. There are beaches much nicer than this one." He grimaces at the shoreline. "You'll have everything at your disposal—cars, yachts, women. I'll give you the summer to get this out of your system before coming to work with me."

I spill half of my drink on my bare chest when I attempt a strong swig, still not speaking.

"Finnegan." My father softens his tone as he perches his Tom Ford suit on the edge of my chaise. "Marriage has been a business contract for generations. Men in powerful positions—men like us—don't marry for love. I'd only put Katelyn in your path because you'd been so determined to find someone. I blame that nanny of yours, filling your head with fairytale nonsense."

My eyes squeeze shut, making the world spin. That was the hardest part, knowing the whole thing had been orchestrated from the start. I'd been overcome with grief at Magda's passing two years earlier. Cordelia and I had been waiting in line to pay our respects when I was bumped from behind by a stunning blonde with blue eyes shining with tears. We made small talk as we moved up the aisle, discovering that Magda had been Katelyn's younger sister's nanny after she'd been mine. It'd been a macabre meet-cute, but I'd fallen for her shortly thereafter when Katelyn had showed up in my classes, also starting her MBA to work for her father's high-end grocery franchise.

"This isn't worth throwing your future away." He stands, brushing off his pants. "I'll pull some strings and get you an extension. Pickle yourself in gin for another week then get on a plane."

I've consumed enough gin that the ripping sensation in my chest shouldn't be this intense. I shouldn't be in this much pain. I shouldn't be this blindsieded to find out that nothing in my life is true, that no one is honest.

"No." I fix my gaze on the ocean waves, feeling my word detonate like a bomb. "I'm done."

"You're an Otto. You don't get to be done."

I tilt my chin up, meeting my father's gaze. "Then maybe I don't want to be an Otto."

"Because..." I clear my throat. "Because I wouldn't let anything happen to you, Cor. Not ever. You know that."

Going from being a billionaire's son to having nothing with a signature had been a rude awakening. Cordelia—not knowing the full extent of the rift between my father and I—smuggled me cash until I got the hang of providing for myself. Her contacting me had been forbidden, but my sister is more resourceful than she gives herself credit for. Even now, Cordelia sends me perfectly tailored designer clothes every season, claiming they're for a guy friend of hers.

The problem is that I'd been stupid—and still a little drunk—when I'd signed the iron-clad contract with my father to walk away from the family. Not because of my choice—that I have yet to regret—but because I'd made the cardinal sin of neglecting to read the fine print. A few months after enrolling in my online library science degree, I used Cordelia's smuggled monthly deposit to pay a lawyer to comb the contract.

And, of course, my father had put in a caveat. I must achieve the highest position in my chosen field by my thirtieth birthday or return to work for my father. Disregarding this contract stipulation would cost Cordelia her trust.

I left that meeting with a renewed hatred for my father and sense of purpose. After that, I clawed my way through every conference, extra certification, continuing education courses, joined every possible professional organization, and networked my backside off. Becoming the person overseeing the operation and strategic direction of a library system that serves half a million patrons in five short years is unheard of in library and information sciences advancement. But if I don't become the library director by my birthday next summer, Dad wins, and my life is his to rule again.

There is no scenario in which Cordelia loses.

"But how, Finn?"

An exhausted sigh leaves my mouth, and I decide it's time to explain everything, even if it means breaking the NDA.

My sister calls my father a few choice adjectives once I'm finished. "I always thought you changed your name to get back at Dad."

"He wanted everyone close to the family to think that."

It also allowed him to control the narrative. Reckless Finn, blowing off his family name and responsibilities. How disgraceful. Let's not speak of it.

"And having contracts with the media so they can't report on you? I always thought it was a little weird that your broken engagement didn't end up in the news or tabloids when I'm reported on for which party I attend."

"Dad is not best friends with the heads of several media franchises because he likes them," I quip, steering around a tight corner.

My sister hums. "And no one knows who you really are? Like, nobody?"

I release a slow exhale. "Stipulations of the contract—I change my name, I lose my trust and any familial connections, and I tell no one."

"This is so messed up." She scoffs. "Even for Dad."

A chuckle escapes me at her indignant tone. It'd been a burden keeping all this to myself over the years. The most I've let it slip was when I'd mentioned I had a sister to Vivian the other night. Even Alec doesn't know I have a sister. When Cordelia calls, I tell him she's an old girlfriend who can't move on, using that excuse to also explain the clothing packages.

"Does Brody know the truth?"

My shoulders tighten until I can feel the muscles pulling at my collarbones. Cordelia mentioned a year ago that Brody had been showing an interest in her for the first time in her life. Though I suspect it's largely due to Brody's girlfriend's influence, the more people in Cordelia's corner, the better. She's got friends, but they're all superficial relationships, much like mine had been.

I open my mouth, not wanting to lie now that I've finally got everything in the open. Before I can answer, though, my left front tire blows. This time, I don't censor my harsh curse.

"What is it?"

"I think I have a flat."

The impending migraine behind my eye pulses like a drum beat. This narrow two-lane road has a steep drainage ditch on each side, making moving out of the way of traffic impossible. Fortunately, not many people are on this part of the road tonight.

"I'll let you go. I need time to process all of this and scrub the toilet with Dad's toothbrush."

Despite the stress swirling around my skull, I grin. "Bye."

My shirt is stained with sweat by the time I free my full-sized spare and prop my car on the jack, having figured out how to do that by watching a quick video tutorial. I'm loosening the lug nuts when my phone rings again. My hands are covered in grime, but I manage to open the call on speaker without smearing my screen.

"Alec, hey. I've—"

"What's taking you so long? I've got these two ladies here, and I promised them that my friend is on his way."

His words are already slurred, which means that if I join him, I'll be taking care of his belligerent mess all night. The tension in my head doubles. Making sure Alec doesn't punch another bar patron is my least favorite part of our friendship. It's one of the many things I wish he would have outgrown over the years.

Alec was the first friend I made upon moving here, the son of two wealthy lawyers. He let me pay a decreased rent for a room in his penthouse apartment in downtown Virginia Beach if I agreed to be his permanent wingman. I feel a little ashamed of it now, but living in Alec's apartment had been too close to my upbringing not to give up. It was professionally cleaned, the kitchen stocked and meals prepped and left in the refrigerator by their family chef, and the building had full amenities. Since I'd never known the cost of anything, it eased the transition.

Look, I know how that sounds. Poor billionaire baby doesn't know how to do anything, but I didn't. I was so lost the first time I entered a grocery store, let alone knowing how to navigate the deli counter. Shortly after that, I ran dry the Aston Martin I had my personal assistant purchase and send to the hotel before the fallout with my father. Everything had always been "handled" before, so I had no clue to watch the fuel gauge.

But I figured it out, just like I'll have to do now with this flat.

"I blew a tire."

"That sucks." Ambient bar noise echoes over the line while the sweat on my brow begins to sting my eyes. "Get here as soon as you can," he says before disconnecting the call.

I press my eyes closed before focusing on the nearby sorghum field. Tiny white butterflies flit between rows, darting in and out of the setting sunlight. It'd be breathtaking if I wasn't in such a foul mood.

I'm halfway through loosening the lug nuts when a nondescript silver sedan slows behind me. I turn to wave it past, but the hazard lights flip on. A second later, Geneva marches from the car in heels and a tight sleeveless dress. Like at the boxing gym, she's wearing head-to-toe black.

"You good?"

Like all our interactions, this seemingly kind question is barked in my general direction. Dark sunglasses cover most of her face as she scans the surrounding area.

"I'm fine. Thanks for checking on me."

She shrugs, still surveying the fields. "Wasn't sure you'd know how to change a tire."

I'd be offended had I not watched an instructional video moments ago.

I level her with a practiced smile. "I'm good. Really."

Her gaze slides to my paused hands. "I only stopped because if Noah found out I'd passed you by, he'd be ticked. And if he gets mad, he bans the other firefighters from coming to class. No sweaty, hot guys punching things, no middle-aged mamas attending my class. It's simple math. Apparently, now that you two are buddies"—Geneva says *buddies* like she's chewing on maggots—"I'm supposed to be nice to you."

"And that's incredibly difficult for you," I deadpan.

The corner of her mouth quirks. "Glad you understand."

A pause settles between us before Geneva leans a hip against my car. I wait for the jack to move, but she must not be applying any pressure.

"You don't have to stay."

"Trust me. I don't want to." Geneva slaps her forearm. "The mosquitos are in full force."

Since it's obvious she's not going anywhere, I continue working.

When we'd been out for drinks, I'd asked Noah about Geneva. He'd laughed and called her his 'grouchy, overprotective half-sister.' His unexpected description made me sift through my memories of Geneva. Even with her surly demeanor, I'd seen her be gentle while correcting someone's form or ensuring a nursing mother stays hydrated during her class.

Now, Geneva keeps peeking at my progress while simultaneously feigning boredom. Nothing about her body language gives off annoyance or impatience. It's like she's looking out for me in her own grumpy way.

When I lower my car until the wheel touches the ground and stand, Geneva bolts into action. "You're not done."

In the time it takes me to mentally run through the video's steps, Geneva crouches to tighten the lug nuts. It's an impressive feat in her three-inch heels. Geneva is already tall, making her eye to eye with me while wearing those.

The shock of this woman, who barely knows me, wrinkling her dress while helping me, makes my stomach swirl. "Stop. Please stop. I can do it."

Geneva makes a dismissive noise, continuing to tighten in an alternating pattern. "Rule number one: Check your ego at the door."

It's something that's painted on the interior wall of her gym in bold letters.

"It's not that," I say, crouching beside her. "It's—"

"Look." She stops tightening to focus on me, but I can't see her eyes through the waning light and her dark sunglasses.

"If you're about to have a moment, I'm going to need you to take that vulnerability and gobble it down like it's the best thing you ever tasted." Her hand grabs a fistful of air and brings it to her lips. "We're just fixing your car. Then we're going our separate ways. I may have ovaries, but I'm not the person you bare your soul to. You got it?"

I nod.

She hands me the wrench and stands. "I've tightened these enough, but double-check them once you fully release the jack." Geneva takes a few purposeful strides toward her car before looking over her shoulder. "And get some air in that tire once you find a gas station. It's a little low. Actually, check all your tires."

The brush-off feels oddly nurturing.

Once I'm back in the car and the AC is blowing full blast, I text Alec that I'm on my way. Sometime tomorrow, I'll need to get the tire replaced since I was lucky enough to have a full-sized spare. I've decided that tonight is going to be about catching up and keeping my friend out of trouble. Maybe if I fill Alec with water and food before I have to leave, he'll refrain from using his muscles in the wrong ways.

Maybe.

Because I'm not interested in kissing anyone tonight. Not unless they let words tumble off their tongue in unexpected ways, or have springy chestnut curls, or give me a large beaming smile that no one else gets to see. I drag my thoughts away from Vivian, rubbing at the goosebumps that trail down my forearms.

It's actually good that Vivian isn't interested in me. It's the best possible outcome. There's entirely too much on the line to get distracted now. Cordelia's call solidified that. I have no doubt that Dad leaked the information to my sister just to rattle me. Little does he know, he just gave me an ally. Now that Cordelia knows, that bone-deep loneliness I've felt for years has shifted.

And when I pull into the parking garage in downtown Virginia Beach just as my sister texts me a smiling selfie of her, a toilet bowl, and an electric toothbrush pinched between her manicured fingers, I actually laugh.

TWENTY

Vivian

Turns out I didn't need to set Finn straight last night because he was uncharacteristically quiet, keeping his distance as he helped me move the dress boxes. And moments ago, when I went on an early morning "walk" which ended at his back door, Finn simply nodded, locked up, and led me to his car. His body jerked toward the passenger side, almost as if it was instinct to open the door for me, before continuing toward the driver's side.

At the beginning of the drive, I assumed Finn wasn't oozing charisma because he wasn't a morning person, but now that we've been sitting in silence for fifty minutes, I'm about to crack. I don't want him flirting with me, and calling me gorgeous, and frying the logical part of my brain, but I miss our easy conversation.

183

His appearance is off too. The dark-gray t-shirt stretched across his shoulders is wrinkled as if he slept in it. The warmth of his eyes hides behind sunglasses and a dark baseball hat. And Finn keeps rubbing his temple every few minutes.

Maybe he's sick?

"You don't have to stay," I remind him.

I told him last night that I only needed help setting up this morning and striking my tent at six. He'd mentioned his recent flat and that he'd need to get it repaired while on the mainland. It'd been so weird hearing Finn talk like an islander, like he belongs here.

Finn nods, saying nothing.

Once we arrive for my eight o'clock check-in, setup goes surprisingly smoothly. The fair doesn't open for an hour, but there are a lot of people already strolling the boardwalk. The scents of fried dough and the sour tinge of beer mingle with the briny sea air. A few blocks down, a guitarist performs a sound check.

My neighboring vendors—a ceramicist to my left and a metal-print photographer to my right—offer cordial good mornings. I focus on unpacking and organizing, trying not to notice how subdued Finn's voice is as he asks for guidance on setup, or how helpful his height is for hanging the banner I had screen-printed with my business name, or how he wordlessly pulls a bag of Skittles out of his pocket and sets it atop my cash box.

The opened flaps of my tent flutter in the breeze as my chest contorts. This 10x10 space feels like the size of a bathroom rug with his large body shifting around to hang dresses on the clothing racks.

I step forward, collecting the hangers from him and hugging them to my chest. "What's wrong?"

"Nothing. I'm fine." Finn bends to pick up more dresses.

As soon as he straightens, I collect those as well, my small hands overfilled with hangers. "You're not fine."

Finn exhales, shaking his head at the ground before rubbing his jaw. "I was up late going over fundraising ideas and didn't get enough sleep. I'm just tired. It's going to be a long day with this and getting my car fixed. And..." He sighs, averting his gaze. "I'm doing my best, Viv."

It feels like he sucker punched me. Finn is helping me, asking for nothing in return, and I'm pestering him.

"I'm sorry. You've done so much for me and—" I nearly fall over, surging forward to grip yet another bundle of hangers. Why is he so quick?

"Go get yourself a coffee—on me." I try to gather all the dresses into one hand so I can reach for the slim card holder in my dress pocket. "There's a shop off 18th."

"In a minute." He takes back the dresses I'm about to drop on the concrete boardwalk.

"Setup is nearly done." I rush to hang up the clothes in my hands and beat him to the rest. "I can finish on my own."

"I don't mind helping. This is important to you. I want it to go well."

I squeeze the last bundle of hangers to my tight lungs. "Why?"

Finn takes off his hat, running frustrated fingers through his hair. "Hero complex. I warned you about that. Remember?"

He shrugs, but there's nothing casual about the way his gaze sweeps my face.

Though the fair hasn't opened yet, a boisterous group of sixty-year-old ladies swing into my tent on a plume of multiple perfumes.

"Oh, these are just darling," one says, sliding readers over her eyes to scrutinize a tag. "Not too expensive either."

The shade of that aqua dress would complement her complexion and the woman's salt-and-pepper bob. I don't tell her, though. I don't mention that I haven't set up my digital payment system yet, or that the fair is not officially opened, or that I was having what felt like a very important conversation before the trio arrived. My mouth opens, but nothing useful comes out.

Panic streaks down my arms. It's not going to be like this all day, with my voice trapped like it's been so many times before. It can't.

You got this. You got this. You got this.

I move to assist the woman looking at the aqua dress when I hear slurred words.

"Diane, tell me how much this one is. I left my eyes at bottomless brunch."

The woman, tugging on a bright-magenta dress, stops when she catches sight of Finn. "Oh, yummy-yum. Please tell me *he's* for sale."

Irritation rakes every cell in my body at her flagrant objectification, but Finn does that thing where all his honesty gets siphoned behind a glossy facade. It's strange, watching the subtle changes he makes, like seeing a person shrug on an ill-fitting jacket.

"I'm afraid not, ma'am." Finn's charming grin cracks at the corners, unable to completely hide his exhaustion, but the woman doesn't notice.

"That's okay. You can help me find the perfect dress."

When Finn flinches slightly as she grabs his biceps with her bony fingers, my vision nearly turns the color of the dress in her other hand.

"Do you have something like this in blue?" a third voice behind me stops me from lurching forward and peeling the woman's ring-laden hand from Finn's skin.

I spin, noting the yellow dress in her fingers. I know I made that one in teal. Depending on her opinion, that might count as blue.

"I think I might," I tell her, taking the yellow dress from her and moving toward the front of the tent to find the teal one.

Each step away from Finn feels like moving against a riptide.

"Will this work?" I ask, holding out the other option. My gaze flits toward Finn, finding his smile restored to its normal wattage as the woman on his arm looks through the racks.

"I think so." She places the hanger beneath her chin, glancing at the full-length mirror I've fastened to one of the front tent poles. "Do you have a changing room?"

"Unfortunately, no." I offer an apologetic smile. "It's against Oceanside Artisan Fair's policy. They want to prevent public undressing."

"I'd like to undress this one." The woman still gripping Finn's arm bounces her eyebrows.

"Joyce! He could be your son," Diane admonishes.

"He could be my third husband." Joyce leans into Finn, and I drop the dress I'm holding to stomp over.

"Let go of him." I don't think I've ever heard my voice so low and angry at the same time. I'm practically growling.

"Oh, honey—" Her rings glint as she waves me off, but I step closer, undeterred.

"Let. Go. Of. Him."

If I was outside of this situation, looking at myself, I'd probably shiver. All five foot five of me is vibrating with furious energy. I don't think I've ever been this outraged in my life. I usually quietly accept whatever life throws at me, but I've started a domino effect with each small change I've made since my ocean wish. Now, I'm a warrior goddess who stands up for what's right.

Joyce's drunken, blotched eyes widen. "But—"

"Let go and get out." My tone leaves no room for argument.

Diane steps between us, corralling her friend and whispering apologies. I follow the trio until they're beyond the borders of my tent and then draw the flaps to "close" the tent. Once secured, I stare at the opaque plastic covering. Those three will probably tell the fair officiants I threw them out. I'm going to get kicked out of this event before it even starts. If that happens, there's no way I'll make enough to give Brynn a day off.

I wait, but remorse doesn't ribbon through my ribs.

"You didn't have to do that." Finn's perfectly neutral voice makes this whole situation worse.

"Aren't you mad?" I ask, twirling around. "Aren't you upset that she was leering at you, touching you? You're a person, Finn, not an object. It doesn't matter that you're ridiculously hot. She should sneak furtive glances at you, like the rest of the world, not treat you like her personal toy."

Finn stares, his chest rising and falling unevenly. His piercing eyes never stray from mine.

Kiss me, my body begs. *I rescued you. March over here and kiss me.*

But then I realize that maybe Finn didn't want to be rescued. After all, I'm sick of people doing that to me. That's why I'm here, doing something way outside my comfort zone that no one from town knows about.

"I'm sorry." I drop my gaze, twisting my ring.

Tension surges as Finn slowly steps closer, and by the time I can see his sneakers in my eyeline, I'm pretty sure my lungs are going to give out.

"Don't be sorry. No one—" He clears his throat of its grit. "No one has ever done anything like that for me before. I've always fended for myself."

I lift my chin, my confidence returning. "Just because you *can*, doesn't mean you always *should*."

Finn's gaze bounces over my face, brows drawn, as if he's trying to understand quantum mechanics.

"Vivian Hutchinson?" a voice calls from beyond the plastic behind me.

My eyes close with an exhale. Time to take accountability for my actions. It's weird that I'm oddly excited to defend my choices to the fair staff member beyond my tent. Now that I've stood up for Finn, it feels that much easier to do it for myself.

"Hi! I'm Wren." The woman in an orange Oceanside Artisan Fair staff t-shirt beams once I've opened the flap. "Just wanted to check in and make sure you're settled. I'm sorry I didn't come by earlier, but I was held up by an incident between two wood carvers." She widens her eyes like I should understand that last statement before quickly continuing, "Anyway, here's your commemorative vendor tote, t-shirt, and my card. Feel free to call if you need anything. Okay?"

I blink at the proffered items, unable to move my leaden limbs. I'm not in trouble? She's not going to haul me away to some artsy jail cell with crocheted bars and a hammock bunk?

"Thanks." Finn accepts the items. "She loves totes—has a whole collection."

"Wonderful!" Wren beams before shuffling off to check in with the metal-print photographer.

My brain feels like it's overheating in the mid-morning sun. Finn knows about my tote collection? Before I can ask, I'm pulled into a conversation with another attendee. Finn gives me an encouraging nod over the woman's head and retreats to the back corner where the cash box sits beneath a lone stool. He looks utterly ridiculous, folding his large frame onto the wooden stool. The woman distracts me for a while, but when I glance back a moment later, Finn is hunched over a hardback library book.

Where did that come from? I've always assumed that Finn is a reader—he's a *librarian* after all—but we've never talked about it. Funny, since we both love books. I wonder if every corner of his room is stacked with books too. Probably not. Finn probably has them properly organized and cataloged into the nicest bookshelves.

His large hands cover most of the book cover, so I can't see what he's reading. Then the corner of his mouth quirks like he's just read something funny, and my stupid heart tries to scale my windpipe and scuttle over to him.

It's several long minutes and two electronic sales later—Yay me!—before I can interrogate Finn about what's occupying his attention. Before I do, I take a moment—okay, several moments—to watch him read. It's probably creepy, but Finn utterly engrossed in a book should be immortalized in marble for future generations to enjoy.

There's also this quietness to him today that's incongruous with the charismatic persona he usually shows the world. It's more appealing than Skittles. And I've dreamt about swimming through a pool of Skittles Scrooge McDuck-style. When Finn is dripping with magnetism, only supermodels and rockstars should be in his orbit. But when he's like this, hunched over a novel, his features relaxed, Finn feels more real.

He doesn't look up until I'm right beside him, and wow, our faces are in perfect alignment with him seated. "What are you reading?"

It's not until my words drift into the sea air that I realize I'm using the pickup line we'd crafted together.

On *him*.

Blood sloshes clumsily in my ears. I'm about to backtrack when I finally catch the book's title.

"Wait. You're reading that?"

<h1 style="text-align:center">TWENTY-ONE</h1>

Finn

"**P**lease tell me you're a fan." Vivian does that bouncy thing she does when she's excited, and my heart twists to the point of pain. This would be so much easier if she wasn't so darn adorable all the time.

Watching her defend me had been an out-of-body experience. It had taken several heartbeats for my sluggish brain to realize that it had actually happened. Vivian might show the world one version of herself, but her strength is always there, simmering beneath the surface. It felt like an honor, having Vivian use that steadfastness on my behalf.

After years of striving on my own, of trying to win this race against time, against my father's puppet mastery, the raw gratitude of having

Vivian in my corner almost capsized me. I wanted to hold her against my chest and never let go. I wanted to whisper thank you over her soft curls. My fingers had flexed at my sides in preparation, but then the fair staff member interrupted.

Instead, I made a decision. I'm not leaving Vivian's side today. Repairing my tire can wait another day. Heck, the rotation of the Earth can wait until Vivian checks this off her list—part two of her self-improvement plan. I firmly stand by my opinion that she's perfect as is, but I also understand the desire to achieve one's goals.

I close the book so we can both see the cover of the Regency romance, using my index finger to keep my place. "I haven't read one of these before," I admit. "But even after a few chapters—"

"You're hooked, right?" Her luminosity nearly burns my retinas.

I'm so familiar with the falsehoods I weave on a daily basis that I almost lie out of habit. This pattern began long before I signed my future away. Early on, my father insisted that no one wanted the nerdy boy who read when they could have a charismatic athlete. Excelling academically was an expectation, but the foundation of true success laid in being likable and making connections—something you can't do while reading at home. Alone.

The sad thing is, Dad was right. I push away the memory of the one disastrous time I thought someone loved the real me. Since then, I've kept everyone out. Even among other librarians, I focus on the social services aspect of librarianship. No one knows about my fascination with historic bookbinding or that once the library closes, I don protective gloves and leaf through Wilks Beach's oldest texts.

But maybe I can start with small doses of truth.

See what happens.

"Yes," I answer.

Vivian barely contains a squeal while touching the cover. "*The Duke's Honor* is the first of eight. And when you're done with this series, you should try Annie Ardent's Wellington series. It's similar to the Worthington series but kisses only."

My forehead wrinkles. "Kisses only?"

"The one you're reading has..." Her voice trails off as that captivating blush stains her freckled cheeks.

Our proximity creeps into my consciousness as I watch the color slip down her neck. With Vivian standing between my spread knees, our eyes and mouths effortlessly align. All I would have to do is slide my palm behind her neck and demolish the remaining distance. I nearly complete my mental plan before remembering Vivian's reaction last time we were this close.

There'd better be an ostentatious medal for willpower, because I earn two of them, leaning back and moving the book between us to create space.

"I admit, I've never read a romance before. I usually stick to non-fiction, the classics, or Pulitzer Prize winners."

Vivian rolls her eyes. "Don't tell me you are one of those snobby literary types that can't be bothered to pick up a book just for the fun of it. Books like this aren't supposed to make you rethink the state of the world. They're supposed to be an escape. A little drop of sunshine on an otherwise dreary day."

The corner of my mouth kicks up. I love when Vivian gets feisty like this.

"I never said I was."

"Oh. Well..." She tucks her hands into her dress pockets. "What made you pick this book up?"

"One of the librarians wanted me to read it." My free hand tightens on my knee to keep it from sliding over Vivian's distracting curves.

"Who?" Her confused gaze falls to the cover as she retreats a small step.

Yes, move backward. In fact, would you mind walking down a block or two so I don't snap and devour those perfect lips?

She's been nervously chewing on them all morning, and I desperately want to soothe them with my own.

Forcing my gaze back to her eyes, I say, "I don't know. They keep leaving it on my desk. A stack of them."

"What do you mean?" Her nose wrinkles, and it's like an imaginary sports commentator laments over my impending loss to my impulses.

I take a slow, controlled breath. "I mean that, every other day, this book and the next three in the series show up on my desk. I don't know who puts them there. They just...arrive. I'm pretty sure I'm being hazed, but to keep them from popping up, I checked them out."

"Finn." Vivian settles her hands on my shoulders, and I nearly swallow my tongue. "Those aren't from your staff."

"They're not?"

Vivian shakes her head, her slow, mischievous smile making me grip the hardback book like it's my lifeline.

"The library is giving you those."

"What?" My brows pinch.

"Remember when I said there's a little bit of magic on our sandy stretch of beach? The library is known to present people with the books they need to read. It's done it to almost every local over the years."

That...that makes no logical sense. The migraine I've been fighting all morning swirls my skull, its tendrils squeezing like taloned claws. My free hand comes to my temple, rubbing as I close my eyes.

"Finn?" Vivian's voice reverberates with concern before I feel her cool fingers on my face.

My hand drops away immediately, her touch infinitely more soothing than my own. I keep my eyes closed as she removes my hat, one thumb holding perfect pressure against my left temple as her other fingertips trace through my hair. An embarrassing, open-mouthed sigh leaves my tight lungs as I sag into the caress.

"There's Tylenol in the first aid kit," Vivian tells me, not moving.

"I have my migraine prescription in the glove box." The truth just leaves my slack lips, effortless.

I wait for my shoulders to bunch, for the unease that accompanies divulging personal information to spike over my muscles. Other people might think it silly, trying to conceal something so insignificant, especially since so many post their unfiltered lives all over social media. But my father drilled into me that one should never reveal a weakness.

Weaknesses could cost you.

Vivian hums, her fingers soothing through my hair again. "You get migraines?"

I open my eyes, expecting to find disappointment or judgment, but there's none in Vivian's evergreen gaze. It makes me want to tell her all my secrets.

Every. Single. One.

"Yes."

She frowns, her hands settling on my shoulders again. "What would you normally do when you get a migraine, besides taking medicine?"

"Lie down. Try to decrease stimuli."

Her lips press into a line as she nods. "I'm sorry we're so far from home, but maybe you can lie down in your car?"

"I'll be fine." I straighten, leaning back so her fingers fall away.

This has all gotten too intimate. I'm supposed to be keeping my distance.

The hard set of her jaw should be a warning. "Finnegan Reynolds, you are going to take your medicine and lie down right now, or I'll sing 'Alouette' at the top of my lungs."

"How did you know my full name, Vivian?" I can't help the flirtatious twitch of my lips. "Did you look me up?"

Her fingers on my shoulders flex. "I swear to the sea, if you pour that fake charm over this, I will blind you with my phone's flashlight."

A chuckle tumbles from my mouth. "You're a stubborn little thing, aren't you? You pretend to be all sweet and quiet, but really, you're a fighter."

Vivian nearly growls.

Though my smile grows, I want to tell her my words are a compliment. If she could see herself the way I do, she'd never doubt her ability to do anything. But instead, I wink, poking the adorable teddy bear.

"Don't."

Vivian moves forward, hands firmly framing my face, and I'm done for. Whatever she wants, she can have. My lashes flutter before I remember myself and meet her steely gaze.

"Don't do that." Vivian hesitates a breath, her tone softening. "I like you like this."

My eyebrows lift. "In pain?"

Her curls bounce with a subtle head shake. "Honest."

The sharp breath stumbling into my lungs is entirely too noisy. In addition to causing mortification to sprint through my veins, it draws Vivian's gaze. I expect her to focus back on my eyes, to continue my talking-to, but her attention fixates. My vision goes a little gray at the edges as Vivian sways forward, her tongue wetting her bottom lip.

"Miss?" An older woman I hadn't noticed stands at the entrance to the tent, clutching a dress. "Could I get this for my granddaughter?" The willowy teen beside her doesn't look up from her phone.

Vivian startles, her blush fierce against her pale skin.

"Of course," she says, moving toward them.

"I'm going to head to the car," I mutter, giving the trio a wide berth as I step into the piercing sunshine.

A hot streak of lightning crosses from my left eye to the back of my skull. I squint, fumbling for the sunglasses tucked into my collar. The entire walk to the car, I focus on the searing pain in my head, not the wobbly uncertainty in my chest.

Because I'm sure my exhausted brain is playing tricks on me.

There's no way Vivian just leaned in to kiss me.

TWENTY-TWO

Vivian

I almost kissed Finn.

The thought keeps repeating itself as I stumble through a conversation with two best friends who end up buying three dresses. *I almost kissed Finn.* When a group of intensely aggressive seagulls attack an abandoned funnel cake at the front of my tent. *I almost kissed Finn.* After I lose one of my favorite designs to a sticky lollipop situation. *I almost kissed Finn.*

I almost kissed Finn. I almost kissed Finn. I almost kissed Finn.

The sentence iterates so many times that it reaches semantic satiation and no longer makes sense. I might as well be thinking, *Dog wearing a peanut butter hat.*

Except, there's the very real problem of what to do now. I was the one who firmly set the friend boundary between us, but earlier, I was ready to sail over it like an Olympic high-jumper securing gold.

A groan escapes me as I press the heel of my palm between my eyes.

Finn texted shortly after he left, saying that if he takes his medicine, he'll probably end up sleeping since it makes him drowsy. Since his Aston Martin is in an interior spot in the parking garage, I didn't worry about him overheating, but I texted him, telling him to crack his windows just in case.

That was four hours ago.

In that time, I've done an excellent job of spiraling. I should join an acrobatic group—I'm that good. What I'm not doing a great job of is selling dresses. I say hi to people as they enter and try to give them the privacy to peruse, but almost everyone leaves empty handed. I'm certain it's because of my awkwardness.

Or it might be because I end up staring off into space, remembering the way Finn's breath see-sawed irregularly when my lips were inches from his, and have to snap myself out of it with a physical shake. Earlier, I startled a five-year-old shopping with her mom, thus resulting in the lollipop situation. One thing is for sure, the low interest in my dresses is definitely not due to foot traffic. There's a standing-room-only throng of people parading past my tent. They look more like cattle than shoppers.

Heading to the back corner of the tent, I pull my spiral notebook from my brand-new tote bag. Even before I open it, I know I'm not close to hitting my goal. Yesterday, I'd written down success milestones with a rainbow of multicolor pens that I could check off during the day. Deducting the cost of dress production, my vendor tent fees, rental costs for the clothing racks, and the gas money I still need to pay Finn, I'm now the proud owner of enough profit to buy Brynn a tuna sandwich.

My nose stings, and I tell myself that the liquid brimming my eyelids is from the ocean breeze picking up. Wind always makes my eyes water. Besides, I never expected this experience to rocket me to some new layer of success. I probably couldn't handle that anyway. It'd be too emotionally stressful, and I'm used to...being small, living small. My shoulders hunch forward as I close my eyes.

I shouldn't even be here.

"I brought sustenance," Finn's voice surprises me.

I slam the notebook closed, tucking it away. A deep inhale fills my lungs before I turn around, grateful for Finn's distraction. The last thing I need is to ugly cry with thousands of onlookers witnessing my abject failure.

Finn looks better. His hat and sunglasses still cover his face, but the ever-present grimace is gone. Then my gaze tracks down his firm chest—purely in a medical assessment kind of way—before I notice the pink lemonade and curly fries in his hands.

A bloom of affection radiates between my ribs. I'd been muttering to myself as we passed the food trucks earlier about having that exact combination for lunch. The Skittles are long gone, but I was too nervous to "close my tent" and potentially lose sales in order to get myself lunch.

"Are those for me?"

Finn's easy smile falls when my voice cracks.

"What's wrong?" He strides forward, setting my food on the stool.

His hands come up as if to brace my arms, but then he slides them into his pockets. It's completely unreasonable for me to be disappointed at the potential loss of contact when Finn is respecting my boundaries.

I blame my hollowing stomach on my low sales numbers, telling him, "Things aren't going as well as I hoped."

Finn looks around the tent, probably noting that it's nearly identical to how he left it. Then, a lopsided grin traces his lips. It's different from his spine-tingly flirtatious one, almost teetering on goofy.

"Permission to turn on the charm to sell dresses?"

I roll my eyes with a huff, but his jokey request eases the tension between my collarbones. I'd actually thought about asking Finn to turn up the charisma when he returned. I mean, I have a gorgeous man at my disposal; why not utilize him to maximize profits? But the idea feels seedy, underhanded, and in direct opposition to what I'd told him before the fair even opened.

I sigh. "I'm supposed to do this on my own, remember?"

Finn nods, a muscle in his jaw ticking.

"Are you feeling better?" I ask to change the subject.

My stomach twists. I should have asked that the minute I saw Finn instead of selfishly dwelling on my lack of sales.

"Yeah." He rolls his neck. "It wasn't a full-blown one, thankfully. That would've put me out for the rest of the day."

"That's good." Awkwardness expands in my throat. It'd been so easy to banter with him earlier, but I'm almost afraid of doing that again. Whenever that happens, we always end up too close.

"And thank you for lunch. You didn't have to do that."

Finn rubs his jaw as he glances at the ground, his ball cap momentarily hiding his face. "It was no trouble."

I open my mouth to ask if he got himself something to eat first, but my ringing phone interrupts. "I should get that."

I'd concocted a simple cover story of spending the day at Wendy's house, but if Brynn figured out I was lying, it'd be better to own up to it sooner rather than later. The idea of my twin sister rallying the town, using the mass texting service that islanders only utilize for emergencies to organize carpools to the mainland to support me, makes my jittery muscles soften. A small smile tilts at the corner of my mouth as I fish my phone out of my tote bag.

Except, it's not my sister calling.

Finn steps behind me when I continue to stare at the ringing device, unmoving.

"Answer it." His voice is low over my ear, sending a shiver down my spine. He's so close I can feel the heat of him through the back of my dress. "I'll help you if you need it."

Right. Because at the end of the day, Finn is still my dating coach, so of course he'd help me answer this call from Atticus. A sour taste stings my tongue as I answer, pressing the phone to my left ear.

"Hello?"

"Vivian?"

"Um…" I falter for a second.

When Finn whispers, "You've got this, gorgeous," my lashes flutter closed. I sway backward unconsciously, putting me dangerously close to Finn's chest.

My eyes pop open a second before I answer Atticus. "This is she."

"Oh, good. Just wanted to make sure because otherwise…well, that doesn't matter now." Atticus sends a noisy snort over the line, and I grimace reflexively. "I was wondering if you wanted to go over your books tomorrow. I have some time in the late afternoon."

"Tomorrow afternoon?"

I push a few wayward strands of hair away from my face, only to have the sea air slap them right back into my eyes. An irritated sound leaves my lips as I tug a particularly unruly lock out of my mouth.

"What's that?" Atticus asks.

"Nothing," I spurt.

"Give me your hair tie," Finn murmurs.

I'm confused until Finn tugs on the hairband around my left wrist. I switch the phone to my right ear so he can slip it over my fingers. Then my knees almost buckle when Finn collects all my hair and gently secures it in the elastic. He does so expertly, like he's pulled up a woman's hair into a ponytail before. I don't have time to fully flesh out *why* he would have this particular skill, because Atticus is giving me details about our business meeting, rambling about the most recent update to my bookkeeping software and inquiring whether I've downloaded it.

"I...uh..." Fainting is a very real possibility when Finn scoops a flyaway from my nape and tucks it into the hair tie. His fingers grazing the back of my neck pull an involuntary hum from me, which Atticus takes as confirmation that I have, in fact, updated my software.

"Excellent," Atticus chirps. Has his voice always been so high-pitched? "So I'll see you tomorrow at 4:30. Bring your laptop." He disconnects the call before I can say goodbye, but I use the abrupt end as an opportunity.

If Finn really didn't want me to lean in and eliminate the space between our mouths earlier, if he doesn't feel this insane electrical spike when we're inches from each other, he won't mind my news.

I spin, my heart leaping when I catch his hooded gaze trained on my neck. Finn's eyes have that dark quality again, his pupils demolishing the tranquil amber of his irises. My breath hitches as his focus stalls on my lips before raising to my eyes.

"I'm meeting Atticus tomorrow."

I'd planned on saying "I have a date with Atticus tomorrow" but chickened out when Finn bit the corner of his lip the second our gazes collided.

A heavy pause settles between us, and I feel weightless, like I imagine someone bold enough to skydive feels for that split second before gravity takes over. Every cell in my body begs for him to kiss me. But then, there's a quick shuttering in Finn's expression, and my stomach sinks to my toes.

"Good," he says, stepping back and swallowing hard. "That's good."

It's petty and childish and several other adjectives ending in *ish*, but I advance into his space. "Is it?"

We hover in suspended animation for only a breath before Finn's decisive nod shatters my foolish dreams.

"Yes. Of course it is. This is what you've been working toward from the start."

My stubborn mouth opens to object, to tell him that plans can change. Whatever my imagination had concocted with Atticus pales in comparison to the many *real* interactions with Finn. I haven't exactly hammered out the details, but suddenly, all of this feels wrong, like sewing a tailored pant cross-grain.

But Finn's phone rings in his pocket, and he excuses himself to answer it. As Finn strides beyond the flaps of my tent, I hear him say, "Perfect timing," before the busy crowd swallows him whole.

TWENTY-THREE

Finn

I'm a complete dirtbag. That's what keeps running through my mind as I wait the following afternoon inside Bayside Table. The mountain of evidence pushes against my neck, oppressively bowing my shoulders. My first offense had been yesterday at the fair when Cordelia's phone call pulled me away from Vivian. Fortunately, there wasn't another crisis in the land of Otto. My sister called to chat like she often does.

The hardest part of my father systematically removing me from our family has been not seeing my sister in person. She'd been fourteen when I left and very much beneath our father's thumb, despite her teenage rebellion in securing a burner phone and sending me gifts. Fortunately, our close relationship had weathered the distance and obstacles—even more of a testament to my sister's cleverness.

Since I'd had to keep so much from Cordelia over the years, I vowed to tell her as much about my life as I could. She always knows the latest library gossip—her favorite topic—how things are going with Alec—she's not a fan—and what projects I'm trying to implement. That's why Cordelia called yesterday with the perfect idea for my library fundraiser.

"A Worthington Ball?" With the ocean wind whipping through the boardwalk, I wasn't sure I heard her correctly.

"They're a whole vibe. Anastasia had one for her twentieth last weekend, and everyone is obsessed. Of course that means I can't use it for my upcoming birthday."

"You'll come up with something better," I say in response to my sister's pout.

"Undoubtedly."

A smile curves my lips until I glance back at Vivian's empty tent. I know Vivian didn't want help today, but the idea of her going home defeated is as appealing as brushing my teeth with cat urine.

The words are out of my mouth before I can second-guess them.

"Cor, I need a favor."

When the owner of a trendy Virginia Beach boutique arrived an hour later, I had to feign surprise. The woman evaluated Vivian's workmanship, pleasantly surprised to find it immaculate. Each of her garments are made of quality fabrics, have incredible structure, and are finished with French seams.

Vivian had done that silent, open/closed mouth thing for a few seconds when the woman suggested taking thirty dresses with her for consignment. The boutique owner warned Vivian that the dresses could be returned if they don't sell in forty-five days, but I'm confident they'll sell themselves. Garments this intricate just need to be in front of the right audience.

Acid burned in my stomach at the underhandedness of the whole interaction. But when Vivian's bright-green eyes landed on mine a second before she launched herself into my arms with glee, I told myself it would be okay. A large part of business is who you know, the connections you've made. Begrudgingly, my father had been right about that too.

"I'm so excited," Letitia says, entering the private room that I reserved for this impromptu meeting and yanking me from my memory. When I sent out a library-wide email last night, almost everyone immediately confirmed.

"The town is going to love this idea," she tells me, pulling several notepads and books from a backpack. "Did you know that, in the fifties, they used the library for public dances all the time? Here." She flips open a weathered book, her fingernail tapping on a black-and-white picture of couples crowded onto the main floor. The photographer must be standing on the stairwell to get the aerial shot.

"I've already coordinated with Margot—she teaches beginning ballet and jazz to most of the Wilks Beach kids out of her garage.

Leading up to the ball, we can host weekly lessons for locals to learn the quadrille, the waltz, and some country dances."

I open my stunned mouth to tell Letitia thank you—this was more than I expected on such short notice—but Patricia speaks first as she sails through the open door.

"I spoke to my eldest daughter," she says, plopping herself next to Letitia and launching right in. "She's in the high school chamber ensemble that meets after school. They've played a few weddings and would happily perform at the ball." Patricia opens her phone to a screenshot and pushes it across the table to me. "Those are the songs they already know, but they are willing to learn more."

Before I can even read the screen, she pulls it back. "Oh, and this is from Robert. He couldn't make it today but wanted you to see this."

I glance at the text message.

Robert

BOUT TIME I GET A CHANCE TO SPIN MY WIFE AROUND AGAIN. BEEN TOO LONG

Letitia and Patricia talk over each other as Trudy and Maxwell, the collections librarian, join us. A server sweeps in and collects drink orders for sweet tea before disappearing again.

"I think a lot of islanders will want to buy their tickets in person, but Greg could whip up a website with event information and a spot for online ticket purchases. We can link it to the main library webpage if patrons in Virginia Beach would be interested in driving out for the event." Patricia tucks her hair behind both ears before tapping on her phone again. "He'd do it pro bono, of course."

Trudy elbows Patricia with a knowing smirk. "More like payment is taken care of since you'll keep him pro—"

"Alright." I stand with a clap, bringing that potential NSFW conversation to an end. "Thanks for meeting on short notice on your day off, but I think the quicker we get this fundraiser coordinated, the better." I quickly make eye contact with each of my staff from my position at the head of the table. "I looked at the calendar, and though it's a tight window, I think it would be best to host the event Saturday, June 24th."

A collective gasp echoes through the room.

"That's in three weeks," Maxwell says.

I raise an outfacing palm. "I know, but our biggest benefactor, Dave Prescott, is taking his wife on a month-long tour of Asia for their thirtieth wedding anniversary in July. It would be best for both of them to attend."

"What about August?" Trudy asks. "That would give us more time to plan."

Directorship interviews are expected to be scheduled in early August. Having a successful—and lucrative—event behind me rather than in the works would be more favorable during my application process.

Patricia makes a dismissive noise. "It's too hot in August. Everyone would be melting in their period dresses and top hats."

"Ooooh, costumes," Trudy coos. "I didn't even *think* of that."

I had. That'd been the second thing that had popped into my mind, imagining how excited Vivian would be by the idea of sewing herself a Regency gown for a ball celebrating the books she adores.

As if my thoughts have conjured her, Vivian walks past the hostess stand and into view, a chatty Atticus on her heels. She is why I'm hosting this meeting at this specific location at this time—and the second reason why I'm a complete scumbag. I acknowledge that it's beyond inappropriate to stalk Vivian while she's with Atticus, but every time I began the email to my staff about meeting on Monday, this location and time kept popping up on my screen.

My tight spine sags at the sight of Vivian in cut-off shorts and an oversized t-shirt, her curls in a messy bun. She didn't dress up for their meeting. Even though this should be a steppingstone to her securing a formal date with Atticus, Vivian didn't wear one of her butter-soft dresses.

My jubilance is efficiently squashed when her hairstyle transports me to the memory of yesterday. It'd been nearly impossible not to drop a kiss on the nape of her neck. And then she'd turned, sucked in that unsteady breath, and reason darn near went out the window as—

"Vivian!"

I flinch at Patricia's loud call through the open door. "Come here, hon."

It's work to keep my hands from fisting. Dragging Vivian in front of a group is going to make her uncomfortable. Patricia should know better.

Vivian glances over her shoulder, and the second our gazes crash, the air is punched from my lungs. Her quick perusal of my attire only takes a millisecond, but I feel stretched beyond the capacity of my skin as it flits from my slacks to my rolled dress shirt to my unstyled hair. Then her nose wrinkles as those expressive eyes drop to her sandals.

"Um." She pauses a beat before stepping toward the door. "Hi."

"Patricia, we don't need—"

"What do you think about making dresses for a Regency ball?" Patricia interrupts me.

Vivian's gaze bounces from Patricia to me, and a burning radiates from behind my breastbone. I wish I'd told her last night. She'd been so effervescent coming home from the fair, and I'd been too torn about my role in it to mention my conversation with Cordelia.

I swallow, reminding myself that my staff is watching. "We're thinking of hosting a Regency ball as a library fundraiser. This is our first meeting to get some ideas in place."

"Doesn't that sound fun?" Patricia asks.

"It—" Vivian's hands loosen their death grip on the straps of her tote bag as her polite smile graces her lips. "It does."

"Can you beautify the fine ladies of Wilks Beach in three weeks?"

Vivian squints, her gaze drifting off. "No. Not in that timeline, but I can alter dresses. I've seen on social media that there are several affordable options online. Annie Ardent did a Regency-themed book signing in Charlotte last year, and almost everyone in attendance dressed up. Perhaps you could coordinate with attendees and make one purchase to save on shipping. If you send them to my shop, I'll make appointments with each guest to have them fitted."

A broad smile splits my face, watching Vivian relax into her savvy business persona. I saw it for the first time yesterday after the boutique owner left with several overfilled dress bags. Vivian had spoken to each subsequent customer with a comfortable grace, selling more than she had in the morning simply from the confidence boost.

"I can do that," Letitia says, scribbling notes. "I'll give locals a few days to decide on a style and pay for their dresses, and I can make a single purchase on my account."

"And if anyone decides to buy their own dress and bring it to me, that is fine too," Vivian adds. "Just have them come by to have it fitted. I'm always available for after-hours appointments too."

"What about the blokes?" Maxwell strokes his trim bread.

Vivian's laugh—her full laugh, not the whisper of one she usually uses in public—bursts from her, sending liquid sunshine weaving through my ribs.

"Same for you. I'll happily alter anything you bring me." She bites the corner of her lip, her joyful expression falling. "Sorry I can't create new garments for everyone."

"Don't apologize." I pause, clearing my throat of its gruff tone and upping the wattage on my grin. "We appreciate any help to make this fundraiser a success. Thank you, Vivian."

Her eyes do a sweep of my face, pausing on my smiling lips before fixating on my hair. Subconsciously, I run my fingers through it, and Vivian's lashes flutter.

"That sounds like an interesting fundraiser." Atticus's voice breaks the tension between us like a boulder crashing through a frozen lake.

"Glad you like the idea." Patricia rises to walk to the doorway where Vivian and Atticus are hovering. "If you'll excuse us, we have a lot of planning to do." She closes the door, staring at it for a second before wheeling on me. "Sit down, Finn. We need to have a chat."

TWENTY-FOUR

"**E**xcuse me?"

That's all I get out before Patricia barks "sit" with her mother-of-five authority. I dutifully do as I'm told, waiting as my staff members exchange loaded glances.

"Do you want to tell me what this is—"

"Uh-huh. Not yet," Patricia interrupts me, holding a finger up in my direction as she and Trudy have a silent conversation.

"I told you. Did you see the way his hands fisted when you hollered at her?" Letitia whispers like I can't hear her.

A wicked grin overtakes Patricia's face. "Why do you think I yelled like that? Everyone knows you don't approach Vivian that way."

My mouth drops open, but I close it the second all four sets of eyes swing to me. Trudy hums, folding her arms and leaning back in her chair. Maxwell leans his elbows on the table with a *Sorry, dude* shrug before placing his chin on his thumbs. The youngest of our staff, he's about five years my junior. We probably could have been friends, except he's an avid surfer, and I despise water.

The air in the room is suddenly more frigid than when they all ignored me for a month.

"I don't mean—"

"Shush," Patricia says, taking a noisy breath before leaning to press her palms on the table.

The hairs on the back of my neck raise. I started out running this room, but it's all hers now.

"First, we want you to know that you've made a good choice. There's no one in this town as good as Vivian."

I'm the recipient of a cutting glare when my lips part, so I quickly seal them. Patricia releases the table to leisurely pace back and forth.

"Secondly, after a private meeting of our own yesterday morning—"

She pauses as a surprised sound escapes my throat.

"You really thought we were going to allow you to have a relationship with *our Vivian* without discussing it?" Patricia raises her eyebrows. "Without it meeting town approval?"

A muscle in my jaw ticks. I've had just about enough of this.

"Vivian is an intelligent and capable woman. She can make her own choices. She doesn't need you to police her life or 'let her' do anything. It's honestly ridiculous the way you all treat her. She's not some fragile creature that needs to be handled with kid gloves. She's so much stronger than any of you give her credit for."

A hushed quiet reverberates around the room after my barking tirade, but I don't care. Forget always being polite, constantly worrying about optics, and being likeable. These people should be *supporting* Vivian, not making decisions on her behalf.

Her plans are incredibly brave. Most people accept what's given to them because it's too hard to do the work of changing your life.

I shoot up, my skin uncomfortably hot, my muscles twitchy. "This is absurd, and I'm not—"

"*Bro.*" Maxwell rubs his forehead, embarrassed for me. "You fell right into that."

A quick glance around the room proves he's right. Every librarian is holding back a smile. Letitia even has her hand splayed over her heart.

I blink, quickly trying to recalibrate.

"I like when they get feisty," Trudy stage-whispers to Patricia. "Shows that they care."

"This one's truly a goner," Patricia says, like I'm not standing at the other end of the table. "Gary skated along while Atticus ran this morning, chatting as they do sometimes, and guess who was thinking about taking on some accounting side projects in addition to his corporate job? I'll give you a hint: Atticus. And wouldn't you know his plans to meet his potential client were at the exact same place and exact same time as our last-minute meeting about the library fundraiser."

I barely keep from muttering "Small towns" like a curse word. I'm used to my life of generalized anonymity, of people knowing me from work and knowing about professional accolades but not paying attention to my personal life.

This is next-level busybody behavior.

But if I'm honest, it doesn't seem like the worst thing to be known, for people to care what happens to you. There's not a warm and fuzzy sense of belonging when you are born to continue a business legacy—you're either a cog in the machine, or you're a problem. Actually belonging somewhere where people genuinely care about you...

I don't even know what a life like that would look like.

My heartbeat slams against my chin, but I slide my hands into my pockets, finally in control of my outward appearance. I'm calm. Unaffected. For all they know, this is merely a coincidence.

"That's certainly an interesting theory," I say with my best smile. "But this is the only business open on Sundays—unless you'd rather have this meeting in Dotty's small produce aisle."

Patricia tsks, shaking her head.

"Maybe it is just a coincidence." Letitia scribbles something on her notepad, ever the peacemaker.

"Good thing," Trudy agrees, "since Atticus's hand dropped *real low* on Vivian's back as he led her away."

My brain knows it's bait, but the signal doesn't get to my tense muscles quick enough. My flinch might as well be a confetti cannon shooting paper hearts embossed with *Finn + Vivian 4eva!*

Maxwell laughs at my tight expression. "If it makes you feel any better, she's just as transparent about her feelings as you are. You should be happy. There's nothing worse than pining for someone and having them not like you."

I don't even have time to process Maxwell's words because the conversation careens on.

Trudy nearly launches herself over the table. "Like the way Atticus has been fawning over Amanda Ratchack since she returned from Sweden?" She snorts. "That'll *never* work out."

"I don't know," Letitia muses. "Stranger things have happened."

"We should ask Camille if she's dreamt about either of them," Patricia adds.

My puzzled expression must show, like every other emotion I seem to be having, since these people are reading me like a large-print book.

"Camille is the middle school art teacher who's also a touch psychic. She 'sees' people together in her dreams, and then they almost always end up coupling off. She's accurately paired off most of the monogamous couples in Wilks Beach, including Gary and me." Patricia taps her chin, her gaze narrowing on me again. "Come to think of it, Camille said she saw Vivian with a man wearing a suit, but she could never get a good look at his face."

All eyes swing to me again. I'd forgone my suit vest today in an attempt to look more casual, but my professional attire revolves around suit pieces—though I rarely wear a jacket.

A collective gasp goes through the room.

"Finn could be him! The faceless man!" Trudy shouts, pointing like a lunatic.

"*Okay.*" I spread my hands in front of my rioting chest. "This meeting has gotten way off topic. Can we focus on the fundraiser, please?"

"I agree." Maxwell leans onto his thumbs again. "The offshore winds are making choice waves. The sooner we get out of here, the better."

Patricia and Trudy grumble, but Letitia just gives me a small smile. "I think it'd be nice if it was you."

"That's kind of you to say," I say evenly, though it feels like fizzy bubbles are shooting down my arms.

"Well, before you *so rudely* shot us down, I was about to tell you that the consensus of our meeting was that we all like you and Vivian together." Patricia adds with a huff.

"You do?"

"You're like her opposite but in the best way—always knowing what to say when she struggles to communicate."

I stare at her, uncharacteristically wordless.

"Not that you need our approval. You'll make your own decisions. It's your life. Yada yada." Patricia waves a hand, sharing a commiserating glance with Trudy.

My brain is buzzing while a strange, yet comforting, sense of warmth infiltrates everything else. I need to figure out this situation with Vivian, but one word keeps ticking at my temple like remnant rain drops falling off a roof—honest.

"I like you like this."

So much of the last several years has been a master class in deceit—mostly out of necessity to protect Cordelia. But there had been a part of me so hurt by Katelyn's actions that it made me want to hide away, especially since she confirmed what my father has always told me.

No one would ever love me as I am.

But he'd been wrong about my ability to thrive without his money, without his last name. What if he'd been wrong about this too? Maybe I could slowly show Vivian parts of who I really am.

"Thank you," I tell Patricia, and then just to needle her, I add my most charming grin. "I'll take your feedback under consideration."

As expected, she rolls her eyes.

"For the fundraiser"—my shoulders settle as I mentally shift gears—"let's start by making a list of actionable items."

TWENTY-FIVE

Vivian

My toes wiggle in the water off the dock behind Bayside Table, my legs kicking leisurely. A boat bobs a few feet to my right, the last to occupy one of the six coveted boat slips. On perfect days like today, this dock brings more mainlanders to Wilks Beach than the road does. Sometimes, early June is cool and breezy, reminding you that summer doesn't officially start until the third week. Other times, it can be humid and scorching, already making you dread August. Today, it's an agreeable eighty with a bright, unmarred sky—warm enough to enjoy my legs in the water as I wait for Finn.

Checking the time on my phone, my face automatically unlocks the screen, displaying my text messages from earlier.

My stomach should be stewing with maggots, but with the breeze coming off the bay, I'm oddly calm. I made a decision the second Finn ran his fingers through his unstyled hair. It'd been an idea I'd toyed with last night when I laid down, too excited about my success to sleep. It'd been the song in the background when I had a relaxing morning with Brynn, deciding to wait to see if the consignment dresses sell before telling her about the fair. At the end of yesterday, I had enough profit to give Brynn the day off, but it'd be icing on the Seabreeze Beans's cinnamon roll if I could also book her a spa day.

When my sister went downstairs to roast beans, I walked here, not even bothering to tell her about meeting Atticus. It's a non-issue because, though this whole endeavor began to win his affection, that's no longer what I want. I'm not even sure if I ever really wanted Atticus but rather *the idea* of Atticus. And after a very cordial meeting with the man, it's clear he's not interested in me in the least. After he helped me organize my bookkeeping software to be more efficient, Atticus unexpectedly pumped me for information about Amanda.

An acoustic guitarist tunes in the background as seagulls float above the restaurant. Clara, the owner of Bayside Table, must be experimenting with adding music on Sunday evenings. The town will be thrilled.

"Hey."

A few escaped strands of hair brush the back of my neck as I turn my head. Finn's expression is strained, his jaw tight like it'd been before he'd taken his medicine yesterday. His back presses against the building, almost as if he needs it for support.

"Are you hurting?"

If he's in pain, this can wait another day.

"No, it's—" Finn draws in a large inhale, holding it for two tense seconds before releasing it in a gush. His focus falls to the dock boards as his forearms flex. I'm about to inquire again when Finn raises his head. Our gazes meet, and then I see it, the subtle shift but in reverse this time. The affable mask Finn wears slips as he takes another steadying breath. "Honest?"

I nod, my chest suddenly tight.

"You're too close to the water."

My eyebrows pinch as I glance at the brackish, near-black water around my calves. I began swimming in the bay, only moving to the ocean when my parents felt I was strong enough to tackle the beach's waves. Most island kids start out that way. That's why the park playground at the south end of the island has a little man-made beach on the bayside.

And after my parents died, swimming became my way to escape the pain that I didn't understand at the time was grief. When the water silenced the noises of the world, I could hear my mom's voice again. I could remember what she sounded like, singing our favorite songs as we danced around the kitchen. I feel safer in the water than I do on dry land most days.

A memory flits at the edges of my mind, a bit hazy at the corners—of us being near water and Finn being uncomfortable. It must have been when he'd been coaching me to approach men at bars. Yes, I'd wanted to say hello to the ocean and...

My chin snaps up, finding Finn practically vibrating, the tendons in his neck popping. I slowly rise, leaving my sandals and my tote on the dock boards.

"I'm perfectly safe here, but I don't mind coming next to you."

"I know." He runs a frustrated hand through those gorgeous locks. "I know how capable you are."

His shoulders drop in ragged increments as I pad over, releasing completely when I'm standing two feet in front of him.

"What is it about water?"

Finn's head shakes, his jaw a steel trap again.

I press my lips together, surveying his body. His knuckles are white from where they grip his laptop. Brynn gets like this when she's stressed. Rigid. Silent. Completely shutdown. With her, I usually make something savory to coax the words out, but I can't do that now.

"Let me just..." I collect his computer, crouching to set it against the exterior wall.

I'm halfway to standing when I remember something else I do with Brynn—talking side by side. When we're walking on the beach or sitting on the couch, she's more willing to open up. I rest my back on the blue siding, my fingers close but not touching Finn's. For a full minute, we watch the boats' fenders bump against the dock, their ropes straining against the galvanized cleats. The guitarist begins the delicate, almost-hypnotic introduction to "Dust in the Wind."

"It's not that I can't swim."

I say nothing, waiting.

"I...I learned young, but then my broth—"

My head turns to catch Finn's eyes closed, his dark lashes firmly pressed to his cheeks.

"I was eight. No one else was around, which almost never happened, and my brother said we should swim. I was just excited that he was taking an interest in me, since he'd spent most of my life ignoring me. It was fun at first—a few cannon balls, a water fight. But then..."

I can't not touch Finn, so I slip my pinky around his.

Finn's throat bobs with a swallow. "I thought he'd let go right away. He'd dunk me. I'd dunk him. I fought when the air got thin, but I couldn't overpower him. He was thirteen and so much stronger than me. When the chlorine burned down my lungs, I—I thought..."

My other hand grips his arm as spikes piston down my legs. I know Finn is fine—he's here telling me this story—but my racing pulse doesn't seem to understand.

"The gardener was tearing into Brody when I came to the surface. I scrambled onto the pool deck, gasping, but Brody just puffed out his chest, looking terrifyingly similar to my father, and told us both that nothing happened. He told the gardener he didn't see anything—not if he wanted to keep his job. Brody hissed that our father would never respect me if I couldn't handle a little roughhousing. I coughed and sputtered for hours afterward, but I...I've never told anyone."

Before his chin drops against his chest, I catch his cheek with my palm. "I—I don't know what to say...I—" Darn my inability to form the right words. "I'm sorry. I'm *so* sorry. That never should have happened."

Finn's shoulders rise and fall before he leans into my touch, his lashes closing. My heart aches as moisture congests at the bridge of my nose. I want to wrap my arms around this giant man, to build a bubble fortress with my body until nothing can hurt him. Standing on my tiptoes, I do just that—slide my hands around him and give Finn the snuggest hug. When his beard scruff burrows in my hair with an exhale, I squeeze tighter.

"I'd felt so lost afterward." His whispered words tickle my neck. "That itchy sensation that I didn't quite measure up had always been there, but I felt the separation even more after that. My father and brother were in one orbit, and I was in another. It became hard to sleep, though I never told anyone the nightmares were about drowning. After that, my nanny took me to my grandmother's library whenever I woke up. Everyone else would be asleep, and she'd snuggle us into a worn leather chair and read to me for hours."

"I like her." I gently slide my fingers into the fringes of his hair, tracing his spine down and then back up again.

Finn's shoulders collapse with another heart-squeezing exhale. "I did too. She was the only person who encouraged me to pursue my interests—until my sister came along, that is."

Was. The glint of sorrow in that word is enough to know that she's no longer with us.

"What was her name?"

"Magda." The reverent way Finn says her name makes my chest tight.

A question about where his mother was in all this hovers on the tip of my tongue, but I don't voice it. Finn has already divulged so much. If his mother had been in the picture, he'd have mentioned it. His casual mention of a gardener and a nanny confirms my suspicions that Finn must have had a wealthy upbringing, though, it seems, an emotionally impoverished one.

After several, long seconds, Finn lifts his head. His eyes bounce between mine before he clears his throat, shifting until I release him.

"Sorry. Um." He rubs the back of his neck. "What did you want to talk about?"

I like you. I want to be with you.

But it doesn't seem like a good time for those words now.

I wave a hand. "It was something about the fundraiser. It can wait."

Finn simply nods, blinking slowly. He's probably feeling as wrung out as I do after one of my epic sobfests. I have the sneaking suspicion that, as hard as public speaking is for me, honesty is challenging for Finn. The fact that he just trusted me with one of his biggest secrets gives me hope for the future, for when I tell him about the adjustments I've made to my four-part plan.

"Do you want me to walk you home? I hear there are ruffians running the streets."

A puff of a laugh leaves his lips. "Sure."

After snatching up my belongings, we amble down Sand Bend Road in companionable silence. I can tell by the way he rubs his temples that Finn is exhausted. My mind whirls with an exciting idea for my shiny, new plan. It's going to put me out of my comfort zone again, but I think it'll be worth it. I think Finn needs to see that *he's worth* the extra effort.

I leave Finn on his doorstep, keeping a respectable distance. "Here you go. Door delivery with absolutely zero muggings."

"Thanks." The corner of his mouth lifts, though his eyes betray his fatigue.

I bite my lip to hide my secret smile. "Have a good night. I'll see you soon."

TWENTY-SIX

Vivian

I swallow down the surge of unease clawing up my throat the next evening and focus on wrapping my hands like Geneva demonstrated. She was surprisingly nice when I stumbled into the boxing gym ten minutes ago, inquiring about trying a class. Now, I'm resisting nervously tugging on the oversized shirt eclipsing my gray bike shorts as I wait for Finn.

The only thing keeping my lunch down is the anticipation of the look on his face when he sees me. I hum one of Raven Sacaria's power ballads as I secure the second wrap around my wrist. Geneva had been very particular about proper wrist support.

"What are you doing here?"

A smile splits my face before I even look up.

And then I'm rewarded for the mental effort of showing up tonight—I seriously repeated *You got this* over a hundred times today. Finn is wearing the same black exercise shorts and snug dark-gray t-shirt he'd worn that first time I went to his house, topped with a backward baseball cap. He looks like a model for a fitness company, but that's to be expected. *My reward* is when Finn palms his neck, and the action raises his sleeve an inch. I spot the slightest edge of ink on the underside of his biceps—undeniably a bookstack tattoo.

My chin lifts in a determined tilt. "I'm going to ask you to do something you're not comfortable with later, so I'm offering my own discomfort first. I hate all non-swimming-related exercises, but I'm willing to try for you. I'm hoping that, later, you'll be willing to try for me."

Finn looks like I sucker punched him in the gut but, weirdly, in a good way.

"*Vivian.*" My name is a breathy whisper, low and intimate, as his fingers curl air.

Goosebumps erupt on my forearms even though the gym's garage doors are open to the warm summer night.

"We're not chit-chatting tonight," Geneva calls out, turning on metal music so loud it vibrates down my spine. "Partner up. Grab a bag. Get going."

I bite the edge of one boxing glove, frantically trying to slide my fingers into the other.

"Do you want help putting on your gloves?" Finn asks, reaching for the one dangling from my mouth.

"New Guy, I'm in no mood," Geneva snaps, rounding on us. She gives me an efficient once-over, all the gentleness she showed me earlier terrifyingly absent. "Though I suppose you're the new one now."

"I guess." My fingertips tremble as I try to shove them into the proffered glove.

Geneva's stern expression infinitesimally softens before she crosses her arms. "What's your preference? Newb. Newbie. Or Rookie."

The way Finn's brows shoot up as he fastens my second glove, I'm guessing name selection is not often extended to new attendees.

"Rookie."

Geneva nods, glancing at Finn with a bored sigh. "I guess you need a new name too."

"Or..." Finn gives her that winning smile. "Just a wild thought here, but you could call me by my name."

Geneva pretends to give it some thought. "What's the fun in that, Pretty Boy?"

When I snort, nearly clocking myself in the face trying to cover my mouth with my gloved hands, the corner of Geneva's mouth quirks. Then she spins on her heel, barking instructions on how to warm up. I bounce on my toes a little, the nervous energy from stepping out of my comfort zone turning over into excitement.

"This is going to be fun."

"Never have I known such torment," I mutter to Finn while refilling my water bottle two-thirds of the way through what everyone else is calling a 'class' but I'm calling pure, unadulterated torture.

"It gets better with time," he says with that flirty little smirk.

I don't know why he's grinning at me like a goon when I'm sure my ruddy face is probably wreathed in a halo of frizzy baby hairs. There are no mirrors here, not even in the bathroom where I spent five minutes hiding after we did fifty burpees, and I thought my heart would explode. Perhaps it's a mercy that I can't see my reflection. If my sweat-soaked shirt and slick legs are any indication, the rest of me is equally disheveled.

The weird thing is, for a boxing class, we've done very little boxing. We warmed up on the bags but then promptly took off our gloves to do my least favorite activity—running. All the way to the library, I huffed like a fish out of water, begging Finn to leave me behind. To save himself. He'd only chuckled, like my *very real* distress was something adorable. To his credit, the covert encouragement he'd murmured whenever Geneva was out of earshot genuinely helped.

Once we returned to the unairconditioned gym, Geneva subjected us to all manner of bodyweight exercises. Push-ups. Planks. Four kinds of squats. Lunges. Mountain climbers. Jumping jacks. Let's just say I'd muttered a silent prayer that the twelve eye-hooks of my decade-old high-impact sports bra wouldn't fail me.

"Gloves on. 1-2-3-2, 1-2-5-2, then 1-6-3-2. Run each combo five times. Let's go!"

Our warm-up consisted of doing each numbered movement independently, but my exhausted brain cannot remember which are which. One is a hook? Or an undercut? Uppercut?

"Rookie." I jump when Geneva's voice resounds from directly behind me. At least she's not yelling.

"I want you here." She jabs before landing a crushing cross that makes Finn reset his position, holding the bag steady. "Jab-cross. 1-2. That's it." My mouth gapes at her effortless show of power. She's not even wearing gloves, just wraps.

When I make no movement, Geneva lifts a dark brow. "Let's see it."

My gloves limply hit the bag before I realize I did the combination backward. I fumble a nearly inaudible apology and try again. Geneva sucks in a slow breath at my effort, and my shoulders scrunch around my ears.

"Let me ask you this." She crosses her arms, looking very much like the Valkyrie she is. "Do you have a nemesis? Someone who really gets under your skin?"

Amanda Ratchack's perfectly sculpted cheekbones flash before my vision, and I scowl instinctively. From behind the bag, Finn's fingers tighten on the canvas. I feel his gaze on me but don't dare take my eyes off Geneva.

"Okay, great. Now think of their face"—Geneva taps the bag—"here."

I turn and move my feet wider with Geneva's gentle corrections. She lets me go another round before using two fingers to lift my elbow. "Don't drop this again. You're losing your power."

This time when I hit the bag, it feels right. A surge of adrenaline swirls in my stomach, and I hit the bag again—harder. It suddenly feels like I'm avenging not only myself but all the underdogs of Wilks Beach. They're all with me, forming an awkward army to take down the people of the world who made us feel less than we are. I lose myself for a minute, my imagination creating elaborate scenarios in which it would be completely appropriate and not at all illegal to punch Amanda Ratchack in her perfect, snarky face. When I finally look up, I'm breathing like I just finished a 25-meter sprint to shore.

Geneva quirks a half smile and walks away.

Finn chuckles, voice low. "I think that's as close to praise that anyone in this class has ever received. Teacher's pet." He winks at me, but it's playful not suave.

He's so unguarded, wearing a backward ball cap and covered with his own sheen of sweat. All class, he's been roguish and flirty but in a more toned-down capacity. Right now, he looks like...

He looks like *my Finn*—the version of himself that comes out in tiny, incremental snippets when we're alone, almost as if Finn forgot to be the polished version of himself tonight. I want to keep him right here, just like this, so I set my lips in a mischievous smile.

"Maybe it's because—"

"Rookie. Exercise your body, not your mouth," Geneva bellows from across the room.

I clamp my lips shut, and then realization spins my world on its axis. The joy encompassing me is so bright and shimmery that there's no way I'm not radiating. Is this what Raven Sacaria feels like bathed in adoring cheers and glowing stage lights? It's got to be close. Because Geneva just yelled at me because I was *talking too much*. Me! Near-silent Vivian, the town's sweet, quiet girl, was just admonished for chatting in class.

A slight chortle escapes me, and then I'm doubled over, heaving with laughter that almost burns my lungs as much as the agonizing run had earlier. In response to Geneva's death stare, Finn shuffles me outside to collect myself. I wave to her as we exit, incapable of apology because I'm laughing so hard that I'm no longer making sounds. Taking her half eyeroll as forgiveness, I allow myself to surrender to the moment. Out here, tucked against the side of the former-auto-shop-turned-torture-chamber, I allow myself to make as much noise as I need to.

Like always, Finn doesn't rush me. He lets me giggle it out, watching with an entertained smile. I yank off my boxing gloves so I can use the collar of my shirt to wipe my face.

"I just— She just—" I give in to the coppery sensation swimming in my veins and laugh some more. "Geneva yelled at me *for talking*."

Finn's expression softens with understanding. "You're right." He braces his forearm on the brick exterior beside his head, voice deepening as he leans toward me. "You know, I'm not surprised. You're quite a chatterbox once you get started. I can see you as the most disruptive person in the class if you keep coming with me."

I like that thought. I like the idea of coming back and challenging myself. Of attending class *with* Finn.

Hope swirls in my chest. "Yeah?"

"Yeah." The corners of his eyes crinkle in the wan streetlight. "You can do whatever you want, Vivian."

His complete faith in me makes my heart skitter and switch directions. What if what I want is to rise on my tiptoes and kiss him? To slide my wrapped hands over his ribs and pull us flush, regardless of our disgusting sweatiness? My gaze falls to Finn's lips, fixating on his slightly uneven cupid's bow surrounded by dark stubble.

I flick my eyes back to Finn's, a smirk curling my mouth. "Thanks for permission."

Then I palm the back of his head and bring his lips to mine.

TWENTY-SEVEN

A surprised sound leaves my mouth, and Vivian chases after it with her tongue. It's impossible not to react, not to flip her against the building and put all my weight into deepening the kiss. This is nothing like the first time. There's a fervor to this kiss, an impatience. It's dangerously explosive, burning through my soul with a ferocity that leaves me stunned.

Vivian's fingers knock my hat off to dive into my hair, and a groan vibrates up my chest. Then realization hits, and I'm turned inside out.

Vivian is kissing *me*.

She's not practicing for some eventual kiss with another man. She's kissing me. She wants *me*. I'm dizzy with relief until a nasty voice reminds me that Vivian doesn't know the real me.

Not yet.

There's time to change that.

Yesterday had been monumental, telling her such a significant piece of my history. The way she'd accepted it—accepted me—and held me afterward makes me think that I could try again. I could let her in piece by piece and hope that when she's holding my heart in her nimble fingers, she'll treat it as delicately as the fabrics she adores.

I pull back slightly. "Vivian—"

"Talk later," she tells me before surging forward, nipping at my lower lip.

Okay, then.

Spreading my fingers wide, I memorize the curves of Vivian's waist. I don't even care that we're both soaked in sweat. If anything, it heightens the sensations against my fingertips. I'm two seconds from slipping my hands beneath her shirt and curling them at the small of her back when Vivian pulls away slightly.

"Maybe you shouldn't— You might not like—" When she bites her lip, I release one hand to soothe it with my thumb.

Her shoulders slump, her gaze dropping to my collarbones. "It's just— I'm not good at *not eating* food."

"Vivian." I give her hips a reassuring pat before sliding my hands to possessively grip her waist. "Do you think I want to hold onto a flat, cement slab while I'm kissing?" My tongue touches my top lip as I let my gaze sweep down her. "I've dreamt about what it would be like to hold you like this."

A truth. A very insistent one.

Vivian's mouth opens and closes twice. "You have?"

"Yes." I set a gentle kiss on her temple before bringing my lips to the shell of her ear. "You, Vivian Hutchinson, are perfect in my book."

I'm not sure what I expected her response to be. A timid smile, perhaps? A breathy "Oh?" I certainly didn't expect all five foot five of Vivian to flip us until she's pressing *me* against the building. An amused sound resonates in my throat before Vivian's kiss knocks all logic out of my brain. I burrow my fingers into her sweaty curls and pour myself into her. When Vivian sighs against my lips, a zip of electricity burns backward through my body, fundamentally changing my cellular structure until there's only one thing I'm absolutely certain of.

I can't give this up. I can't give *her* up.

I need to find a way to incorporate Vivian into my plans and hope to all that is good in the world that when she finally gets under all my layers, she'll like what she sees.

"Dang, Vivian," a voice calls out, tone mirthful. "I didn't know you had it in you."

We separate enough to see two firefighters in station uniforms—Jonas and Carson, I think?—walking out of the open bay doors of the fire station. They're both carrying folding beach chairs and energy drinks.

Carson slugs Jonas in the shoulder. "Never mind him," he calls over the distance before saying to Jonas, "We should have just sat out front."

"Naw. The bay view is the best perk of being at this station." Jonas drops into his chair, stretching his legs out toward the water.

We disentangle from each other, my pulse thick in my throat when Vivian frowns at the two men. I should have thought of how we were in the eyeline of anyone outside of the fire station or, really, anyone on the road if they'd been looking between the two buildings. Heck, a fellow class attendee could have wandered out while I was distracted by the soft noises Vivian makes when my lips tug at hers.

"This is going to be all over town tomorrow," I tell her.

I don't love the idea of creating another secret when, for the first time in my life, I'm trying to be authentic, but if Vivian needs me to, I'll do it. I'm beginning to think I'll do anything when it comes to her.

"I don't care. This is my life, and I am finally—*finally*—taking control of it." She lets out a punchy exhale with a nod, but then, those gorgeous green eyes snap to mine, and the uncertainty in them slices me open. "I mean, unless...unless you—"

"*No.*" My tone could cut through granite, but my thumbs are gentle over her freckled cheeks as I frame her face. "Let them talk."

A bubble of a laugh leaves her lips open. "Tell me how you really feel about it."

"Don't tempt me, gorgeous." My head tilts as I give her a seductive smile.

Vivian's eyes go wide as she sucks in a stuttered breath. It's not until this moment that I realize I've never unleashed my full flirtatious power on Vivian. What fun it would be to watch her squirm under the attention. I hover my lips an inch from hers, teasingly, when a loud whistle sounds.

Jonas takes two fingers out of his mouth. "Maybe pack it in? A lot of people walk the road in the evenings."

Vivian drops her forehead onto my shoulder with a giggle. The sound is oddly addicting. I not only want to hear it again, I want to be *its source*.

"It's not that we're not happy for you both, but you know..." Carson points east toward the rest of town.

I nod at the two men, raising an open palm to them before setting it at the base of Vivian's spine to steer her back to class.

Tomorrow, there will likely be some sort of small-town social payment for getting caught up in the moment, but I don't give a single care. Vivian makes everything better by just breathing. Whatever is coming our way, I'll handle it. I've already weathered this town's cold shoulder. Let's see them do their worst.

TWENTY-EIGHT

Vivian

Pepper's fluffy tail swats my face, waking me. I split open one eye and groan when I catch the first strands of early morning light beyond my curtains. It's way too early for me to be awake, especially since I was up late replaying that incredible kiss. I thought embarrassment over being caught would seep into the memory and taint it, but nope. I would kiss Finn Reynolds in front of Santa and everyone during the town's Christmas tree lighting ceremony if given the opportunity.

A happy hum harmonizes with Pepper's purring as I turn over, burrowing deeper beneath my floral duvet. I only get two seconds of snuggly warmth before my bedroom door flies open.

"We need to talk." Brynn plops herself on the edge of my bed, one leg tucked under her. My cat skitters to the floor and out my open door, but Brynn softens my rude awakening by extending an iced coffee in my direction.

It seems it hasn't taken long for news of last night's events to reach gossip central. My eyes catch the time as I push myself up against the headboard—5:55 a.m. Honestly, it's shocking it took almost a half hour for someone to report to Brynn.

"Thanks." I take the proffered coffee with one hand while rubbing my eyes with the other.

"Well?" Brynn prompts.

"Well, what?"

Annoyance brews in my veins because her tone and body language are giving stern-sister-talkin'-to vibes, not oh-my-gosh-you-kissed-a-hot-guy-I'm-so-excited-for-you energy. I was so happy for her when she and Noah hit it off years ago. And yeah, that ended in a dumpster fire, but it's been her choice not to date any of the other eligible men in Wilks Beach since. If Brynn chose to, I'd be ecstatic for her. Why the heck can't she be happy for me?

"Why the heck can't you be happy for me?"

My twin's face mirrors the shock resonating down my arms. I just said that out loud? Wait. You know what? Yeah. I'm leaning into this new chapter of not only speaking in general but speaking my mind.

Doubling down, I add, "I refuse to feel shame for sharing a kiss with someone I really like—even if it was in public."

Brynn reaches to tug at the hem of her t-shirt, but it's trapped beneath an aqua Seabreeze Beans apron. "It's just confusing because I thought you liked Atticus."

The hurt in her words has me dropping my tense shoulders and stretching my fingers to settle over her knee.

"I did, but"—the smile lifting my lips has its own energy—"things changed. Have you eaten?" I know she hasn't. Brynn typically gets too busy and forgets to eat. "Let me make you an omelet, and I'll explain everything."

After quickly using the bathroom, I crack eggs into a glass measuring cup. I wish I had the time to make Brynn tater tots—our favorite food—but I know she wouldn't wait for them to be ready. Her jittery knee is already bouncing against the underside of our round two-person kitchen table. She hates being away from the coffee shop during the morning rush.

"Do you remember my ocean wish?"

She nods. "You wanted to talk to Atticus."

"It turned out I needed a little help, so Finn offered to be my dating coach..." I give my sister the rough details of how he took me to Virginia Beach to talk to men, leaving out our practice kiss and how Finn helped me at the Oceanside Artisan Fair, because I still want to surprise Brynn with that later.

I cross the kitchen, setting a simple spinach-and-swiss omelet in front of my sister.

"And then you kissed?"

"Take three bites, and I'll tell you."

My twin rolls her eyes but compiles, shoving half the omelet into her mouth like an uncivilized frat boy. Food bribery was something Aunt Tammy used to do growing up when Brynn's weight dipped into dangerously low territory. Brynn learned the quickest way to get to whatever activity was on the other side of the meal was to gobble it up like a competitive eater.

"I kissed him." Her fork pauses halfway to her mouth, but I encourage her to continue the action. "I wasn't quite sure how it would go, but I needed to try."

"And he kissed you back."

I bite my lip, remembering how enthusiastically Finn returned my kiss. "Yeah."

Brynn sets down her fork and stares out the window.

"I really like him, Brynn. He's obviously gorgeous and incredible at his job, but there's this soft underlayer that's even more attractive than what he shows anyone else. I can identify with that—keeping your true personality to yourself." When my sister doesn't respond, I feel as small as I had before I started this process of self-improvement. "It'd be really nice for you to be happy for me."

Brynn's dark-brown eyes catch the downturn of my lips, and she shoots to standing, nearly toppling the vase of hydrangeas I put on the table on Friday. Her arms come around me so fiercely an involuntary squeak escapes me.

"I am. I will be. I want to be." Brynn squeezes me even tighter. "I'm sorry. It's just...a change."

Understanding dawns like the sunrise beaming over the ocean each morning.

Brynn does everything the same way every day. It's as if she's afraid if she deviates one iota, the world will come crashing down. Our apartment decor and the furniture arrangement hasn't changed since Tammy moved out. The same goes for the styling of the coffee shop. She only purchases updated equipment when it becomes searingly necessary.

That's one of the reasons why I waited so long to ask for the space for my store. I knew that separating the family business into two would be hard on her. But when I'd told her how important it was to me, she agreed, and we worked through the renovation together.

I should have considered that making these changes in my life would upset her balance.

"It is," I say, hugging her back. "I should have warned you so you could process it. I'm sorry."

Brynn leans back, shaking her head. "Don't apologize. I'm in the wrong here."

A part of me wants to joke about immortalizing her words on a plaque and hanging it over the TV, but since we're actually talking for what feels like the first time in forever, I don't dare.

"I've wanted this for a long time, Brynn. I wanted to prove that I could do something more than smile and nod." My lungs feel tight, but I fill them anyway. "No one expects much of me on this island. I know they're trying to be kind, but it makes me feel like I'm still that terrified little girl who just lost her parents. Like I'm trapped in this tight little box."

Brynn's hands rub my shoulders, almost too roughly, but I know it's her way of consoling me.

"But once I made that wish...things started being different. It was hard at first, but I feel like I'm growing and stretching in ways I didn't even plan to." A bark of laughter escapes me. "Last night, I went to a boxing class."

My sister's eyes fly wide.

"I know, right? Me voluntarily attending an exercise class is akin to mermaids walking on land. Every muscle I didn't even know I had is on fire, and it hurts to breathe, but I might go again. Geneva appears terrifying but is secretly sweet, and there's something undeniably cathartic about punching out your frustration."

Brynn's lip twitches at the corner. "Maybe I should join you."

"You should!" I grip both her hands in between mine. "It'd be so much more fun with you there. Though I should warn you that Geneva's class should be classified as torture not exercise."

My sister chuckles before falling into silence, thinking. "So what's next for you?"

"I don't know." There's a breathy giddiness to my words. "I want to keep trying new things. Maybe I'll croak out a Raven Sacaria song at karaoke on Thursday. That'll keep the town guessing."

A part of me wants to tell my sister about part three of my plan, but Brynn needs some time to digest this news before I launch something *that big* on her.

My sister's smile fades as she chews the inside of her cheek. "I'm sorry I didn't see that you needed this. I know that I can be"—when my confident sister struggles for words, my heart cracks—"too rigid, but I don't want you to be unhappy because of me. I love you. I want what's best for you."

"I love you too. You don't make me unhappy."

Brynn doesn't answer, her hands dropping from mine.

"You don't." My words come out firmly as I stoop to catch her gaze. "You know that, right? You're the most important person to me."

It takes a few halting seconds for my sister's eyes to meet mine. "You might not feel that way when you fall in love with Finn."

I snort, even though a small part of my heart whispers I might already be there. "You didn't feel that way when you were in love with Noah. You two were all moonpie, heart-eyes for each other for years, but you still loved and made time for me."

"Point taken." Brynn's hands fist at her sides.

Oops. While distracted by baring my soul, I'd forgotten our pact to *never* speak of Noah.

"Want to go to karaoke with me?" I ask, quickly changing the subject.

I nearly faint with shock when Brynn tilts her head, considering. "I'll think about it."

"Really?"

Fizzy bubbles shoot through my veins. Maybe my changes will encourage Brynn to make a few of her own—when she's ready, on her own timeline. Whenever that is, I'd be more than happy to hold her hand along the way.

"We'll see. I should get going," Brynn says, already sliding back into work mode. She's halfway to the staircase before she pauses and pivots.

"Oh, and what's this about a dance at the library? Joe said it was a sock hop?"

A grin lifts my lips. As much as Wilks Beach residents love to gossip, they occasionally get their information twisted.

"It's a Regency ball," I correct her. "Finn is organizing it as a fundraiser to update the media room."

My sister straightens. "A Regency ball? He's doing that for you?"

"No." I feel my blush staining my cheeks. "Not for me, for the town."

"But you love everything Regency."

"So do millions of *Worthington* viewers."

"But those people didn't model their business after a modiste's shop."

I turn to the sink, turning on the water to scrub the dishes. "This fundraiser idea is better than Carol Cook's suggestion for a topless fire station car wash."

My sister scoffs. "That's just an excuse for Carol to gawk at shirtless men without having to walk down the beach."

"Too true. Her ocean wish would be twenty uninterrupted minutes with Henry Cavill's abs." When my sister's surprised laughter fills our small apartment, my smile grows. "Though, I'll never understand why she lives in a beach town when she hates sand."

"She's a local. Like us. We're born here. We belong here."

"And every once in a while, we let new people into our ranks." I glance at my sister, thinking about the various mainlanders who've made Wilks Beach their home over the years. Maybe, with time, I can convince Finn to consider the town his too.

Just like we can have an entire conversation with eyebrow lifts and head tilts, Brynn understands what I'm asking for here.

"We do." Her mouth is firm, but my sister nods. "We do."

TWENTY-NINE

Finn

I'm not sure what I expected the town's response to be the morning after kissing Vivian. Picketing? Tomato throwing? General upheaval over me locking lips with the local sweetheart? For the most part, I'm met with knowing grins as I walk to the library. Then I'm darn near accosted by back slaps and exuberant hugs from my coworkers. Even Robert says, "I'm excited as all get out," with absolutely no change in facial expression.

I never thought I'd be grateful for small-town gossip and how *up in your business* people can get after being at the receiving end of everyone's disapproval when I moved here. The fact is, I would have kissed Vivian back even if I was still the town villain. I'd have been helpless not to.

But I have to admit, the external validation is...nice. It's akin to the sense of belonging that comes when I enter the market and someone calls me by name or when everyone on my morning run smiles and waves back.

When Carol Cook barges into my office a few minutes after the library doors open, I grin, almost excited to see what she'll throw at me. "Are you going to make an honest girl of our Vivian?"

I barely restrain a chuckle. "Excuse me?"

"Don't pretend you didn't hear me." Carol cane-walks through my door and attempts to slam it closed but, due to the fact that the glass door has a hefty hydraulic system, fails miserably.

"That was anticlimactic," she murmurs before spinning to me with a pointed finger. Today's nail polish matches her smudged lipstick—a purply mauve. "Much like your love life will be without my help."

"Mrs. Cook," I begin, my tone cordial, though a flick of irritation courses through me.

She rolls her eyes. "Spare me." Then she deepens her voice. "I'm young and handsome, but all foam, no beer, and can't see a good thing when it's right in front of me."

My slow inhale pulls my dress shirt taut against my chest. "I can assure you that—"

"Bap bap bap." Her interrupting sound is akin to one you'd use to stop a wayward dog from jumping up on bed. "You know nothing about how things work in this town."

Since Carol clearly needs to say her fill, I slide my hands in my pockets. "Enlighten me."

It takes several seconds for Carol's lips to fully curl in a smile, almost as if drawn out for dramatic effect. Clearly being the holder of the town's information is a position she relishes. I take one hand out of my pocket, rolling it in the air to hurry her along.

She makes a dismissive noise before hobbling over to my desk chair and making herself comfortable. Once Carol has adjusted her pink trousers and matching blouse, she catches my gaze.

"You may have run around, slobbering on others in the past—"

"I did not slobber—" Carol silences me with a single tattooed eyebrow.

"You may have had casual dalliances in the past, but Vivian is an old-fashioned girl—"

"Woman," I interrupt, unable to keep the slight edge out of my tone.

Carol tilts her head but keeps her smile of approval muted. "Vivian is a woman who deserves more than kisses against the sides of buildings for everyone to see." She tugs at the collar of her shirt as if to steady herself, but I'm sure it's part of the performance. "The next course of action is clear. It's time you asked her to the ball. You're obviously infatuated with her. She's clearly enticed by"—Carol pauses, flicking her open palm over my appearance—"all of this, so there's no time like the present."

It's my turn to smirk at the indomitable Carol Cook.

"It seems I mistook you as an observant woman..." I see the exact second Carol stops herself from taking the bait. "Because someone who clearly has their thumb on the pulse of this town would know that I am not a man of questionable character. It is my full intention to ask Vivian to the library fundraiser."

"Glad we're on the same page," she continues, a mischievous gleam in her eye. "I don't like mainlanders, but I've made an exception for you because Vivian likes you. Everyone thinks Vivian is naive, but she's a good judge of character—you end up being one when all you do is observe. Though I trust her judgment, believe me when I say I will rip you limb from limb if you ever do anything to hurt her."

"I would rather drown than cause Vivian pain."

The truth escaping my mouth feels like a sucker punch to the stomach, but its veracity rings like a reassuring pulse throughout my body. A soft four-letter word slips through my mind, but before I can analyze it, Carol makes two attempts to stand, distracting me. I cross behind the desk, but she's successful before I can help her up.

Carol quirks her lips as if to dismiss me but then rests a hand on my shoulder. "Life is full of uncertainty. You can plan and plot, but you never know what's around the corner," she says, giving me a little pinch. "That's why I start every day with a cinnamon roll. You've got to enjoy things while you can."

The moment is almost as sweet as the dozens I shared with Magda. A wave of nostalgia washes over me as my lips slip into a smile.

Carol's face softens into a small grin before she uses her cane against my shins.

"Now move out of the way. I've got to get to Dotty's and inform her that *her grandson* was the one who vandalized the lifeguard towers. Shameful behavior." Though her words are admonishing, the corners of her lips quiver as if restraining a delighted smile.

The next hour is a whirlwind of planning for the fundraiser, but I manage to break away a little after ten. Carol is right. I should have done this the second Vivian's lips fell from mine. The morning's stagnant haze has been burned off by the bright sun, but the oppressive humidity threatens to turn my shirt into a sodden mess during the short walk to Vivian's Alterations.

"Be with you in a minute." The words come out muffled, her mouth occupied by several color-tipped pins as Vivian hunches over a men's shirt when I enter her shop.

A song whispers in the background as my heart tries to beat out of my chest at the sight of her. Her hair is half up, a few springy tendrils kissing her temples. She's wearing the same green sundress she had on the day we met, when she crashed into me and everything changed. I'd initially thought the lingering pressure in my lungs that morning had been from the force of her hitting me, but now I realize it was her. Vivian's effortless beauty had captivated me even when I'd been trying to dismiss her out of habit and self-preservation.

Vivian finally glances up, two pins tumbling from her mouth and pinging on the polished cement floor. "Finn."

When she doesn't instantly smile, I self-consciously run a hand over my vest. "Good morning."

Her lips part, but Vivian doesn't speak, only tucks her bottom lip between her teeth.

A thousand questions swarm my head like hornets. Does she regret last night? Is this the end? Do I need to carve my heart out of my chest with a melon baller?

Out of habit, I set a flirty smile to my lips, straightening a pile of button boxes on her large worktable. "I assume you'll be incredibly busy with everyone's alterations, and I wanted to make my appointment first."

Coward. Just ask her out.

I ignore the unhelpful thought and stride forward, sliding my hands into my pockets and deciding to up the ante.

"I've ordered everything I need, but if you haven't noticed"—I pull my shoulders back, subtly broadening my chest—"I prefer garments to fit me perfectly."

Heat flashes in her eyes, and the relief is so overwhelmingly sweet that my knees nearly buckle. Vivian sets aside the shirt and stands, her yellow measuring tape dangling around her neck. "I'll need to take some measurements so when your clothes arrive I can adjust them accordingly."

"Of course." It takes effort to keep my voice even. I started this flirty exchange, but Vivian is in control now.

She pauses beside me for millisecond, her gaze flicking to mine before gesturing to her octagonal step riser. "Face the windows please. Stand off the riser so I can use it first."

It feels like the AC just went out, and the room floods with summer heat as I await her touch. Her fingers start at the back of my shoulders first, sliding the measuring tape from one edge to the other. The puff of breath at the nape of my neck has me pressing my eyes closed, struggling to keep composure. Every movement is slow and deliberate, her touch a tad heavier than innocent. Vivian measures my arm length next, followed by biceps and wrist circumference. Having my measurements taken isn't a new experience, but it's a challenge to keep my heart rate from ratcheting when Vivian's fingers pause at the pulse point on my wrist.

"Turn around, please." With her still on the riser, our faces perfectly align.

"Um—" She licks her lips, her confidence flickering, and gestures to her own neck. My chin lifts in understanding as her fingers close the measuring tape around my bobbing Adam's apple. I try not to flinch when her fingertips dip into the notch between my collarbones, her eyelashes fluttering slightly. The moment hovers for what feels like years until the measuring tape slides from my neck.

I lift my arms so Vivian can place the tape around my back, lowering them when she gathers the yellow band around my chest. My ribs are expanding too quickly, though. I know I should breathe normally so she can get an accurate measurement, but it feels like thunder is building in my veins. When her hands collect over my heart, I'll lose the battle I've been waging with my impulses. I won't be able to stop from sliding my fingers beneath that beautiful tangle of curls, from using my other hand to tilt her jaw up.

Her hands freeze, the measuring tape six inches away from the buttons of my shirt, almost as if Vivian knows. Those gorgeous green eyes meet mine, an uneven breath skittering between her parted lips.

"What color is your tailcoat?"

My fingers flex at my sides, poorly dissipating the debilitating tension. "Green," I grit out.

"Green?"

My body is too strained for this conversation inside a conversation. I ache to touch Vivian, but more importantly, I need her to understand that what's happening between us isn't like the other relationships I've had since my broken engagement. Those I kept superficial to focus on my professional goals and to keep myself protected. Though my heart thrashes in my ribcage, I choose this moment not only to be honest, but vulnerable.

"I assumed that was the color you'd choose for your gown, since you look gorgeous in it. Though I probably should have consulted you on the exact hue so we don't clash. It's hunter green, but..." I rub the back of my neck with a soft chuckle. "It seems I've gotten ahead of myself."

I drop my hand, focusing on Vivian's expressive eyes. "Vivian Hutchinson, would you do me the honor of accompanying me to the Wilks Beach Regency Ball?"

My sternum burns with the desire to promise more, but I don't want to do that without being certain that I'm here to stay.

I expect Vivian to give me that smile of hers, maybe tease me with a coy reply, so when she jumps and wraps her legs around my waist, I'm almost too slow to catch her. *Almost.* My palms settle under her thighs as Vivian's lips crash to mine, her fingers greedy on my jaw. It's an incendiary continuation of last night. Fire burns down my spine until the soles of my feet sting. I groan into her mouth as her fingers burrow through my hair.

A kaleidoscope flashes behind my closed eyes as her fingers twist the strands, slight pain chasing the pleasure. I barely have time to adjust to the new sensation before Vivian's lips come over the edge of my jaw, below my ear. I don't think I've ever felt so possessed in my life, so helplessly at a woman's mercy. Whatever Vivian wants from me, I'll give it to her and ask if she needs more.

Her lips return to mine, and Vivian uses her firm grip on my hair to slow the pace. She's almost teasing me now. Each time our lips separate, I can feel her smile.

"Set me down, Finn."

The gentle command is in exact opposition to everything I want, but I find myself complying anyway. My hands sliding to hold her soft waist is a small consolation. Vivian takes her time righting my hair with languid caresses. My eyelashes flutter, fighting to stay open. The only thing keeping me from closing them is how breathtaking Vivian looks like this, moving with assured confidence, taking what she wants.

"I was just curious."

An entertained puff of breath escapes me. "Were you doubting my ability to carry you, gorgeous?"

"No." Her eyes flick to mine, and a cloud passes over them before she focuses on her feet. "Maybe."

Vivian is many things: mind-bendingly beautiful, delightfully quirky, professionally proficient. But one thing she's not...or at least one thing she's not *with me*...is shy.

I use a knuckle to gently lift her chin. "I don't doubt your ability to do anything. Trust that I'm just as capable."

The way Vivian surveys me, accepting my words after a few beats, is unexpectedly intoxicating. Her small nod and ghost of a smile make my legs tremble slightly. I don't think I've ever felt for a woman the way I do about Vivian. It's simultaneously the best sensation I've ever experienced and terrifying beyond comprehension. My thoughts start to spin out of control, but then Vivian's grin deepens, drawing my attention.

"I just realized I haven't answered your question."

I smirk, slipping from the heartfelt back into flirty territory. "Don't worry, gorgeous. I got the message loud and clear."

Vivian's giggle lights up the space between us, and my heart beats double-time when she rests her fingers on my chest with a mischievous smile. "I'll go with you...on one condition."

THIRTY

Vivian

The following Saturday, I fidget as I sit behind a small table facing Seabreeze Beans's entrance. I'm somehow more nervous about this than when I spoke to strange men in bars weeks ago. I think my anxiety is twofold. I'm doing this in the epicenter of town gossip, and if I fail here, everyone will see.

To keep myself busy while I wait, I text Finn. Though we haven't seen much of each other this week because of our grueling schedules, we've texted every day. I've been slightly overwhelmed with the sheer amount of work, since every adult on Wilks Beach plans to attend the fundraiser. My end-of-day exhaustion had me skipping music trivia and not even contemplating karaoke. Finn has been just as busy, missing his boxing classes for after-closing planning meetings with his fellow librarians.

Vivian

I can't wait to see you tonight after the library closes.

Finn

I can.

A shocked sound comes out of my open mouth.

Finn

Wait, that came out wrong. I can't wait to see you, but I think after the hard week we've both had, we should have dinner at Bayside Table instead.

I chuckle at my phone. This isn't the first time Finn has attempted to get out of his condition for taking me to the fundraiser—swimming lessons.

My mind floats back to Tuesday morning after he'd asked me to attend the ball with him.

"I'll go with you...on one condition. I want to teach you to swim."

Finn hesitates, his jaw working. "I don't think so."

My hands smooth up his neck to frame his face. "I know how hard it is doing something out of your comfort zone, but I fully understand that our fears aren't the same. What happened to you was horrible, but if you want to try to let go of that fear, I'm here. We can go as slow as you need, and if you decide it's not worth it, I won't push.

But Finn..."—my thumb slides across his cheek with a featherlight touch—"I believe you can do this."

His forehead comes to mine, rocking back and forth. "I don't think I've ever trusted anyone the way I trust you." After a long moment in which my heart can't decide to soar or shatter at his sweet words, Finn leans back with a heavily drawn breath. "Okay. I'll try."

A tight tug pulls at the center of my chest at the memory.

Vivian

Remember, you're just sitting in your bathtub. I looked at the pictures on Rebecca's realty website of your rental, and the antique clawfoot tub looks barely big enough for you to fit, so there's no way you'll be submerged. And we don't have to fill it all the way. We'll start out small.

Dots hover and recede, hover and recede as I wait for Finn's response. He'll probably write something flirty and distracting like he's been doing all week.

Finn

I'm scared, gorgeous.

A squeak escapes me as the bridge of my nose congests with unexpected tears. I wonder how upset Summer would be if I stood her up so I could rush to the library to wrap Finn in a large hug. I'm half rising, my thighs hitting the edge of the round wood table when the door jangles, and Summer strides through. She beams at me from across the shop, pushing sunglasses atop her blonde bob.

"Hey, Vivian."

"Hi." I return her smile, trying to ignore the blood rushing in my ears from Finn's text. "I know it's bad timing, but I've got to make a quick call. Grab something on me, and I'll be right back."

Before Summer can answer, I break into the mid-morning sunshine and dial Finn. He doesn't answer, but that doesn't mean he's ignoring me. I've seen the way Finn gives undivided attention to whomever is in front of him. With how busy the library has been in the wake of the fundraiser announcement, he's probably speaking to a patron. Wilks Beach residents can be an opinionated bunch.

"Hey," I say softly when his voicemail message ends. "I know I can't take that feeling away from you, though I really, *really* want to. I can tell you that I'll be right there with you. It'll be just like you encouraged me when we went to Virginia Beach. Remember? Just walk down the bar? Just sit in shallow water. That's it. Afterward, I'll take you to Bayside Table, okay?" I sigh loudly. "I wish I could give you a hug, but Summer is waiting. I'm nervous about talking with her, but I'm going to push through. Let's both do something we're scared of today, and we can celebrate afterward, okay? I lo—" I cut myself off just in time. "I look forward to seeing you later."

I hang up the call as my pulse sprints. That word—the *big* one—has been hovering in the periphery of my mind every time I think of Finn. I'm not sure if I'm ready to attach that modifier to the way I feel about Finn, but I do know I want a relationship like the one my parents had. My mom would count the hours until Dad would drive home from the mainland on weekdays. My father used to surprise her with little gifts—unique stationery was Mom's favorite. Then they'd dance in the kitchen after they thought we'd gone to sleep, and Brynn and I used to sneak to the top of the stairs and watch them. A twinge of sadness twists my belly, and I take a deep breath to release it.

As I re-enter the coffee shop, something resting on the receiving counter snags my attention. A gnome floats on a flamingo raft, holding a pineapple cocktail, right beside the sign that says "Pick Up." I lift the figurine, clutching it to my chest with a gleeful squeal. Sandy relieves Brynn at the espresso machine, and my sister walks over, setting down a mug topped with whipped cream.

"I've been thinking about all the changes you've been making and thought I'd try a few of my own." The uncertainty in my sister's gaze makes my lungs ache.

"He's perfect." I reach to squeeze her hand over the counter before replacing the figurine in his place beside the chalkboard-style sign still adorned with Aunt Tammy's handwriting. "Did you name him?"

The corner of her mouth quirks. "Roasty McToasty."

I burst into laughter so loud that Summer and a few others glance over, but I can't find it in me to care. I'm done with hiding. I'm finally ready for this town to know the real me.

Brynn's returning smile feeds my soul. "Take this to Summer, will you? And apologize for the wait. I had to dig in the back to find another peppermint syrup to make her latte."

"On one condition," I start—apparently, I'm full of conditions lately.

My sister's brows tweak as she waits for me to finish.

"Let's go swimming after you get done today. It's been forever since we've had a beach day. We can relive our childhood bests—building sandcastles, body surfing, the whole nine."

Brynn crosses her arms, and my stomach sinks. I know the suggestion deviates from her schedule, but tonight's plan is already altered with me spending the evening with Finn instead of us watching movies at home.

Hope soars as my sister's lips give the slightest tug. "I'm not going unless we play mermaids."

"Oh, we're playing mermaids." I beam. "And afterward, I'll make you your favorite green chili egg casserole before I leave."

"With tots?"

Brynn and I operate under a simple philosophy: if you don't like tater tots, something is fundamentally wrong with you. That and not smiling at dogs. If a dog passes you while being walked and you don't at least crack a small grin at their happy, furry face, you shouldn't be friends with us. Speaking of friends, I should be getting back to the one I'm trying to make.

"Of course with tots."

My sister nods with a deep, steadying inhale, no doubt calming the anxiety that change brews in her bloodstream. She's so strong in so many other ways, but this has always been her Achilles heel.

A weird swell of pride ribbons through my ribs at being the one helping Brynn with this after a lifetime of her always helping me.

I reach across the counter to squeeze her fingers again. "It'll be fun. Trust me."

Brynn's returning grip is a bit too firm, but I smile reassuringly.

"Here you go." Sandy drops off my iced coffee with an unexpected treat—a plate of iced sugar cookies shaped like surfboards.

I balance all three items, carrying them to where Summer has been politely waiting. She sighs wistfully as I set down her coffee.

"Is it as magical as I imagine having unlimited access to delicious coffee and sweets every day?"

A laugh bubbles from me, unrestrained. "Absolutely."

Summer takes a large gulp of her coffee, licking whipped cream from her upper lip. "I'm so glad you called me."

My cheeks hurt from smiling. "Me too."

It's not until I'm seated across from her that I notice Summer has a smear of paint across her brow. Speckles of sky blue also dot her running tank.

"Are you working on a home project today?"

Summer has been slowly repairing her grandmother's dilapidated cottage, often with her boyfriend, Nick's, help.

"I'm repainting the bathroom." She nods before gripping her mug with both hands and leaning in. "But can we talk about your crush upgrade? Nothing against Atticus, of course, but"—Summer lets out a low whistle—"if I wasn't madly in love with Nick..."

I chuckle as her sentence drops off.

"You seem really happy," she adds, her smile softening in that maternal way of hers even though Summer is only a few years older than me. It's probably a trait she's gained from being a beloved pediatrician.

"I am." The honesty of the statement feels revolutionary, like some crucial change clicks behind my breastbone.

We chat about her work and mine, gossip about the rumors about Atticus and Amanda, and by the time Nick's phone call interrupts with Mariah Carey's "All I Want For Christmas Is You" ringtone, asking if she needs anything from the mainland, my heart is so full I feel short of breath.

And when I give Brynn a quick hug after Summer leaves and head back to my shop, Lidia Prescott arrives with a sumptuous Regency gown for me to alter. I take her measurements, easily chatting all the while. Then I crank my Raven Sacaria playlist and get to work. As I adjust the decadent bodice, a small grin lifts my lips. After all these good things happening today, I'm going to end the day with another big "first."

I just haven't told Finn yet.

THIRTY-ONE

Finn

As I walk home after work, the warm summer air feels like it's congealing in my lungs. I suck in a deep breath, reminding myself of Vivian's words—that I won't be submerged. Though I haven't been inside a bathtub since I was eight, she's right in that my larger size makes drowning impossible.

Over the years, I've tried to get over this fear. But whenever I wade to my waist, searing panic has me retreating toward my towel. Since then, I make excuses for not getting all the way in at the pool or the beach. It's surprisingly easy to avoid swimming, even when you live oceanside.

Thoughts of canceling swirled all morning. After all, Vivian said I didn't have to go through with this if I didn't want to. But when I returned to my office after lunch, three children's board books—each about learning to swim—were stacked neatly in the center of my desk. The mystical library hadn't been wrong steering me toward Regency romances, so as odd as it feels, I'm going to trust its guidance once more.

As I turn the corner of my rental into the open backyard, lingering panic abates. In its place, my heart stumbles off a balcony and falls six stories. Vivian has foregone the deck furniture and stretches out on the topmost stair, bracing her arms behind her. The most decadent expression graces her features as she tilts her chin toward the evening sun. Her lashes fan on her cheeks as a blissful smile graces her mouth. My phone is out before I think twice about it, snapping a quick picture.

Vivian must hear me approaching, because she tilts her head in my direction, a few curls tumbling over her simple purple dress as I pocket my phone. "Hey."

It requires effort to keep my pace casual and not sprint to her side when that broad smile—the one just for me—splits her face.

"Hey." My words are chalky, so I clear my throat. A dozen flirty remarks present themselves, but I end up saying the thought that won't leave me alone. "Just sit in shallow water?"

Vivian's gaze turns tender as she pats the space beside her. I set aside my shoulder bag and accept her invitation, gazing at the tranquil bay water but not feeling calm in the least.

"Do you ever sit out here and read?"

"All the time." It's no longer a surprise when I answer with the truth. Vivian is about to see the most raw and vulnerable part of me. I'd thought my love for literary antiquities was something that needed to be hidden, but nothing is as revealing as the fear Vivian is about to witness.

"Would you be interested in watching the *Worthington* series with me?"

"Sure," I tell her, unsure where this line of questioning is going. I'd assumed I'd change into a swimsuit the second I got home so we could get the aqueous torture done before we could both finally relax after a long week.

"You don't mind period dramas?"

I brace my elbows on my knees, leaning forward. "I'm honestly interested in seeing the director's interpretation, particularly of book two."

"I *love* book two," she says with an airy sigh. "I can't wait for that season to drop."

We sit in companionable silence for a few moments before Vivian asks, "And your thoughts on holding hands as we take a quiet evening stroll down the beach?"

A grin lifts my lips as I turn my head. "What's with the questions?"

"Just making sure you're as perfect as you seem," she says to the bay.

"I'm not." My tone is suddenly harder than steel.

Vivian glances at me, her features soft, the corner of her mouth tugging upward. "See, that's the best part. You don't get to decide if you're perfect for me. I do."

I find myself opening and closing my mouth, words trapped in my throat, like Vivian used to do. She squeezes my forearm, leaning her head against my shoulder. We watch an osprey dive into the water, snag a fish, and fly into the marshy distance.

After a beat, she asks, "What did She-Who-Must-Not-Be-Named do to break your heart?"

The idea of concealing the answer doesn't even register. Whatever Vivian asks, I'll answer.

"She never even liked me. The sole reason she wanted to marry me was for my father's money."

I expect Vivian to express sorrow on my behalf, maybe wrap me in a hug, especially since I alluded to an engagement. Instead, she hums.

"And ever since, you've made yourself hard to know so something like that could never happen again."

I almost chuckle. What did Carol say about Vivian being a good observer?

"Something like that," I murmur.

Vivian lets out a satiated breath, snuggling against me. "Good thing I like you for other reasons—none of them having anything to do with money."

"Is that so, gorgeous?"

She tilts her chin up with such a joyful grin my heart gives a heavy thud. "Yes. I mostly like you because you smell like books."

This time, I do laugh, leaning down to give her smiling lips the lightest brush. We gaze at each other for a long moment, the sea air stirring the tiny hairs around Vivian's face. The adoration in her gaze never wavers, and I find myself momentarily lost.

I love this woman.

I'd thought that I'd loved Katelyn, but that emotion was a joke compared to how I feel about Vivian. I want to simultaneously vanquish all her enemies and relax next to her, watching the stars wink into existence as the sky turns dark. Never in the years after leaving my family had I entertained the idea of *forever* with anyone.

But I want that now.

I want everything she asked me about earlier, a thousand times over, but I also want *more*. I want a beach wedding with everyone in this town in attendance. I want to show her my long-hidden book collection and create a personal library with her, blending our books like we'll blend our lives. And eventually, I want tiny little versions of Vivian with curly chestnut hair and sprays of freckles across their cheeks.

And I want her to have a husband who can partake in one of her favorite hobbies.

I drop my lips to hers again for a long but chaste kiss. When I raise my face, Vivian senses the change in me. She gives my forearm another squeeze before using me as a lever to rise then extending her hand.

"Ready to try this?"

"No," I answer, gripping her fingers and standing. "But for you, I will."

The threat to my male pride is making it a challenge not to do something reckless like grab Vivian's twitchy fingers and run them over my abs. Was it a bit cocky to slowly peel my shirt off before I lowered myself into the twelve inches of water in the tub? Sure, but I haven't had standing water touch my ribs in decades. I needed some advantage. Vivian's slight puff of breath at seeing me shirtless for the first time was the ego boost I needed to sit down.

"How are you doing?"

"Fine, gorgeous. How are you? You look a bit *warm*." My gaze intentionally rakes over the flush streaking down her neck into the collar of her sundress as I bite the corner of my lip.

The suave response is all an act. My pulse is entirely too fast, and my shoulders are tense from short, inefficient breaths, but I place a confident, flirtatious smile on my mouth. I'm playing the part of *fine* like my life depends on it.

Vivian moves from her position leaning against the bathroom vanity, almost distracted. It seems she's taken my muscled bait. My smile quirks higher as I pull my shoulders back, peacocking...just a little. All I need is for her to kiss me, and I'll surge out of this water, distracting her and myself from this misery. But then Vivian surprises me by combing her fingers through my hair and setting a gentle kiss on my forehead.

"I'm so proud of you."

My lashes flutter closed as my entire body riots. I've already been struggling to keep it together, but with one sentence, Vivian has decimated what's left of my defenses.

I don't think anyone has ever told me that. Not my father. Not teachers. Not even Magda.

No one.

I don't respond. I can't. All I can do is swallow over the boulder that somehow got in my throat.

"You know," she starts, her quiet words giving me something to focus on. "I've never been on a date."

This information has me opening my eyes and looking up.

Her small grin isn't shy. It's almost...peaceful? "I was kind of hoping you'd be my first first date tonight."

I want to be your LAST first everything. Your last first kiss. Your last first date.

"I would be honored."

Vivian does that bouncy thing, and I feel my chest relax for the first time since I lowered myself into the water.

"Okay, but five more minutes first." She kneels beside the tub, extending her hand with her thumb up. "In the meantime, we thumb war."

I chuckle. And the astonishment running through me is nothing short of a miracle. I, Finn Reynolds, who has avoided swimming for years, am sitting up to my chest in a tub of water, *laughing*. All because of Vivian. My love for her doubles in that instant, and it's work to keep the words off my tongue. Since it's far too early for declarations, I fall back on a tried-and-true standard—flirting.

"I don't know, gorgeous. I have an unfair advantage being that my hands are a lot bigger than yours." The suggestive tone has the effect I'd hoped for, staining Vivian's cheeks crimson as she wrinkles her nose.

"Less talking, more warring."

Another laugh escapes me. "Alright."

After five minutes, my legs are jelly as I stand. I try not to let Vivian see the slight tremble, flexing unnecessarily as I reach for a nearby towel—because lifting a one-pound towel really requires full biceps contraction. Vivian's gaze snags on my arms before slipping to my abs as I dry my torso and then tuck the towel around my waist. I can't help but smirk at her blatant appreciation.

"What should I wear tonight?"

There's a second delay before her focus returns to my face, getting stalled on my chest as I take an intentionally large breath.

"Um...something casual?"

Vivian heads downstairs while I get changed. As I pull a polo over my head, an insidious thought worms its way into my brain. There's no way I can continue a relationship with Vivian if I fail professionally. If this all goes horribly wrong and I have to return to work for my father, I'll have to leave Wilks Beach. The smart thing would be to keep my distance, to stay emotionally withdrawn.

But then I recall the exact phrasing of my father's contract.

The Signatory agrees to attain the highest position in their chosen field by their thirtieth birthday. Failure to do so shall require the Signatory to return to employment under their father's direction, under terms and conditions to be determined at that time.

My twenty-ninth birthday was a week before I met Vivian. I'd spent it celebrating with Alec, though it'd felt like a noose had been tightening around my neck.

A rough breath shakes free of my lungs. A year. Even if I fail, I have a year to love the most unexpectedly enchanting, irresistible, and astonishing woman I've ever met. And if I am successful and Cordelia's future is secure, I'll stay here. Either way, I'll come clean to Vivian about my identity once the directorship position is finalized. Until then, I'm not going to waste a second of time in her presence.

I quickly don shorts and shoes, thundering down the stairs to start what will hopefully be Vivian's *last* first date.

THIRTY-TWO

Vivian

"**I**'m doing this all wrong," Finn grumbles. "I should be picking you up at your door with an obscenely large bouquet of flowers and then driving you to the finest restaurant on the mainland."

The way Finn pouts like a despondent puppy is the *cutest* thing. And my heart can't help but do a happy little skip at his casual use of "the mainland" when referring to the city where he used to reside. Maybe Finn is a step closer to considering this small stretch of beach home?

"I don't want any of that. I want this," I say, squeezing our interlaced fingers as we walk to Bayside Table.

"You could have at least let me get you flowers," he mutters under his breath.

I pull us across Sand Bend Road into Judith Abernathy's front yard. Blue hydrangea bushes form a hedge around her white siding exterior.

"Just pinch one of those."

His mouth drops open, but there's a teasing flash in his gaze. "Vivian Hutchinson, town sweetheart, are you encouraging me to steal from one of your neighbors?"

"If it'll keep you from whining on my first first date." I place my free hand on my hip, firming my lips in a mock stern expression.

Finn instantly softens, using his other hand to tuck a curl behind my ear. "Sorry, gorgeous. No more complaining from me." He brushes a quick kiss over my cheek before hovering his lips over my ear. "But next time, your flowers will be nothing short of opulent."

I lean back with a teasing smirk. "I'd expect nothing less from someone as dramatic as you."

Finn laughs, and I want to bottle that carefree sound and wear it in a locket around my neck.

"Come on." I tug him toward the restaurant.

At Finn's hesitation as I bypass the restaurant's main door in favor of the expansive outdoor space, I send him a challenging glance. He rubs the back of his neck with an audible sigh, pulling a laugh from my belly. Before we can even make it around the corner to the green space, Finn's hand is on my jaw, tilting my lips up to his. The kiss is inexplicably hot and sweet at the same time. A delectable sense of satiation corkscrews down my spine.

"I love when you do that," he murmurs against my lips.

"What?" My answer is little more than a puff of breath.

"Laugh. Smile." He tilts back so I can see the curve of his mouth. "Exist."

My entire body feels awash with starlight, and for the first time in a long time in Finn's presence, I'm speechless. Something changes in his expression as my parted lips shudder on a halting exhale. His strong features become sharper, more reverent.

"Vivi—"

"Hey! Are you two here for the dance lessons?" Patricia and Gary step behind us on the path around to the patio space.

We separate a polite distance, but my chest soars when Finn doesn't release our intertwined fingers.

"Dance lessons?" My brow wrinkles as I glance at Finn.

"Sorry. I forgot to mention it." He winces slightly. "Letitia coordinated with Margot to give waltz lessons tonight since she'd been unable to host on Wednesday."

Finn probably forgot because he'd been distracted by his terrifying fear of being immersed in water. It'd been profound to watch such a confident, capable man lay his vulnerability bare. I'd been flitting around the bathroom, filling the tub, making jokes to lighten the mood. The split second when Finn met my gaze, the panic plain in his eyes, before he stepped in the tub anyway, a concentric pulse thrummed through my body. I was proud of him for taking that risk, for being brave enough to do so with an audience. In the moment after, when Finn lowered himself with a held breath, all the while trying to distract me with his sculpted torso, I realized the emotion I hadn't been sure about already thrived in every cell of my body.

Patricia pats Finn's arm. "We've all been working like dogs this week. Time for a little revelry!"

"To be sure!" I beam, leaning into Finn's arm.

His eyes catch mine, enjoying our shared joke over my fondness for Regency words and phrases.

The four of us turn the corner as an eight-piece 80s rock band, complete with neon clothes and big hair, begin their set. The keytar player is completely in her groove during the opening bars to Europe's "The Final Countdown."

"How are we going to waltz to a rock band?" I ask through a laugh. "Not that they aren't incredible."

I've only heard the immensely popular 80s group *The Deloreans Band* playing from my apartment window, since Brynn and I don't venture out on Saturdays. One of the vocalists begins the lyrics as Patricia leans in to answer.

"We're going to learn the basic steps with Margot in the grassy area, and then the band is supposed to play "Open Arms," "Take it to the Limit," and "Electric Heartbeat." Those all should have a waltz feel to them so we can practice. Next week, we'll have a more formal lesson at the library."

I grin at the last song title. It's one of my Raven Sacaria favorites. Just as the band is really getting into their song, the audio cuts out.

They continue a few beats acoustically before the bassist yells out to the crowd. "Give us a second, and we'll be right back!"

Several hoots and hollers arise in response. *The Deloreans Band* usually pulls more mainlanders to our island than the regular Saturday night bands.

Geneva strides by in her signature black heels and snug black dress. She gives Finn a tight nod, but the corner of her mouth quirks when she catches my gaze.

"I'm surprised to see Geneva here," Finn says after she's passed us by.

"Why? She's here almost every Saturday night." Not that I know this information firsthand, but it's well known throughout town. "I've heard she enjoys shooting down the mainlanders who try to hit on her."

As if on cue, an unfamiliar man sidles up to the bar where Geneva is speaking to Cynthia. The mustached man says a greeting over her ear, setting his hand on Geneva's back. Except, his hand is so low he's essentially cupping her backside. Finn drops my hand as he surges forward, but before he can intervene, the man is met with a whip-quick elbow to the solar plexus. Geneva doesn't even take her attention away from the tattooed bartender during the movement. She just keeps chatting with Cynthia like nothing happened.

"Hey!" one of the man's friends shouts as he rushes to aid his doubled-over friend. "That was uncalled for."

The crowd turns from watching the band resetting the audio to the scene at the bar.

"What was?" Geneva blinks at the second man with doe-eyed innocence, her voice artificially airy. "Me flinching when he touched me? There's no way I could have hurt him with a little twitch."

He glares. "That was way more than a twitch."

"Looked like a flinch to me," Cynthia says, setting two orange crush cocktails in front of the couple to Geneva's left.

The man looks around, but no one—absolutely no one—offers him backup. Since his friend is still wheezing, he human-crutch-walks him to a picnic table by the water. Barely restrained chuckles echo in the bar area before the strum of an electric guitar diverts everyone's attention back to the stage.

Finn continues to frown. "I hate when men do that—take advantage just because they can."

"It's disgusting," I agree, my stomach churning as Geneva lets out a slow deliberate breath.

I want to go over and talk to Geneva, preferably wrap her in a hug, but I'm pretty sure she wouldn't want to be approached. If she'd been giving don't-talk-to-me vibes before, she's giving poison-barbed-angry-wolverine vibes now.

"Fortunately, Geneva is a force to be reckoned with."

"Yeah, but..." I tilt my head. "As much as she projects that *Live, Laugh, Toaster Bath* exterior, I think she's really all marshmallowy gooeyness inside."

I don't share the observation I made on my way to Finn's house earlier. Geneva had been working out in her gym alone. One of the garage doors had been half open, *Paramore* pouring out into the air.

She'd been *absolutely destroying* a punching bag with not only hits but a series of barefooted kicks. But then there'd been this moment I wasn't supposed to see. Geneva placed one glove on the bag, bracing herself as her head hung low. I'd thought she was just resting, but then she used her other forearm to wipe away tears.

Of course, she could have been wiping sweat out of her eyes.

Either way, I made a decision at that moment. Geneva is officially added to part four of the plan: make new friends. Things went great with Summer this morning, but somehow, I know I'll need to tread lightly in befriending Geneva. When she'd arrived, out of the blue, five years ago, it'd taken Noah over a year to finally convince her that he was nothing like their estranged father. Luckily, I'm three thousand times more lovable than that cheating dirtbag.

Finn chuckles at my description of Geneva before offering his elbow like a proper gentleman. "Shall we, my lady?"

"Yes, let's." I wrap my fingers around his strong arm, and he escorts me toward the people awaiting dance lessons.

We're exactly three steps into Margot's instruction when I snort. "You already know how to waltz."

"It was expected." Finn keeps his gaze over my shoulder, his expression too stony for the relaxed atmosphere.

I'm carefully considering my next question when Karen's ring-laden hand slaps me in the ribs after Todd sent her out in a sloppy spin. The two are in rare form tonight, overly affectionate as they waltz along. Usually when they're out in public, they're fighting.

"Sorry," Finn murmurs, pushing me closer to him with one broad hand between my shoulder blades and effortlessly steering us away.

"Why are you apologizing?"

"I should have kept you out of the reach of those menaces. I don't know how everyone puts up with them."

"They're locals." I shrug.

Finn makes a disapproving sound in his throat, turning me again until we're even farther away, almost to the edge of the property. The proximity to the darkening bay makes a muscle in Finn's jaw twitch.

"Have I told you part three of my self-improvement plan?" I ask him, hoping to distract him.

Finn finally looks at me with a whisper of a smile. "You've been surprisingly closed off about that, which is strange because you usually spill your secrets with little prompting." His lips brush my ear. "I believe all that is required is rosé."

I'm ill-equipped to be in this man's arms when he's flirting with me. This is my first first date, but I'm ready for it to be over before we even order food in favor of kissing his lips for the rest of the night. Who needs sustenance when you've got a flirty librarian to kiss, am I right?

"At this point, you just need to waft this scent under my nose, and that'll be just as effective." I nuzzle Finn's throat, taking a noisy inhale.

Finn laughs, his chest rising and falling against me. Suddenly, it occurs to me how strange this situation is. *This is* my first first date.

I should be a ball of nerves, barely able to function, but being in Finn's arms is as natural to me as the breaststroke.

The way he effortlessly leads me through the grass in perfect sync with the music has me even more excited for the ball than I already was. Since I'll be living out my Regency dreams, that level was astronomically high to begin with. I smile, imagining the way the skirts of my dress will swish with each practiced turn. My gown is already patterned in muslin—just to be absolutely certain I love it before I start construction. With all the alterations I'm doing for the town, I won't have time to start over.

"So what's part three?" Finn's question pulls me from thinking about embellishment details.

I lean back to catch his gaze, steadying myself as I tell someone my last secret. This is something I have wanted for longer than my foolhardy crush on Atticus, longer than I wanted an independent store of my own, longer than I envisioned selling my work to anyone other than fellow townspeople. I'd honestly never thought I'd have the opportunity, but then the singer-songwriter I love so much decided to come out of retirement for a six-month residency in Vegas.

"I want to see Raven Sacaria perform. Her residency starts in July, and I'm hoping to convince Brynn to come to Vegas with me. Neither of us have ever vacationed outside of Wilks Beach with the exception of the YMCA camp Aunt Tammy sent us to in Virginia Beach as kids."

Almost instantly, I feel guilty for complaining. Lots of families don't go on lavish vacations, only to visit family. It's just that all my family lived in the same apartment as me.

"To be fair, we live in a prime vacation destination, so there's no reason to leave—"

Finn gently kisses me. "You should be able to do whatever you want, Vivian. If you want to travel, travel."

My grin triples in size, causing Finn's to grow, the corners creasing in near-perfect parentheses.

"I'm looking forward to flying for the first time. When Raven's show was announced eight months ago, I started saving. I've got enough for bargain airline tickets, and with all the extra work from the fundraiser, I should be able to book a room off-strip instead of the budget motel I'd been planning on," I say, nearly breathless with excitement.

His smile fades as a flicker of something dark slips across his brow. Before I can ask, Finn tucks it away.

"I'm sure you and Brynn will have a great time."

I take my hand off Finn's impressive deltoid to tuck a curl behind my ear with a nervous laugh. "I have to tell her first." I hesitate a moment, not wanting to betray my sister but also needing to be honest with the man I've fallen in love with. "Brynn doesn't like change."

His expression softens. "I'm sure she'd make an exception for you."

"She usually does," I tell him, the corner of my mouth quirking.

Finn's relaxed grin lifts his lips as he expertly guides me through the dance. Since I didn't know waltzing would be part of tonight, I abandoned my sandals at the start of the lesson. The cool grass is soothing on my bare feet, and the outdoor string lights behind Finn's head give him an ethereal quality. A fizzy sensation tickles down my chest. Now would be just as good a time as any to tell him I love him, but it's also *our first date*. I have zero experience, but I'm pretty sure that's frowned upon.

Instead, I say, "This is the best date I've ever been on."

Finn leans me closer until my cheek is nearly resting on his chest, whispering something in my hair.

I can't quite make out the words over Raven's soulful voice belting the heartfelt lyrics of "Electric Heartbeat," but it sounded a lot like, "Last first date."

THIRTY-THREE

Finn

The last two weeks have been a complete whirlwind while simultaneously the best fourteen days of my entire life. The extra planning meetings and coordinating with vendors didn't even feel cumbersome because firstly, I'm used to hard work, and secondly, the entire town kept pitching in.

The Wilks Beach Garden Society insisted on making all the floral arrangements for the event, refusing to take payment. Similarly, Jeremy, the single dad who bakes all the goodies for Seabreeze Beans assembled a team of grandmothers to help him create delectable mini cakes and tarts for guests. Maxwell insisted that his cousin, who moonlights as a DJ, also help because "No one wants to listen to chamber music for two hours straight, even if they play Ariana Grande's 'Thank You, Next.'"

I've seen Cordelia's mother organize fundraisers for various charities, but her involvement had been signing a check and overseeing the planner who was doing all the real work. This event will not be as lavish as any of those fundraisers, but I think the floral-outline dance cards that Trudy had the storytime children color are far more meaningful than lush cardstock from a professional printer.

Though the planning for the fundraiser has been largely smooth-going, the best part of the past fortnight—as a Regency fellow would say—was time spent with Vivian. The day after our date, I sent an obscenely large bouquet to her shop. Since Vivian's Alterations was open Sunday afternoon for appointments, half of the town gawked at the opulence. Then I scoured the internet for original Raven Sacaria vinyls and surprised Vivian with a turntable for her shop.

My heart had nearly stopped when she'd gripped me by the shoulders and leveled me with a resolved stare.

"These gifts are wonderful, and I'm grateful for them, but being with you is what matters to me. I'd rather have a purloined hydrangea bloom and the memory of us laughing like hyenas as we flee the scene, or snuggle with you on the couch as we listen to Raven's musical genius out of my phone's tinny speaker than something flashy."

I'd never seen an example of true love in real life, only read about it. It hadn't occurred to me until Vivian said something that expressing love is more than the stuff of fiction—large purchases and showy proclamations. At its center, it's the tender, everyday moments shared between two souls.

That simple conversation shifted my perspective.

After that, I made sure we knocked everything off Vivian's question list, from long beach walks to reading on my deck. We even binged the first season of *Worthington* in preparation for tonight. I'd also brought her to the library after hours to view the town's archives. Since Vivian didn't think my near panic attack the second time we attempted swimming lessons by wading into the bay water was off-putting, I hoped she wouldn't mind my fascination with rare books.

At Vivian's complete and utter acceptance of who I am, I realized there is only one course of action left.

My pulse thrums against the fabric wrapped around my neck as I walk the short distance to Vivian's apartment. Fortunately, tonight is unseasonably cool, since we're all dressed from chin to toe in layers. To distract myself from my rambunctious nerves, I revel in the memory of Vivian's reaction to my final fitting in her shop. My smirk deepens, remembering how she'd drawn her heavy curtains and then kissed me to within an inch of my life. Hopefully, there'll be a continuation of that tonight, but only after I tell her who I really am.

I can't wait a day more.

The plan had been to reveal everything after I knew about my promotion to library director, but I love Vivian too much. She should know all the variables that go along with being with me.

If she finds out my true identity and decides not to continue our relationship, I'll understand.

I'll be decimated, but I won't blame her.

My phone rings in my pocket, and I answer it without looking at the contact, assuming it's another last-minute emergency call from one of my staff.

"*Finn.*" My name is slurred, and loud bar music echoes in the background. "I need some help tonight. There's this leggy redhead that won't give me the time of day, but if you were—"

"I told you I have a work event tonight." I also told Alec that was the reason I couldn't go out these last two weeks. I'd mentioned that tonight was important for my career advancement, though without any of the behind-the-scenes details.

"All you ever do is work." He sounds like a petulant child.

I rub the bridge of my nose. "That's what adults do, Alec."

"I liked you more when you were fun."

Yeah, well, I didn't like me.

The thought resonates like a bomb blast, my ears ringing in the aftermath. I'd been living an inauthentic life when I'd been working in Virginia Beach. Professionally, I was making strides in the field I'd chosen, but every other facet of my life had been incomplete. I'd assumed that was due to my father's contract stipulations and that I'd needed to conceal so much, but really, I was choosing not to be me. Living in Wilks Beach, being encouraged by Vivian to open up, showed me how small my life had been until now.

For the first time, I feel like I don't have to hide. I honestly believe that when I tell Vivian all my secrets, everything will be okay. And even if it isn't, at least I won't be living a lie.

The weight falling from my shoulders brings a relieved inhale into my lungs.

"I can't do this anymore. I thought I was being a friend, but..."

It isn't until this moment that I realize living in this tiny town has taught me more about friendship than anything from my upbringing or the professional networking I'd done since. Sorrow drops in my chest that I'm nearly thirty and finally learning what having true friendship means.

"I've only been enabling you, and I can't do that anymore. You need help." A thought occurs to me. "I've met a man here who got sober. I'll ask him about some resources to send you, but I can't be your wingman anymore."

The tirade I receive in response is so loud and venomous I pull the phone away from my ear. I'd expected bargaining, more whining, not a fury of expletives coming through the line.

"You can forget you ever knew me. I'm blocking your number," Alex finishes before the line goes dead.

I close my eyes with a steadying breath, making a mental note to talk to Noah and send resources to Alec's email later. I don't want anything bad to happen to my former roommate, but I finally understand that I deserve healthy relationships in my life.

When Brynn answers the apartment door in running shorts and a faded high school track shirt, my eyebrows raise. "You're not coming?"

"Someone has to take pictures." She raises her phone.

Before I can argue that she could easily do both, Vivian appears at the top of the stairs. To say my soul leaves my body is a grave understatement. All the lyrical lines in all the novels of the world could never compare to how breathtaking Vivian is in this moment. Her Regency gown matches the exact shade of my tailcoat, but a subtle sheen makes the fabric almost liquid as she descends the stairs. The dress's bodice is adorned with delicate beadwork that must have taken Vivian hours, and the lace cap sleeves ending in elbow gloves make my fingers itch to touch them. Costume jewelry adorns her freckled collarbones as well as accents her elaborate updo.

"I— You—" I chuckle and palm the back of my head. "I was going to compliment you with Regency words, but I can't think of a single one."

Vivian arrives beside us, her smile just this side of wicked. "For someone who loves books, that's quite a compliment in itself."

I almost swallow my tongue. There is *nothing* sexier than a confident Vivian. When my feet move forward unconsciously, Brynn clears her throat.

"Why don't you both stand on the stairs for pictures?"

The tension in my body loosens as Vivian goofily insists we do classic prom photos after her sister takes a few nice ones. By the time we're done, everyone is cracking up. I help Vivian step out of the door before Brynn catches my arm. Vivian gives her sister a small grin, lifting her skirts and walking away to give us some privacy.

"I wanted to apologize for how we got on in the beginning. I can see now that I was wrong about you."

Years of practice at schooling my facial expression comes to my advantage as I nod instead of displaying my shock. Hadn't Noah said that Brynn never apologizes?

"Thank you."

She slides her shoulders back with a nod of her own. "Have fun tonight."

When we arrive, the library is like I've never seen it, and I'd left it largely decorated only an hour ago to get dressed. With all the finishing touches, like the battery-operated candles atop nearly every surface, the high school chamber orchestra setting up as the DJ plays classical covers of popular songs, and the rest of the town in Regency finery, it's a perfect culmination of weeks of diligent work.

"This is incredible," Vivian breathes as we enter the central area after picking up her dance card.

"Thank you. I want to give the other librarians congratulations. Do you mind?"

"Not at all." She wraps her gloved fingers around my arm, encouraging me to lead the way.

"Vivian, hi!" We're waylaid by Cade, the town masseuse, and her boyfriend, William, who's a doctor I think? I've actually never seen him in person before. "I wanted to say thank you again for the custom dress." Cade pulls out the skirts of her bubble-gum pink dress that matches the color of her bob hairstyle.

"I thought you didn't have time for custom dresses?" I ask.

"It's not technically custom. I just dyed it for her." Vivian grins. "It looks great, especially with the purple accents."

"Thank you." Cade fluffs the oversized purple ostrich feathers in her hair and tugs at her purple wrist gloves.

I offer my hand to William, formally introducing myself while Cade stage-whispers with an eyebrow bounce, "Carpe diem? More like carpe date-him."

It takes us a few moments to make the rounds, finally thanking and chatting with my staff at the refreshment table loaded with tiny, personal-sized treats and plastic wine glasses filled with lemonade. Once the orchestra completes its final tuning, the DJ cuts the music. I set down my glass and extend my palm to Vivian with a slight bow.

"I believe I have this dance."

I wanted to write my name in all the slots on her dance card but knew that Regency romance-loving Vivian would understand the significance of claiming her first waltz.

Vivian accepts my hand with a teasing grin. "So you do. I trust you will prove a most accomplished partner."

I lean close, dropping the formal speech as my lips brush the shell of her ear. "You have no idea, gorgeous."

Pleased with the scarlet staining her cheeks, I lead Vivian to the dance floor as many of the couples we've seen at Margot's lessons join us. As the lilting music surrounds us and we gracefully glide into the first steps of the dance, I'm confident that the rest of the night will go just as smoothly.

THIRTY-FOUR

Vivian

I should be used to the blissful sensation of dancing in Finn's arms since we practiced with the rest of the town and then on our own under the stars on his deck. Of course, that last session ended up being more kissing than dancing, but...something feels different tonight.

Revelatory.

It takes me two turns of the floor before I realize that I can't hold my feelings in anymore. I've had so many near misses these past two weeks, but with Finn smirking at me as we glide around the room, his black hair loose and playful over his forehead, I can't *not tell him* I love him.

"I want to tell you something," I begin.

His flirty expression falls, sincerity replacing it. "I do too."

The tight line of his lips makes my heart smack the underside of my chin, but I swallow to force it down and continue. "I, um...I've really enjoyed our time together. This has been the best month of my—"

Finn's smooth steps falter, nearly stomping on my dress. "Are you ending us?"

"What?" An unhinged cackle flies from my mouth. "No. That would make me an absolute dunderhead."

"A dunderhead, huh?" When Finn smiles at me with that twinkle in his eyes, my words get stuck in my throat.

"Well, yes...because I, uh..."

Though I've run through this scenario in my head each night before I fall asleep, I can't seem to organize my thoughts now. Not when all my bookish dreams are coming true and the man I love is effortlessly guiding me around the dance floor surrounded by my favorite locals. The only thing that would make this night more perfect is if Brynn decided to attend.

Since my sister would rather wear sweats than formal anything, I'd known she wouldn't be interested in the ball. The only reason we'd gone to our senior prom was because we'd both had dates, and Aunt Tammy insisted it was a life milestone we'd regret if we skipped it.

Also...I kinda dropped a pretty big bomb on her earlier, and Brynn needs time—and miles under her feet—to process everything. When I'd told her about the Oceanside Artisan Fair, she'd been floored. My sister had given me a hug so tight I almost had to tap out. And when Brynn told me how proud she was, I happily spilled about everything else: the consignment deal with the dress shop on the mainland, my plans to give her a weekend off with a spa day, and my goal to take us both to Vegas.

I should have been paying attention as I gushed about my plans, then I would have noticed how Brynn had gone silent, how her foot began fidgeting. That much change at once probably made my sister feel like her skin was peeling off. I'm honestly surprised she waited until after Finn picked me up to start pounding the pavement. Once Brynn can wrap her head around everything, I know she'll be one hundred percent on board.

"May I go first?" Finn's gentle question brings me back to the room.

Since Finn has always waited for me when I've struggled to speak and is gazing at me like I'm the only person in this room, I nod.

"I want you to know that I've never been honest with anyone the way I am with you. Not even with my sister."

Finn had shared a few more stories from when they'd been kids, including a hilarious recounting of a stubborn seven-year-old Cordelia refusing to go to school unless her big brother put her hair in a ponytail. Every day for three months, she demanded he style her hair. During the memory, Finn had mentioned that he hadn't gone to boarding school like his older brother but stayed at the local academy to be close to Cordelia, knowing he'd leave her soon enough for college.

Finn takes a deep breath. "By the time she was born, I'd already internalized my father's insistence that something was wrong with me. I'd known that survival meant keeping my innermost thoughts hidden. But with you"—his gloved thumb traces my cheek—"everything is different. It doesn't make sense, but you seem to like the unpolished parts of me best."

My fingers tighten around Finn's arm. I will explode—just become a puffball of shredded lace and beading—if I don't tell this incredible man how valued he is, how wonderful he is, and how much my heart belongs to him.

"Finn—"

"I never want to interrupt you, gorgeous, but let me finish this."

I press my lips together, nodding.

"I'm not who you think I am." A shudder racks his body as if he expected the air to liquify at the release of those words.

"Let me guess. You're Batman?"

The joke lands just as I had hoped, pulling a genuine smile across Finn's delectable beard scruff and an unexpected chuckle from his lips.

Then all the joy dies as he releases a slow exhale. "Kind of."

Kind of?

"I'm the son of Patrick Otto, of Otto Hotels." Finn pauses, surveying my confused brow for a beat before he continues.

"My father is a shrewd businessman, exceedingly wealthy, and ruthlessly callous—in both work and his personal life. In college, I had a girlfriend who I thought loved me for who I was and not for the billions tied to my name, so I asked her to marry me. But the whole thing was a farce. My father had put her in my path...after she signed a contract." A humorless puff of air leaves his mouth as his lips twist into a sneer. "That's my father's favorite thing—contracts. He loves those more than his children, his wives, probably more than his money..."

Finn takes a steadying breath, and my mind threatens to overheat, processing this information.

"The terms were simple. Marry me, bear one child, leave before said child turns five, and she walks away with one hundred million." Finn shakes his head in disgust. "The saddest thing is, he could have easily parted with a billion and not even blinked. After discovering my father's deceit, we had a falling out. I was done with all of it. Call it a quarter-life crisis, but I'd figured out that money didn't solve anything. In my family's case, it ruined everything good. Before I could leave, my dad made me sign a contract, forcing me to change my name, threatening to sue me if I disclosed anything about my true identity, and unknowingly bound me to my sister's future."

My eyebrows hurt from being pinched together. None of this makes any sense. It sounds like the plot to a Wellington novel, not real life.

"In order for my sister to keep her trust, I either need to become the library director or return to work for my father."

My mouth opens and closes, doing that ridiculous goldfish thing I thought I'd outgrown.

Finn glances over my shoulder before fixing me with a pleading stare. "I wanted you to know now. Assuming I get this promotion at the end of summer, everything will stay as it is. But if I don't, I'll only have a year with you before I have to leave to work for him."

"But you're a librarian, not a billionaire." These are the only words my frazzled brain can put together.

A sad smile graces his lips. "Yes. This career and this life is what I traded my billions for, and there's not a day I regret it, but I need you to understand that as much as I love you, I promised to ensure Cordelia's future first."

My chest tightens. "You love me?"

"More than I ever thought possible."

The honesty in Finn's amber eyes is unmistakable. For all the times I've encouraged him to tell me the truth, he's offering this freely. It's a breathtaking thing, seeing this man open his tender heart up to me. I blink, stunned to the marrow but just as determined to prove to Finn that I feel the same. My fingers curl around his wrist, breaking the dance and dragging him into the stacks.

"Then I'll go with you."

"I don't understand." His large body blocks everyone from view, the bafflement between his brows achingly sweet.

How could he not understand that I'd follow him anywhere?

"When— If you have to work for your father, I'll go with you. I'll move wherever you need to be."

"*Vivian.*" My name sounds like a prayer and the first breath of air in an infant's lungs and the sound of rain saturating an arid desert all at the same time.

"I can't ask you to do that. You'd be leaving your town, your sister, your business." Though his words hold undeniable truths, his fingers curl around my waist, almost like he can't let go.

I brush a lock of his hair aside before setting my palm against his cheek. "I'm choosing you, Finn, because I love you too. I love you for exactly who you are in here." My hand moves to rest over his heart. Even through all the layers of fabric, I can feel its solid beat. "Nothing else."

Finn's fingertips tremble as they rise to frame my face. "I never thought this would be possible for me."

Tears spring to my eyes. "I know. But if you'll let me, I'll spend the rest of my life showing you how much you deserve it."

When Finn's lips crash over mine, the overhead lights flicker and burn out. Only the overlay of white twinkle lights—interlaced with silk flowers—remains over the dance floor. The approving murmur of the crowd fades to silence when Finn deepens the kiss. I am two seconds from pushing us farther into the recesses of the library for some real privacy when a throat clears behind Finn.

"Sorry to interrupt, but I need to speak to you." A bespeckled woman with what looks like a dead badger around her shoulders focuses on Finn. "It's urgent."

"Lynnette." Finn straightens his cuffs, sliding into his magnetic persona. "Good to see you. Let me introduce you to my—"

"Girlfriend," I supply, offering my hand to the older woman. "I'm Vivian. Nice to meet you."

After receiving a limp handshake, I glance back at Finn. The heat in his gaze could melt the polar ice caps in two seconds flat. An unsteady breath slips into my lungs as my neck flushes. I'm still not used to the immensity of Finn's intense focus. It's intoxicating and disorienting at the same time. Finn's gaze slips down the column of my throat, the corner of his lip tucking between his teeth.

"I have information." She leans toward Finn, snagging his attention before bouncing her eyes pointedly at me. "About Ralph."

It's subtle, but I notice the way Finn's shoulders raise a fraction of an inch, how his spine firms. Whatever news Lynnette has about this Ralph person, it's obviously very important.

I move to excuse myself. "I should—"

Finn's palm against my waist stops me. "Stay," he whispers over my ear. "Please."

His second word is almost tortured, making my fingers twitchy. I want to run them over his temples and through his hair until his lashes flutter closed, relaxed. Only when I give a small nod does Finn return his attention to Lynnette.

"You can tell us both."

She shoots me a dubious look before speaking. "You were going to find out on Monday, but I figured since you've been striving toward this goal for so long, you'd like to know now. That and I'm a fan of Regency romance, so I already had tickets to this event." Lynnette straightens the collar to her dowager dress. "Ralph, it seems, has changed his mind about retirement. I overheard a call with the mayor that he's decided to stay on for another two years. I still think you'd make a great replacement, but it seems you'll have to wait a bit longer."

Finn's hand tenses over the small of my back, and I lean into him to quietly offer support. With what he's just told me, this news decimates the plans he's been working toward for years.

His lips tip into that practiced smile. "I appreciate your vote of confidence. And for letting me know. It—" The exhausted exhale leaving his mouth makes my forearms tense. "It certainly changes things."

Lynnette offers a tight nod before stepping away.

Finn waits until she's out of sight before pinching the bridge of his nose. "I should have seen this coming."

"Seen what coming?"

He strides to the end of the stack, collapsing into a wingback chair and bracing his forehead with his palm. "I have no doubt that my father paid Ralph off to stay on longer."

I hesitate a beat, processing this, before ripping off my gloves. I need to touch him, proper period attire be darned. One hand slides through Finn's hair as I use the knuckles of my other to lift his chin. "It doesn't matter, remember?"

"It does. That world is toxic, Vivian. It'll destroy us. I was so confident that I'd win this, but I should have known better. I should have kept my distance. I should have been stronger in resisting that insatiable tug whenever I saw you." Finn's pained expression steals my next inhale. "I'm sorry. I know what you said earlier, but that was when—"

"You're forgetting a few key things," I interrupt. "How incorrigibly stubborn I am. How strong you believe me to be."

"You are." His focus darts all over my face. "You're incredible."

A soft grin lifts my lips as I lean down until our noses brush. "And how much I love you. That conniving blackguard is powerless against us."

I don't give Finn a chance to argue. My lips take his in a bruising kiss. Finn pulls me onto his lap, returning the kiss with a desperation that sends waves of goosebumps down my legs. The world drops away until this whirring sound drowns out everything else. I ignore the noise, knowing that the only thing that matters is the two of us together. The island's magic might make it seem like there's an electrical shortage or stormless thunderclap when, really, it's the perfect synchronicity of two souls finding each other.

I've just decided to spend the rest of the evening right here, on Finn's lap, when Maxwell runs up to us. "You gotta see this."

Our eyes catch as we break the kiss, unwavering for a second before reality comes crashing in. The music has ceased, half the guests have already fled the dance floor, and the rest are rushing toward the exit. Overhead, the building shakes. It feels like the stained-glass ceiling is seconds from caving in. What I thought was an auditory hallucination or a trick of the island's magic is actually the unmistakable roar of a helicopter.

And it sounds as if it's trying to land right outside the library.

THIRTY-FIVE

Finn

By the time Vivian and I push through the throng of genteel-dressed attendees outside the library, the helicopter blades have come to a complete stop, and my sister's executive protection agent, Jax, is helping Cordelia down from the cabin. A helicopter shouldn't fit in the small cross section between the business road leading to the library parking lot and Sand Bend Road, but there sits a sleek black Sikorsky with my father's insignia on the tail.

Cordelia smiles brightly at the crowd, familiar with awaiting paparazzi flashbulbs wherever she goes. Only a few teenagers film the ordeal. Every other local seems baffled as to what's going on.

"Dearest Finnegan!" My sister catches sight of us and strides over, the golden skirts of her elaborate Regency gown swishing behind her.

"What are you doing here?" I squint at the metal behemoth, double-checking I'm not hallucinating.

We've always been allowed to schedule flights at will, but every itinerary is shared with our father. There's no way he'd permit Cordelia to fly to the city where I've been living if we're not even supposed to be talking on the phone. Adrenaline surges through my veins, thinking about how he'll retaliate against my sister's blatant defiance and how I might be helpless to stop him.

"I wasn't going to miss this soirée. Not when it benefits such a good cause." Though Cordelia has always been comfortable in a crowd, there's an extra zip of energy surrounding her tonight.

"But...the repercussions."

"Dad is a heartless jerk. It brings me immense joy to disobey him." Cordelia's focus drifts to my left, and her smile doubles. "You must be Vivian! Oh, Finn, she's just as beautiful as you mentioned. You"—Cor waggles her gloved finger at Vivian— "are very hard to cyberstalk. There are literally no pictures of you on the internet. How is that even possible?"

Vivian opens her mouth, but Carol Cook interrupts, nearly jabbing me in the toe when she slams her cane against the ground. "Does anyone care to explain why a helicopter is blocking the only road in and out of town? Who is she? And who exactly are you?" Carol's age-spotted finger points an inch from my nose.

Shoot. Optics.

Freaking optics.

I should have thought about how this would look, maybe pretended to not know Cordelia, but it's been over five years since I've seen my sister in person. My heart clenches just looking at her. Suddenly, I don't care about the fallout. And *there will* be fallout. Cordelia is here. My smart, tenacious, hilarious baby sister is right in front of me. I've seen her grow up over our video calls, but this is...

I step forward, engulfing my sister in a large hug. "I missed you, Cor."

"I missed you too." Her voice scratches like she's fighting off tears, so I tighten my grip.

For once, Carol doesn't keep asking questions, only utters an appraising hum and waits.

When I release Cordelia, she blinks at the cloudy night sky, dabbing the edge of her eye with a silk handkerchief from her reticule.

"Sorry about blocking traffic," Cordelia tells Carol, her smile still a little wobbly.

"I'll handle it," Jax says, ducking away to speak to the uniformed pilot while keeping his gaze trained on Cordelia.

As my sister leans closer to Carol to answer a question, Vivian grips my arm. "I'll make sure they leave you alone. Take as much time as you need to catch up."

"Who?"

"The town." Then Vivian winks, puts two fingers in her mouth, and whistles so loud even the pilot pauses his climb into the cockpit. "Everyone inside! It's not safe to be out here when that thing takes off."

The crowd stares, slack-jawed. Meanwhile, my love for Vivian grows boundless. I wonder if she'll ever stop surprising me. I can't wait to spend the rest of my life figuring it out.

"When have I ever asked you for anything?" The woman of my dreams narrows her eyes and sets her fists on her hips when all of Wilks Beach remains frozen. "Get. Inside. The. Library."

"You heard her." Carol takes Vivian by the elbow, turning them toward the building. "Toot sweet!"

The rotors begin their slow rotation once everyone recedes a safe distance. The rest of my library staff corrals the curious guests like sheepdogs as Carol and Vivian lead the way back inside. Once the wind speed picks up, I use my badge to steer Cordelia into the circulation room so we can talk. My sister and Jax have a wordless conversation before he nods, positioning himself just outside the door.

I lean against the automated book return system, still not believing what I'm seeing. "How is this possible?"

Cordelia's smile turns wicked. "Turns out I'm almost as good at scheming as Dad."

"And that means..."

She props herself against a table, grinning like a fiend but not elaborating. My fingers slide through my hair with an exhale. My sister enjoys a slow reveal almost as much as she relishes a grand entrance.

"It all started with some well-timed eyedrops in Dad's scotch and a teensy-tiny fire."

I rub my jaw. "*Cordelia.*"

"Okay, okay," she says before muttering something that sounds like *killjoy*. "Since you're so impatient, I'll spare you the delicious details and cut to the chase. I gained access to Dad's contract room, and let's just say I had a lot of fun in there."

My eyebrows hit my hairline. Most billionaires have something they like to protect, be it a priceless piece of art or family heirloom. My father protects his triplicate-printed contracts in a walk-in vault hidden behind a bookcase in his study. Every business dealing of his career, after being digitized, is filed in that room. I think Grandmother's Harry Winston collection is locked away in there too, but it's mostly a shrine for his favorite thing.

Once, when I'd been home from college, he'd taken me in there, showing me the organization system like a proud king flaunting his prized possessions. "Words," he'd said, "have the power to make or break a person." He'd meant contractual words used in a legal sense, but I'd interpreted it under my own lens. For me, literature, and the families found within, had given me the reprieve I'd needed when my reality had been an emotional wasteland.

"How'd you get past the retinal scan?"

Cordelia sends me an impish grin. "I thought you didn't want details."

"I'm reconsidering my stance."

"No. You're right." She waves me off as the orchestra begins playing in the main room. "We've got a party to get to."

I glance at the closed door behind my sister. "Jax helped you, didn't he?"

Ever since Jax started protecting my sister two years ago, he's been a little *too attentive* of her needs.

"I'll have you know that the plan was ninety-nine percent mine. Jax just helped with cutting the security feed, but you're missing the takeaway, which is…I have it all."

"All of what?"

"The contracts. Yours. The contract Dad had with Katelyn." She pauses when I involuntarily flinch. I don't have a shred of emotion for my ex, but I'll never get over the sting of my father's manipulation. "It was the progeny clause of Katelyn's contract I found interesting. The bit requiring her to leave before the child turned five. Sound familiar?"

My brows furrow as Cordelia continues.

"When did your mom divorce Dad? Do you remember?"

"I was almost…" My words drop off as a sickening sensation swirls in my stomach.

"Me too. So I pulled the contracts with our mothers—all three of them. How banal of Dad to reuse the same wording in each one, and how predictably cruel of our mothers to willingly sign away their children." Though Cordelia's expression remains blasé, the crack in her voice gives her away.

"Cor." I gather her to my chest.

I don't say anything else because what is there to say? We already knew that our father is a controlling scumbag, but discovering that our mothers traded money for the children they were supposed to love leaves me hollow. The only thing making this situation mildly tolerable is the relationship Cordelia and I forged in spite of our toxic upbringing.

Which brings me back to my original question...

"How are you here?" I ask, releasing her.

My sister sighs, her palms tapping her cheeks a few times. It's a motion she only does when she's exhausted. For the first time, I notice her swollen eyelids, the dark circles under her eyes despite her immaculate makeup.

"I told him off."

All I can do is blink.

"Once the documents were secured, digitized, and given to trusted backups in case something really crazy happened, I marched into Dad's office and informed him that I'm done playing his games. Because of Jax's help during my little heist, he hadn't known I'd raided his vault. He also didn't know that I'd taken all our trust documents as well." A small tug lifts one side of her mouth. "Yours and Brody's match—one-third distribution at twenty-five, thirty, and the rest at thirty-five, a bazillion terms and conditions, but I discovered something very unusual about mine."

I'm about to shake her when she pauses again, that Cheshire grin widening.

"Dad has been in breach of fiduciary duty for almost a year since my trust terms state I should've received a single lump-sum payment at eighteen. But more importantly, my trust is irrevocable."

My knees feel like they're seconds from giving out. "Are you saying..."

"Dad's collateral is fake." Cordelia is luminescent. "He was probably going to sabotage your chances of getting the directorship, but now—"

"He did." I barely get the words out, struggling to breath. I should be relieved, elated, but it feels like my heart is exploding. "I just found out that he set me up."

A string of very unladylike words bursts from my sister's mouth, incongruous with her regal attire.

"This is some next-level *Dynasty* nonsense." She grits her teeth. "That makes me feel even better about telling Dad to shove it after dropping the lawsuit on his desk. Turns out there are a lot of former enemies who were more than happy to offer their legal counsel to see the great Patrick Otto take a hit."

My head shakes in amazement.

Cordelia frames my shoulders. "None of this would have been possible without you. If you hadn't loved me when no one else had, if you hadn't continued to raise me from afar, I'd probably be riddled with addictions or debilitating psychosis. And that's why"—a fizzy energy lights her face as she gives me a little squeeze—"you, my tender-hearted brother, are a billionaire again."

"What?" My eyes fly wide.

"Well, you will be. Once I get my lump sum..." Cordelia uses her index finger to tap my chest. "You'll get half."

"You can't do that."

"You know what, Finn?" My younger sister looks more mature and confident than I've ever seen her. "I'm just figuring out that not only am I completely capable, I can do *whatever* I want."

It's hard to argue with Cordelia when it's clear she's finally surfacing the ocean of fear and control that our ruthless father dropped us in at birth—*before birth.*

My mouth lifts in a grin. "Okay, Cor. You're the boss."

"Boss." She gives her shoulders a little shimmy. "I like the sound of that."

My spine relaxes as I grin. It's impossible not to absorb Cordelia's infectious spirit, like spring flowers tilting up toward long-awaited sunrays.

"So what are you going to do now?" she asks through a broad smile.

I go to slide my hands in my pockets then laugh when I remember that I'm wearing pocketless breeches. "I like my life, especially since moving here and—"

"And falling *in love*," she chimes in, sounding more like her teenage self.

A chuckle escapes me. "And falling in love. Honestly, I'll probably let that money sit in the bank, accruing interest, until you want it back."

Cordelia pouts. "No. You're supposed to use it!"

My gaze flows over the dilapidated circulating room. Everything in here besides the sorting machine is circa 1975 or earlier. "Perhaps some donations are in order."

"Now you're talking."

"And I suppose…" I begin, thinking of Vivian's plans to see Raven Sacaria and how I might be able to convince her to embrace a little extravagance—just this once. "I've got a girlfriend to spoil."

THIRTY-SIX

Vivian

A flight attendant unintentionally interrupts Cade's story about an ostrich chase through the Texas desert when she arrives by our plush leather seats with a tray of crystal flutes.

"Yes, please!" Cade says before accepting the proffered glass of champagne.

I'm glad I invited Cade to join us on this trip, because not only is she a literal ball of light but Cade keeps saying everything we're all thinking. It'd been Brynn's idea to expand our trip to Vegas to include our newly acquired friends since Finn changed my simple long weekend away into an exorbitant affair.

When Finn told me at the ball, over a month ago, that his sister would shortly be inheriting her billions and giving him half,

I thought I'd been caught in one of my imagination's elaborate fantasies. But nope, I'd pinched the underside of my arm until it turned pink and never woke up.

"It doesn't have to change anything, just make things easier. When you let that much money pollute your life, it corrupts you." Finn's flirty grin loses some of its light before his gaze meets mine and softens. "I still want to live in my rental. I want to walk to work as this library's manager. I want to shop at Dotty's like nothing happened tonight, but..." He sucks in a slow breath.

"There are a few things I'd let that money change. I'd love to buy you whatever fabric your heart desires. I am absolutely going to replace that glitchy button machine before it permanently damages your fingers." He brings my fingertips to his lips for a soft kiss. "And it would make me immensely happy to cover everything for your trip to see Raven Sacaria. Can you let me do that?"

Other than the library receiving a donation amount that Dave Prescott couldn't match in three lifetimes, the last month of being a billionaire's girlfriend has felt just like normal life. So much so that I'd been completely unprepared for the luxury of the chauffeured SUV picking me, my sister, Geneva, and Cade up from Seabreeze Beans earlier today. Summer is speaking at a pediatric conference in Florida and keeps texting how she's kicking herself for not getting out of it.

"This is the best bubbly I've ever tasted." Cade arches her light eyebrows at Felicia, who's been taking excellent care of us during our cross-country flight. "Though, it's not bubbly, is it?"

Due to Cade's outgoing nature, we've learned that Felicia and her pilot husband have been flying Cordelia to various locales for most of her life. We've also learned that the co-pilot is their twenty-eight-year-old *very single* son.

"No, miss." The breathtakingly beautiful middle-aged woman barely restrains a smile. "This is a 1999 Salon Blanc de Blancs."

I don't even have the slightest clue what that means, but I'm sure, like everything about this trip, it's expensive. My phone lights with a video call from Finn, and I excuse myself from the table and four seats facing each other to one of the single seats toward the back of the plane. The disorienting goodbye kiss he gave me this morning is still on my lips, more decadent than that champagne I just tasted.

"Hey, gorgeous." He leans back in his office chair, running his fingers through his loose hair. "How's the flight so far? Are you keeping your promise to me?"

After kissing me into oblivion, Finn made me promise to let go and enjoy this experience.

"Yes," I tell him. "I'm squeezing every ounce of joy out of each moment."

The corner of my ridiculously hot boyfriend's mouth quirks. "And everyone else?"

"Cade would be happy at the bottom of a paper bag, so she's elated. Her stories keep making us all laugh. Geneva is completely comfortable, acting as if she belongs in this opulent world..." I make a mental note to investigate why later. "And Brynn has finally realized that she doesn't have to be in charge, making sure everyone is taken care of, since you've already done it. I haven't seen her this relaxed in years, and I can't thank you enough, Finn. This has been so incredible, and we're not even at the concert yet."

"I'm so glad to hear that. You all deserve a break, but…" A coil tightens in my core when Finn's smile turns devious. "I'm actually calling because I've got another surprise for you. I've been working on it for weeks but just got confirmation."

I suck in a scattered breath. "What is it?"

"You not only have front row seats and backstage passes, but you'll be meeting Raven before the concert."

A bark of disbelief leaves my mouth. "I'll what?"

"You can't go all the way there and not say hi to your favorite musician." His eyes twinkle. "It's only for five minutes before she does her final show prep, but—"

"Finn, that's amazing!"

Even though it's probably inappropriate on this posh plane, I stand, squealing and jumping. Finn's laughter over the phone makes my heart three thousand times lighter. The rest of our group asks what's going on, cheering when I tell them about Finn's secret plans for us.

"Miss?" Felicia says. "Sorry to interrupt, but we're beginning our descent. If you wouldn't mind ending your call and fastening your seatbelt."

I rush back to the seat next to my sister, buckling quickly. "I love you. I can't even—" Happy tears flood my vision, blurring the phone screen. "I'm supposed to hang up, but I don't want to."

Finn's gaze softens, his playful expression dropping. "I love you too. Call me after the concert tonight when you're back in the room. No matter the time. I want to hear about everything."

As I hang up, I can't help kicking my feet like a thrilled three-year-old. Around me, my sister and new friends share my joy, excitedly talking over each other. My cheeks already sting from smiling, and we've only just begun.

"My throat hurts," I say, my voice little more than a scrape from scream-singing along all night.

My destroyed mascara is giving hungover-racoon vibes, my face in opposition to my beautiful midnight-blue, sequined fit-and-flare. I'm so glad that we met Raven before the concert when we were all glittering from prepping for the night in the sumptuous penthouse suite. The whole thing is larger than any of our homes or businesses with a full dining room, en suite bedrooms for each of us, and a grand piano *and* a fountain in the main living space.

I'm also glad I didn't completely burst into tears when Raven hugged me earlier. Hearing her soulful voice as she kindly answered questions is one of the highlights of my life. She was so nice as we all took pictures and gushed over her influential career, her signing whatever we put in front of her. Our trip coordinator, Mateo, who'd been spoiling us since we landed on the private airfield, handed me a picture frame Finn sent for Raven to sign. That way, I could put the photo of the two of us in it with her signature across the bottom.

"I know we talked about ordering a pizza and chilling in the hot tub on our terrace after the show, but I'm getting a second wind," Brynn tells us as we climb into the hotel golf cart waiting to take us back to our room.

"I'm game," Cade says, beaming.

"Wherever you ladies go, I go." Geneva tugs down the skirt of her tight black dress as she sits.

"I could arrange for a VIP table at any nightclub," Mateo offers from the front seat beside the driver. "I can give you a rundown of each establishment's merits to help you decide."

Everyone looks to me, waiting. I'm a little emotionally exhausted from such an incredible evening, but the buzzing energy resonating down my forearms doesn't make me want to turn in yet. Regardless, a nightclub sounds like a lot. But if everyone else wants to go, I'm not about to ruin the fun.

"Why don't we save the night club for tomorrow," Brynn answers, her eyes clocking my twisting pinky ring. "How about we explore the casino tonight. Maybe get some dessert?"

She says it as a question, her dark eyes simultaneously nurturing and assessing as they fix on mine. A wide grin splits my face. Though I used to get frustrated when Brynn would answer for me, this time, my sister has suggested the perfect solution before my tired brain could think of it.

I cross my sparkly ballet flats at the ankle, leaning back in the leather seat. "That sounds like a perfect end to our evening...*after* we stop by a bathroom so I can fix this."

My friends chuckle as I wave my hand over my face.

After Mateo coordinates a dessert-tasting table with a stop-by from the celebrity chef for whom the restaurant is named, we wander the casino floor, trying our luck at slot machines. Brynn is determined to win her twenty dollars back, not understanding that as much as she hates losing, her tenacity might not help her here. Geneva wanders toward a small circular bar amid the noisy floor where a boxing match is on two of the six screens behind the bartenders' heads. Cade and I follow, both wincing when the redheaded man takes a hard punch to the jaw.

"Left hook," Geneva barks at the screen. "Simmons is weak to defend on that side."

A man at the bar, hunched over a fruit-topped hurricane glass, says nearly the same thing at the same time. When he looks over his shoulder, an unmistakable zip of electricity laces his gaze as it crashes with Geneva's. A slight shiver racks her athletic frame before Geneva snaps her focus back to the two boxers on the screen.

"Did you see that?" Cade clutches my arm, giddy.

"I *did*."

"He looks familiar. Isn't he the one that was dancing and singing behind us the whole concert?"

A noisy inhale fills my lungs. "Yes! With the Southern accent. He's got quite a voice."

The three women who were seated to his left leave their seats in a fit of giggles. Cade tugs me over, leaving the stool directly next to the stranger open. "Geneva, come sit. Let's get another drink!"

We had champagne with dessert, but I see through Cade's ploy. Geneva's attention remains locked on the last round of the match, so she barely acknowledges the man—or us as we all do a shot of vodka. Cade gives me a defeated shrug, her gaze darting between Geneva and the stranger. I think she's going to try something really outlandish to get the two to talk when a deep voice hovers over my ear.

"I was going to ask to buy you a drink, but it looks like I'm too late."

I nearly topple the stool, jumping off it to wrap my arms around Finn's neck. "What are you doing here?"

That captivating smirk lifts his beard scruff. "I realized that I could arrange a flight whenever I wanted, so I decided I'd rather hear about your concert experience firsthand."

My mouth drops open, speechless, before I glance at Cade. "Would you mind..."

She waves a hand. "Not at all. We're good here. Mateo is hovering over there in case we need anything. Brynn is sucked into that machine. Go catch up."

Finn leads me to a quiet bar so entrenched with plants it resembles an elegant jungle, ordering us both waters after we've sat in a secluded corner. "Tell me everything."

I love the way Finn's eyes glint with amusement as I recount the evening. I want every night to end this way, with us telling each other about our days, listening to the little details.

"I'm so glad it was everything you wanted." Finn leans back in his plush chair, one ankle crossed over his knee, the picture of sophisticated decadence.

It's not until this moment that I register that Finn is wearing a tailored three-piece suit, black as his hair. He's still missing the tie, the dip between his tanned collarbones prominent. My gaze lingers on his neck, noting the uptick in his pulse.

"Where are you staying tonight?"

"I'm not."

My brows knit. "What do you mean?"

"This is your trip with your sister and friends. I'm not staying and interrupting that. I just knew how important this concert was for you and wanted to hear about it directly."

My heartbeat skitters in my ears, nearly blocking out the un-intrusive jazz in the background. "You're telling me you flew all the way across the country just to have a conversation with me?"

Finn's eyes flash, his fingers tightening on the arm of the chair. "I would do anything for you, Vivian."

It's impossible not to kiss him, not to carefully set my glass aside and shift from my lounge chair to his lap. Finn watches each slow motion, his chest rising and falling in short irregular breaths. My fingers slip through his hair before firmly framing his jaw. I'm mere millimeters from touching his lips with mine when a crazy thought occurs to me.

"Want to get married? I hear people do it all the time in Vegas."

Finn's hands shift from the chair to my waist, squeezing.

"No," his gritty voice rasps against my lips before giving me a kiss so passionate I forget to pout over his refusal.

When we finally break apart, Finn's earnest gaze meets mine. "We're getting married in Wilks Beach, on the sand at sunset, in front of everyone you love, after I've proved I'm worthy of you."

My shoulders slump. "You've already—"

Finn silences me with another devastating kiss. "Let me have this. *Please.*"

I can't deny Finn when he asks like that, so I only nod, brushing my lips against his temple. When Finn exhales, gathering me to his chest in a snug hug, I smile. We relax like that for a long while, my fingertips trailing up and down his neck.

"I don't want you to leave yet," I say, leaning back to catch his gaze. "I'll tell everyone that we're spending the rest of the evening together, and I'll see them back in the room later."

I return to my seat to grab my clutch, texting the group chat we created for this trip. Cade sends me a winky emoji followed by a thumbs up. Brynn doesn't respond, but she's probably still sucked into that slot machine. Geneva hates texting, so I'm not surprised when it's radio silence from her.

Once my phone is tucked away, Finn interlaces our fingers. "What do you want to do?"

Since I've already kissed him until we're breathless, I rack my brain. "It sounds boring, but can we stay here and talk?"

There's a tug at the corner of his mouth. "Nothing is boring with you. This is perfect."

A soft smile slips over my face as my gaze drifts around the room. My fingers buzz with energy when I see the decorative stones across the room, eerily similar to the ones used in the landscaping around Wilks Beach Library. I shoot up from my chair, collecting a flat white rock from a trendy planter display. When I plop back down, I leave my shoes on the ground, criss-crossing my legs on the chair and giving Finn a peek of my black bike shorts.

"I had it all wrong. I thought my wish had come true because I spoke to Atticus," I say, turning the stone over in my fingers. "But it was you."

"What do you mean?" Finn's forehead wrinkles adorably. How can this man be sexy and endearing at the same time? It should be illegal.

"*I wish I could talk to the man of my dreams.*" I recite the words I'd written in black permanent ink before tossing the stone into the sea on my birthday.

My heart pounds in my chest, but the rest of my body almost sighs with comprehension.

Of course.

It'd been Finn all along.

My toes unfurl, and my shoulders settle as a bright smile lifts my lips. "I made that wish, and then I ran into you—quite literally—in my sister's coffee shop and then again at the library."

"Vivian." My name is little more than a gruff whisper. "Are you saying..."

"We were always meant to be together," I tell him, pressing the stone into the center of his twitchy palm.

Finn takes a deep inhale as he slides the rock into the inside chest pocket of his suit, his hand pressing it against his heart. Then he leans back, the subtle upward tilt of his chin and curl of his fingers an unmistaken invitation. Blood shimmies in my veins when I forsake my chair for his.

Looks like we're not quite done kissing.

Finn

EPILOGUE

One year later

It's a habit by now to forgo my front door and wind around the side of my rental after leaving work on a Saturday. I know my gorgeous girlfriend will be waiting for me on my back deck before we walk to Bayside Table and enjoy whatever band is playing tonight. I'd given her a spare key months ago when the weather chilled, but Vivian prefers to relax outside whenever she isn't building new dress collections for the boutique on the mainland or seeing to the tailoring needs of Wilks Beach.

There are two distinct reasons a broad smile splits my lips when I see Vivian. The first is that she's engrossed in a paperback copy of the latest Wellington novel. Since it released yesterday, I'm surprised Vivian hasn't finished it already. Earlier today, I'd found her tucked into the reading nook overlooking the nature preserve at the library, unable to resist a covert kiss before returning to work.

Vivian likes to pop by the library unexpectedly, usually demanding kisses. It's always been one of my favorite parts of our relationship but has become a bit of an issue lately. Since the library has been pretty demanding about placing wedding planning books on my desk at every opportunity, it forces me to quickly stash them in awkward places when Vivian arrives unannounced. Even Letitia asked, after an impromptu meeting, why *The Ultimate Wedding Planner* was face down under my office trash can.

The second reason my ribs feel pumped full of helium is that Vivian isn't sprawled out on a deck chair. She's perched on the far edge of the floating dock that stretches into Back Bay, her legs kicking leisurely in the water.

My fingers pat the ring box that's been in my pocket for weeks. The ring is a perfect marriage of antique styling around the largest center diamond I think Vivian will accept without fighting. I don't want her stubborn tornado tendencies to come out in the middle of our proposal. I'd almost asked Vivian to marry me earlier today when the late-afternoon sun had haloed her chestnut hair, but it hadn't felt quite right. Since I know Vivian wouldn't want an outlandish proposal, I've been waiting for the perfect intimate moment—something that's uniquely us.

I set my shoulder bag down at the edge of where the dock connects to my backyard, toeing out of my shoes and tucking the ring box inside one. I consider removing my suit vest but figure that will give me away. Vivian doesn't even look up when I hover above her, just murmurs a quiet, "One moment." Since she's clearly finishing the last page of the book, I wait, sliding my hands into my pockets and surveying the peaceful bay surrounding us.

Being this close to water used to make my heart spin circles in my chest. My heart is racing now, but it's out of sheer joy and anticipation, not out of fear. Overcoming my fear of drowning had been slow going, requiring not only Vivian's encouragement but also the help of a licensed professional. Two months ago, on a warm May day at the beach, when I hadn't panicked after a wave capsized us both, I realized I was finally ready to ask Vivian to be mine forever.

Vivian sets aside her book, giving me that smile—the one just for me—as she tilts her head back. "That one was sooo good. I can't believe I have to wait a year for the last in the series."

"Maybe you can pump the author for information when you meet her next month."

I booked us tickets to Annie Ardent's Regency-themed book signing in Wilmington as soon as Vivian told me about the event. Though she prefers to live our everyday lives like normal people, Vivian lets me spoil her when we travel. I've already begun tentative plans for an elaborate and extended tour of Europe for our honeymoon.

"Are we re-wearing our outfits from the ball or fashioning something new?"

When Vivian simply bites her lip, I laugh.

"Something new it is."

"I was thinking an almost jewel-toned navy for you, with a white damask waistcoat, and using a complementary wedgwood blue for my dress. There's this beautiful brocade I've been eyeing online, and I just need the right project for it."

"Sounds like you found it," I say, bending down to kiss her. "You already know my favorite thing is coming in for a fitting."

When Vivian's lips drop from mine with a delicious pop, I send her a devilish wink. Instead of her nose wrinkling, my girlfriend's stunning green eyes grow unfocused with the sizzling memory of her tailoring my spring/summer wardrobe. Cordelia still likes to send me clothes, saying it gives her something to do besides starring in the reality TV show that has America hooked to their screens.

Satisfaction races through my bloodstream as I straighten, tugging at the collar of my shirt. "It's a bit hot out here."

Vivian watches me with a curiously pinched brow as I back up a few steps. I've gotten into the water whenever Vivian has asked me, but I've never initiated it myself.

"I think I'll go for a swim."

Then I rush forward, launching myself off the dock and into a flip before disappearing beneath the surface.

The cool bay water inundates every sensation, nearly blocking out the sound of Vivian's bright laughter and her coinciding splash as she jumps in. I find myself smiling as I resurface, quickly wiping my eyes and looking for the love of my life. She pops up a bit to my right, her grin luminescent.

"I can't believe you did that."

"How many times do I have to tell you I'd do anything for you?"

It only takes one sure stroke before Vivian is kissing me again. I tug us closer to the dock so I can use one hand to hang onto the edge and the other to palm the small of her back, bringing her close. Her legs wrap around my waist, her fingers framing my jaw as she pours herself into me. The fact that water is surrounding my chest should make anxiety spiral down my spine, but I've never been happier.

We play a bit after catching our breath—her splashing me, me setting a hot kiss over her neck before darting away, her chasing me and starting the whole thing over again. When my abs hurt from laughter, I subtly lead her toward the aluminum dock ladder.

"Come on. We'll have to get cleaned up and changed before we can head out."

Vivian pauses, keeping one hand on the ladder to set her smiling lips on mine. "Worth it."

We hold hands walking to shore, our sodden clothes dripping on the wooden planks. I pause beside my belongings, dropping onto my knee instead of crouching to pick them up. Vivian's fingers fly to her lips, her eyes misting immediately.

"Finn?"

"Yes, gorgeous. I'm asking you to marry me."

"I do!" Her hands clasp over her heart as she bounces slightly.

A chuckle rumbles from my chest. "Let me ask you properly first."

When Vivian bites her lip, I transfer the ring box to one hand, using my other thumb to soothe her bottom lip.

"I never expected a love like ours." My thumb traces her freckled cheekbone, tucking away a saturated curl. "How I feel about you rivals the most poetic words ever printed on paper. I debated collecting some of the best quotes on love but decided that honesty is better. Because I know, in the depth of my bones, that you and I are forever, Vivian. You're what my soul needs to be happy. All I want is to spend the rest of my life loving you." I open the box, the ring glistening in dwindling sunlight. "Will you, Vivian Hutchinson, do me the immense honor of being my wife?"

She hiccups a happy sob. "You had to be dramatic, didn't you?"

"Just a little bit," I say, my grin doubling.

Her trembling fingertips trace my cheeks, my temples, before sliding into my wet hair. The hue of her eyes deepens as she slowly leans closer to whisper, "Yes," over my lips. I shoot to my feet, banding my arms around her and taking her with me. Vivian laughs, tears shaking free before we settle into a soft kiss. There's an understanding with this subtle brush of lips, an agreement between her heart and mine.

"I love you."

I loosen my grip until Vivian slowly slides to the ground. "I love you," I tell her, my words a throaty rasp.

My hands shake as I slip the ring over Vivian's finger.

She briefly glances at it before her fingertips frame my face again, her gaze steady on mine. "You know all I want is you, right?"

The corner of my mouth quirks with a flirty smirk. "Come on, gorgeous. We all know you're just fulfilling your bookish dream of marrying the sexy librarian."

Vivian fights the grin trying to lift her lips. Then my heart nearly incinerates when she gives me that nose wrinkle.

"You smell more like marsh water than books right now." She leans into my throat, taking a noisy inhale. "I might have to rescind that yes."

When Vivian giggles, making a move to bolt toward the house, I scoop her into my arms, holding on to her like I plan on doing for the rest of my days.

Acknowledgements

Firstly, I want to thank **YOU**, my incredible reader! I'm so honored that you spent your time enjoying Vivian and Finn's story. I love these two and I sincerely hope you do too!

Thank you to my amazing beta readers Hannah, Randi, Cassondra, Moni, Sara, and MacKenzie. Your insight into this book and enthusiasm for these characters is so valued! Thanks again to Jenn for her immaculate copy edit—you're seriously the best. I'm grateful for my awesome Street and ARC teams—thanks for reading and shouting out this book! Thank you to Lauren for launch help. And again, the talented Enni designed the beautiful cover for this book. You captured Finn's flirty smile perfectly!

I'm so grateful for my supportive family and friends who cheer me on. I'd be a mushy crumble without you. A huge thank you to my husband and sweet kiddos for always being there for me. I love you more than I could write in a thousand books.

About the Author

Laura Langa is an award-winning sweet romance and romcom author, receiving the HOLT Medallion Award and Booksellers' Best Award. Laura strives to write stories that make readers laugh while tugging at their heartstrings, and to create relatable characters you'd want to befriend. Laura loves trees and all things green, hates flossing but forces herself to do it every night, has a concerning addiction to sugar, and believes that salt air can often cure a bad mood.

www.LauraLanga.com
www.LauraLanga.com/newsletter
Instagram @LauraLangaWrites

www.ingramcontent.com/pod-product-compliance
Lightning Source LLC
Chambersburg PA
CBHW011317310726
48973CB00011B/2957